THE LAIRD'S LUCK

THE LAIRD'S LUCK

AND OTHER FIRESIDE TALES

BY

A. T. QUILLER-COUCH

(Q)

CHARLES SCRIBNER'S SONS

NEW YORK 1901

CONTENTS

THE LAIRD'S LUCK

*[In a General Order issued from the Horse-Guards
on New Year's Day, 1836, His Majesty, King
William IV., was pleased to direct, through the
Commander-in-Chief, Lord Hill, that " with the
view of doing the fullest justice to Regiments,
as well as to Individuals who had distinguished
themselves in action against the enemy," an
account of the services of every Regiment in the
British Army should be published, under the
supervision of the Adjutant General.*

*With fair promptitude this scheme was put
in hand, under the editorship of Mr. Richard
Cannon, Principal Clerk of the Adjutant General's Office. The duty of examining, sifting,
and preparing the records of that distinguished
Regiment which I shall here call the Moray
Highlanders (concealing its real name for reasons
which the narrative will make apparent) fell to
a certain Major Reginald Sparkes ; who in the
course of his researches came upon a number
of pages in manuscript sealed under one cover
and docketed " Memoranda concerning Ensign*

1

THE LAIRD'S LUCK

*D. M. J. Mackenzie. J. R., Jan. 3rd, 1816 "—
the initials being those of Lieut.-Colonel Sir
James Ross, who had commanded the 2nd
Battalion of the Morays through the campaign
of Waterloo. The cover also bore, in the
same handwriting, the word "Private," twice
underlined.*

*Of the occurrences related in the enclosed
papers — of the private ones, that is — it so
happened that of the four eye-witnesses none
survived at the date of Major Sparkes' discovery. They had, moreover, so carefully taken
their secret with them that the Regiment
preserved not a rumour of it. Major Sparkes'
own commission was considerably more recent
than the Waterloo year, and he at least had
heard no whisper of the story. It lay outside
the purpose of his inquiry, and he judiciously
omitted it from his report. But the time is
past when its publication might conceivably have
been injurious; and with some alterations in
the names — to carry out the disguise of the
Regiment—it is here given. The reader will
understand that I use the* IPSISSIMA VERBA *of
Colonel Ross.—Q.]*

2

THE LAIRD'S LUCK

I

I HAD the honour of commanding my Regiment, the Moray Highlanders, on the 16th of June, 1815, when the late Ensign David Marie Joseph Mackenzie met his end in the bloody struggle of Quatre Bras (his first engagement). He fell beside the colours, and I gladly bear witness that he had not only borne himself with extreme gallantry, but maintained, under circumstances of severest trial, a coolness which might well have rewarded me for my help in procuring the lad's commission. And yet at the moment I could scarcely regret his death, for he went into action under a suspicion so dishonouring that, had it been proved, no amount of gallantry could have restored him to the respect of his fellows. So at least I believed, with three of his brother officers who shared the secret. These were Major William Ross (my half-brother), Captain Malcolm Murray, and Mr. Ronald Braintree Urquhart, then our senior ensign. Of these, Mr. Urquhart fell two days later, at Waterloo, while steadying his men to face that heroic shock in which Pack's skeleton regiments were enveloped yet not overwhelmed by four brigades of the French infantry. From the others I received at the time a promise that the accusation against young Mackenzie should be wiped off the slate by his death, and the affair kept secret between us. Since then, however, there has come to me an explanation which—though hard indeed to credit—may, if true, exculpate the lad. I laid it before the others, and they agreed that if, in spite of precautions, the affair should ever come to light, the explanation ought also in justice to be forthcoming; and hence I am writing this memorandum.

It was in the late September of 1814 that I first made acquaintance with David Mackenzie. A wound received in the battle of Salamanca—a shattered ankle—had sent me home invalided, and on my partial recovery I was appointed to command the 2nd Battalion of my Regiment, then being formed at Inverness. To this duty I was equal; but my ankle still gave trouble (the splinters from time to time working through the flesh), and in the late summer of 1814 I obtained leave of absence with my step-brother, and spent some pleasant weeks in cruising and fishing about the Moray Firth. Finding that my leg bettered by this idleness, we hired a smaller boat and embarked on a longer excursion, which took us almost to the south-west end of Loch Ness.

Here, on September 18th, and pretty late in

4

the afternoon, we were overtaken by a sudden squall, which carried away our mast (we found afterwards that it had rotted in the step), and put us for some minutes in no little danger; for my brother and I, being inexpert seamen, did not cut the tangle away, as we should have done, but made a bungling attempt to get the mast on board, with the rigging and drenched sail; and thereby managed to knock a hole in the side of the boat, which at once began to take in water. This compelled us to desist and fall to baling with might and main, leaving the raffle and jagged end of the mast to bump against us at the will of the waves. In short, we were in a highly unpleasant predicament, when a coble or row-boat, carrying one small lug-sail, hove out of the dusk to our assistance. It was manned by a crew of three, of whom the master (though we had scarce light enough to distinguish features) hailed us in a voice which was patently a gentleman's. He rounded up, lowered sail, and ran his boat alongside; and while his two hands were cutting us free of our tangle, inquired very civilly if we were strangers. We answered that we were, and desired him to tell us of the nearest place alongshore where we might land and find a lodging for the night, as well as a carpenter to repair our damage.

5

"In any ordinary case," said he, "I should ask you to come aboard and home with me. But my house lies five miles up the lake; your boat is sinking, and the first thing is to beach her. It happens that you are but half a mile from Ardlaugh and a decent carpenter who can answer all requirements. I think, if I stand by you, the thing can be done; and afterwards we will talk of supper."

By diligent baling we were able, under his direction, to bring our boat to a shingly beach, over which a light shone warm in a cottage window. Our hail was quickly answered by a second light. A lantern issued from the building, and we heard the sound of footsteps.

"Is that you, Donald?" cried our rescuer (as I may be permitted to call him).

Before an answer could be returned, we saw that two men were approaching; of whom the one bearing the lantern was a grizzled old carlin with bent knees and a stoop of the shoulders. His companion carried himself with a lighter step. It was he who advanced to salute us, the old man holding the light obediently; and the rays revealed to us a slight, up-standing youth, poorly dressed, but handsome, and with a touch of pride in his bearing.

"Good evening, gentlemen." He lifted his

bonnet politely, and turned to our rescuer.
"Good evening, Mr. Gillespie," he said—I
thought more coldly. "Can I be of any service
to your friends?"

Mr. Gillespie's manner had changed suddenly
at sight of the young man, whose salutation he
acknowledged more coldly and even more curtly
than it had been given. "I can scarcely claim
them as my friends," he answered. "They are
two gentlemen, strangers in these parts, who have
met with an accident to their boat: one so serious
that I brought them to the nearest landing, which
happened to be Donald's." He shortly explained
our mishap, while the young man took the lantern in hand and inspected the damage with
Donald.

"There is nothing," he announced, "which
cannot be set right in a couple of hours; but we
must wait till morning. Meanwhile if, as I gather,
you have no claim on these gentlemen, I shall beg
them to be my guests for the night."

We glanced at Mr. Gillespie, whose manners
seemed to have deserted him. He shrugged his
shoulders. "Your house is the nearer," said he,
"and the sooner they reach a warm fire the better
for them after their drenching." And with that
he lifted his cap to us, turned abruptly, and

pushed off his own boat, scarcely regarding our thanks.

A somewhat awkward pause followed as we stood on the beach, listening to the creak of the thole-pins in the departing boat. After a minute our new acquaintance turned to us with a slightly constrained laugh.

" Mr. Gillespie omitted some of the formalities," said he. " My name is Mackenzie—David Mackenzie; and I live at Ardlaugh Castle, scarcely half a mile up the glen behind us. I warn you that its hospitality is rude, but to what it affords you are heartily welcome."

He spoke with a high, precise courtliness which contrasted oddly with his boyish face (I guessed his age at nineteen or twenty), and still more oddly with his clothes, which were threadbare and patched in many places, yet with a deftness which told of a woman's care. We introduced ourselves by name, and thanked him, with some expressions of regret at inconveniencing (as I put it, at hazard) the family at the Castle.

"Oh!" he interrupted, "I am sole master there. I have no parents living, no family, and," he added, with a slight sullenness which I afterwards recognised as habitual, "I may almost say, no friends: though to be sure, you are lucky enough

8

to have one fellow-guest to-night—the minister of the parish, a Mr. Saul, and a very worthy man."

He broke off to give Donald some instructions about the boat, watched us while we found our plaids and soaked valises, and then took the lantern from the old man's hand. "I ought to have explained," said he, "that we have neither cart here nor carriage: indeed, there is no carriage-road. But Donald has a pony."

He led the way a few steps up the beach, and then halted, perceiving my lameness for the first time. "Donald, fetch out the pony. Can you ride bareback?" he asked: "I fear there's no saddle but an old piece of sacking." In spite of my protestations the pony was led forth; a starved little beast, on whose over-sharp ridge I must have cut a sufficiently ludicrous figure when hoisted into place with the valises slung behind me.

The procession set out, and I soon began to feel thankful for my seat, though I took no ease in it. For the road climbed steeply from the cottage, and at once began to twist up the bottom of a ravine so narrow that we lost all help of the young moon. The path, indeed, resembled the bed of a torrent, shrunk now to a trickle of water, the voice of which ran in my ears while our host led the way, springing from boulder to boulder, avoiding pools, and pausing now and then to hold his lantern over some slippery place. The pony followed with admirable caution, and my brother trudged in the rear and took his cue from us. After five minutes of this the ground grew easier and at the same time steeper, and I guessed that we were slanting up the hillside and away from the torrent at an acute angle. The many twists and angles, and the utter darkness (for we were now moving between trees) had completely baffled my reckoning when—at the end of twenty minutes, perhaps—Mr. Mackenzie halted and allowed me to come up with him.

I was about to ask the reason of this halt when a ray of his lantern fell on a wall of masonry; and with a start almost laughable I knew we had arrived. To come to an entirely strange house at night is an experience which holds some taste of mystery even for the oldest campaigner; but I have never in my life received such a shock as this building gave me—naked, unlit, presented to me out of a darkness in which I had imagined a steep mountain scaur dotted with dwarfed trees—a sudden abomination of desolation standing, like the prophet's, where it ought not. No light showed on the side where we stood—the side over the ravine; only one pointed turret stood out against the faint moonlight glow in the upper sky: but feeling our way around the gaunt side of the building, we came to a back court-yard and two windows lit. Our host whistled, and helped me to dismount.

In an angle of the court a creaking door opened. A woman's voice cried, "That will be be you, Ardlaugh, and none too early! The minister——"

She broke off, catching sight of us. Our host stepped hastily to the door and began a whispered conversation. We could hear that she was protesting, and began to feel awkward enough. But whatever her objections were, her master cut them short.

"Come in, sirs," he invited us: "I warned you that the fare would be hard, but I repeat that you are welcome."

To our surprise and, I must own, our amusement, the woman caught up his words with new protestations, uttered this time at the top of her voice.

"The fare hard? Well, it might not please folks accustomed to city feasts; but Ardlaugh was not yet without a joint of venison in the larder and a bottle of wine, maybe two, maybe three, for any guest its master chose to make welcome. It

11

was ' an ill bird that 'filed his own nest ' "—with more to this effect, which our host tried in vain to interrupt.

" Then I will lead you to your rooms," he said, turning to us as soon as she paused to draw breath.

" Indeed, Ardlaugh, you will do nothing of the kind." She ran into the kitchen, and returned holding high a lighted torch—a grey-haired woman with traces of past comeliness, overlaid now by an air of worry, almost of fear. But her manner showed only a defiant pride as she led us up the uncarpeted stairs, past old portraits sagging and rotting in their frames, through bleak corridors, where the windows were patched and the plastered walls discoloured by fungus. Once only she halted. " It will be a long way to your appartments. A grand house! " She had faced round on us, and her eyes seemed to ask a question of ours. " I have known it filled," she added —" filled with guests, and the drink and fiddles never stopping for a week. You will see it better to-morrow. A grand house! "

I will confess that, as I limped after this barbaric woman and her torch, I felt some reasonable apprehensions of the bedchamber towards which they were escorting me. But here came another surprise. The room was of moderate size, poorly

12

furnished, indeed, but comfortable and something more. It bore traces of many petty attentions, even—in its white dimity curtains and valances—of an attempt at daintiness. The sight of it brought quite a pleasant shock after the dirt and disarray of the corridor. Nor was the room assigned to my brother one whit less habitable. But if surprised by all this, I was fairly astounded to find in each room a pair of candles lit—and quite recently lit—beside the looking-glass, and an ewer of hot water standing, with a clean towel upon it, in each wash-hand basin. No sooner had the woman departed than I visited my brother and begged him (while he unstrapped his valise) to explain this apparent miracle. He could only guess with me that the woman had been warned of our arrival by the noise of footsteps in the courtyard, and had dispatched a servant by some back stairs to make ready for us.

Our valises were, fortunately, waterproof. We quickly exchanged our damp clothes for dry ones, and groped our way together along the corridors, helped by the moon, which shone through their uncurtained windows, to the main staircase. Here we came on a scent of roasting meat—appetising to us after our day in the open air—and at the foot found our host waiting for us. He had donned his Highland dress of ceremony—velvet jacket, phillabeg and kilt, with the tartan of his clan—and looked (I must own) extremely well in it, though the garments had long since lost their original gloss. An apology for our rough touring suits led to some few questions and replies about the regimental tartan of the Morays, in the history of which he was passably well informed.

Thus chatting, we entered the great hall of Ardlaugh Castle—a tall, but narrow and ill-proportioned apartment, having an open timber roof, a stone-paved floor, and walls sparsely decorated with antlers and round targes—where a very small man stood warming his back at an immense fireplace. This was the Reverend Samuel Saul, whose acquaintance we had scarce time to make before a cracked gong summoned us to dinner in the adjoining room.

The young Laird of Ardlaugh took his seat in a roughly carved chair of state at the head of the table; but before doing so treated me to another surprise by muttering a Latin grace and crossing himself. Up to now I had taken it for granted he was a member of the Scottish Kirk. I glanced at the minister in some mystification; but he, good man, appeared to have fallen into a brown study, with his eyes fastened upon a dish of apples which

14

adorned the centre of our promiscuously furnished board.

Of the furniture of our meal I can only say that poverty and decent appearance kept up a brave fight throughout. The table-cloth was ragged, but spotlessly clean; the silver-ware scanty and worn with high polishing. The plates and glasses displayed a noble range of patterns, but were for the most part chipped or cracked. Each knife had been worn to a point, and a few of them joggled in their handles. In a lull of the talk I caught myself idly counting the darns in my table-napkin. They were—if I remember—fourteen, and all exquisitely stitched. The dinner, on the other hand, would have tempted men far less hungry than we—grilled steaks of salmon, a roast haunch of venison, grouse, a milk-pudding, and, for dessert, the dish of apples already mentioned; the meats washed down with one wine only, but that wine was claret, and beautifully sound. I should mention that we were served by a grey-haired retainer, almost stone deaf, and as hopelessly cracked as the gong with which he had beaten us to dinner. In the long waits between the courses we heard him quarrelling outside with the woman who had admitted us; and gradually—I know not how—the conviction grew on me that they were man and wife, and the only servants of our host's establishment. To cover the noise of one of their altercations I began to congratulate the Laird on the quality of his venison, and put some idle question about his care for his deer.

" I have no deer-forest," he answered. " Elspeth is my only housekeeper."

I had some reply on my lips, when my attention was distracted by a sudden movement by the Rev. Samuel Saul. This honest man had, as we shook hands in the great hall, broken into a flood of small talk. On our way to the dining-room he took me, so to speak, by the button-hole, and within the minute so drenched me with gossip about Ardlaugh, its climate, its scenery, its crops, and the dimensions of the parish, that I feared a whole evening of boredom lay before us. But from the moment we seated ourselves at table he dropped to an absolute silence. There are men, living much alone, who by habit talk little during their meals; and the minister might be reserving himself. But I had almost forgotten his presence when I heard a sharp exclamation, and, looking across, saw him take from his lips his wine-glass of claret and set it down with a shaking hand. The Laird, too, had heard, and bent a darkly questioning glance on him. At once the little man—

whose face had turned to a sickly white—began to stammer and excuse himself.

" It was nothing—a spasm. He would be better of it in a moment. No, he would take no wine: a glass of water would set him right—he was more used to drinking water," he explained, with a small, nervous laugh.

Perceiving that our solicitude embarrassed him, we resumed our talk, which now turned upon the last peninsular campaign and certain engagements in which the Morays had borne part; upon the stability of the French Monarchy, and the career (as we believed, at an end) of Napoleon. On all these topics the Laird showed himself well informed, and while preferring the part of listener (as became his youth) from time to time put in a question which convinced me of his intelligence, especially in military affairs.

The minister, though silent as before, had regained his colour; and we were somewhat astonished when, the cloth being drawn and the company left to its wine and one dish of dessert, he rose and announced that he must be going. He was decidedly better, but (so he excused himself) would feel easier at home in his own manse; and so, declining our host's offer of a bed, he shook hands and bade us good-night. The Laird ac-

17

companied him to the door, and in his absence I
fell to peeling an apple, while my brother drummed
with his fingers on the table and eyed the faded
hangings. I suppose that ten minutes elapsed
before we heard the young man's footsteps returning through the flagged hall and a woman's voice
uplifted.

"But had the minister any complaint, whatever
—to ride off without a word? She could answer
for the collops——"

"Whist, woman! Have done with your clash-
in', ye doited old fool!" He slammed the door
upon her, stepped to the table, and with a sullen
frown poured himself a grass of wine. His brow
cleared as he drank it. "I beg your pardon, gentlemen; but this indisposition of Mr. Saul has
annoyed me. He lives at the far end of the
parish—a good seven miles away—and I had invited him expressly to talk of parish affairs."

"I believe," said I, "you and he are not of the
same religion?"

"Eh?" He seemed to be wondering how I
had guessed. "No, I was bred a Catholic. In
our branch we have always held to the Old Religion. But that doesn't prevent my wishing to
stand well with my neighbours and do my duty
towards them. What disheartens me is, they

18

won't see it." He pushed the wine aside, and for a while, leaning his elbows on the table and resting his chin on his knuckles, stared gloomily before him. Then, with sudden boyish indignation, he burst out: " It's an infernal shame; that's it—an infernal shame! I haven't been home here a twelvemonth, and the people avoid me like a plague. What have I done? My father wasn't popular—in fact, they hated him. But so did I. And he hated me, God knows: misused my mother, and wouldn't endure me in his presence. All my miserable youth I've been mewed up in a school in England—a private seminary. Ugh, what a den it was, too! My mother died calling for me —I was not allowed to come: I hadn't seen her for three years. And now, when the old tyrant is dead, and I come home meaning—so help me! —to straighten things out and make friends— come home, to the poverty you pretend not to notice, though it stares you in the face from every wall—come home, only asking to make the best of of it, live on good terms with my fellows, and be happy for the first time in my life—damn them, they won't fling me a kind look! What have I *done?*—that's what I want to know. The queer thing is, they behaved more decently at first. There's that Gillespie, who brought you ashore:

19

he came over the first week, offered me shooting, was altogether as pleasant as could be. I quite took to the fellow. Now, when we meet, he looks the other way! If he has anything against me, he might at least explain: it's all I ask. What have I done?"

Throughout this outburst I sat slicing my apple and taking now and then a glance at the speaker. It was all so hotly and honestly boyish! He only wanted justice. I know something of youngsters, and recognised the cry. Justice! It's the one thing every boy claims confidently as his right, and probably the last thing on earth he will ever get. And this boy looked so handsome, too, sitting in his father's chair, petulant, restive under a weight too heavy (as anyone could see) for his age. I couldn't help liking him.

My brother told me afterwards that I pounced like any recruiting-sergeant. This I do not believe. But what, after a long pause, I said was this: "If you are innocent or unconscious of offending, you can only wait for your neighbours to explain themselves. Meanwhile, why not leave them? Why not travel, for instance?"

"Travel!" he echoed, as much as to say, "You ought to know, without my telling, that I cannot afford it."

"Travel," I repeated; "see the world, rub against men of your age. You might by the way do some fighting."

He opened his eyes wide. I saw the sudden idea take hold of him, and again I liked what I saw.

"If I thought——" He broke off. "You don't mean——" he began, and broke off again.

"I mean the Morays," I said. "There may be difficulties; but at this moment I cannot see any real ones."

By this time he was gripping the arms of his chair. "If I thought——" he harked back, and for the third time broke off. "What a fool I am! It's the last thing they ever put in a boy's head at that infernal school. If you will believe it, they wanted to make a priest of me!"

He sprang up, pushing back his chair. We carried our wine into the great hall, and sat there talking the question over before the fire. Before we parted for the night I had engaged to use all my interest to get him a commission in the Morays; and I left him pacing the hall, his mind in a whirl, but his heart (as was plain to see) exulting in his new prospects.

And certainly, when I came to inspect the castle by the next morning's light, I could understand

21

his longing to leave it. A gloomier, more preten-
tious, or worse-devised structure I never set eyes
on. The Mackenzie who erected it may well have
been (as the saying is) his own architect, and had
either come to the end of his purse or left his
heirs to decide against planting gardens, laying
out approaches or even maintaining the pile in
decent repair. In place of a drive a grassy cart-
track, scored deep with old ruts, led through a
gateless entrance into a courtyard where the slates
had dropped from the roof and lay strewn like
autumn leaves. On this road I encountered the
young Laird returning from an early tramp with
his gun; and he stood still and pointed to the castle
with a grimace.

"A white elephant," said I.

"Call it rather the corpse of one," he answered.
"Cannot you imagine some *genie* of the Oriental
Tales dragging the beast across Europe and dump-
ing it down here in a sudden fit of disgust? As a
matter of fact my grandfather built it, and cursed
us with poverty thereby. It soured my father's
life. I believe the only soul honestly proud of it
is Elspeth."

"And I suppose," said I, "you will leave her
in charge of it when you join the Morays?"

"Ah!" he broke in, with a voice which betrayed his relief: " you are in earnest about that? Yes, Elspeth will look after the castle, as she does already. I am just a child in her hand. When a man has one only servant it's well to have her devoted." Seeing my look of surprise, he added, " I don't count old Duncan, her husband; for he's half-witted, and only serves to break the plates. Does it surprise you to learn that, barring him, Elspeth is my only retainer?

" H'm," said I, considerably puzzled—I must explain why.

I am by training an extraordinarily light sleeper; yet nothing had disturbed me during the night until at dawn my brother knocked at the door and entered, ready dressed.

" Hullo! " he exclaimed, " are you responsible for this? " and he pointed to a chair at the foot of the bed where lay, folded in a neat pile, not only the clothes I had tossed down carelessly overnight, but the suit in which I had arrived. He picked up this latter, felt it, and handed it to me. It was dry, and had been carefully brushed.

" Our friend keeps a good valet," said I; " but the queer thing is that, in a strange room, I didn't wake. I see he has brought hot water too."

" Look here," my brother asked: " did you lock your door?"

" Why, of course not—the more by token that it hasn't a key."

" Well," said he, " mine has, and I'll swear I used it; but the same thing has happened to me! "

This, I tried to persuade him, was impossible; and for the while he seemed convinced. " It *must* be," he owned; " but if I didn't lock that door I'll never swear to a thing again in all my life."

The young Laird's remark set me thinking of this, and I answered after a pause, " In one of the pair, then, you possess a remarkably clever valet."

It so happened that, while I said it, my eyes rested, without the least intention, on the sleeve of his shooting-coat; and the words were scarcely out before he flushed hotly and made a motion as if to hide a neatly mended rent in its cuff. In another moment he would have retorted, and was indeed drawing himself up in anger, when I prevented him by adding—

" I mean that I am indebted to him or to her this morning for a neatly brushed suit; and I suppose to your freeness in plying me with wine last night that it arrived in my room without waking me. But for that I could almost set it down to the supernatural."

I said this in all simplicity, and was quite unprepared for its effect upon him, or for his extraordinary reply. He turned as white in the face as, a moment before, he had been red. "Good God!" he said eagerly, "you haven't missed anything, have you?"

"Certainly not," I assured him. "My dear sir——"

"I know, I know. But you see," he stammered, "I am new to these servants. I know them to be faithful, and that's all. Forgive me; I feared from your tone one of them—Duncan perhaps . . . ."

He did not finish his sentence, but broke into a hurried walk and led me towards the house. A minute later, as we approached it, he began to discourse half-humorously on its more glaring features, and had apparently forgotten his perturbation.

I too attached small importance to it, and recall it now merely through unwillingness to omit any circumstance which may throw light on a story sufficiently dark to me. After breakfast our host walked down with us to the loch-side, where we found old Donald putting the last touches on his job. With thanks for our entertainment we shook hands and pushed off: and my last word at parting was a promise to remember his ambition and write any news of my success.

II

I ANTICIPATED no difficulty, and encountered none. The *Gazette* of January, 1815, announced that David Marie Joseph Mackenzie, gentleman, had been appointed to an ensigncy in the —th Regiment of Infantry (Moray Highlanders); and I timed my letter of congratulation to reach him with the news. Within a week he had joined us at Inverness, and was made welcome.

I may say at once that during his brief period of service I could find no possible fault with his bearing as a soldier. From the first he took seriously to the calling of arms, and not only showed himself punctual on parade and in all the small duties of barracks, but displayed, in his reserved way, a zealous resolve to master whatever by book or conversation could be learned of the higher business of war. My junior officers—though when the test came, as it soon did, they acquitted themselves most creditably—showed, as a whole, just then no great promise. For the most part they were young lairds, like Mr. Mac-

26

kenzie, or cadets of good Highland families; but, unlike him, they had been allowed to run wild, and chafed under harness. One or two of them had the true Highland addiction to card-playing; and though I set a pretty stern face against this curse—as I dare to call it—its effects were to be traced in late hours, more than one case of shirking "rounds," and a general slovenliness at morning parade.

In such company Mr. Mackenzie showed to advantage, and I soon began to value him as a likely officer. Nor, in my dissatisfaction with them, did it give me any uneasiness—as it gave me no surprise—to find that his brother-officers took less kindly to him. He kept a certain reticence of manner, which either came of a natural shyness or had been ingrained in him at the Roman Catholic seminary. He was poor, too; but poverty did not prevent his joining in all the regimental amusements, figuring modestly but sufficiently on the subscription lists, and even taking a hand at cards for moderate stakes. Yet he made no headway, and his popularity diminished instead of growing. All this I noted, but without discovering any definite reason. Of his professional promise, on the other hand, there could be no question; and the men liked and respected him.

Our senior ensign at this date was a Mr.
Urquhart, the eldest son of a West Highland
laird, and heir to a considerable estate. He had
been in barracks when Mr. Mackenzie joined; but
a week later his father's sudden illness called for
his presence at home, and I granted him a leave
of absence, which was afterwards extended. I
regretted this, not only for the sad occasion, but
because it deprived the battalion for a time of one
of its steadiest officers, and Mr. Mackenzie in
particular of the chance to form a very useful
friendship. For the two young men had (I
thought) several qualities which might well attract
them each to the other, and a common gravity
of mind in contrast with their companions' prev-
alent and somewhat tiresome frivolity. Of the
two I judged Mr. Urquhart (the elder by a year)
to have the more stable character. He was a good-
looking, dark-complexioned young Highlander,
with a serious expression which, without being
gloomy, did not escape a touch of melancholy. I
should judge this melancholy of Mr. Urquhart's
constitutional, and the boyish sullenness which lingered on Mr. Mackenzie's equally handsome face
to have been imposed rather by circumstances.

Mr. Urquhart rejoined us on the 24th of
February. Two days later, as all the world knows,

Napoleon made his escape from Elba; and the next week or two made it certain not only that the allies must fight, but that the British contingent must be drawn largely, if not in the main, from the second battalions then drilling up and down the country. The 29th of March brought us our marching orders; and I will own that, while feeling no uneasiness about the great issue, I distrusted the share my raw youngsters were to take in it.

On the 12th of April we were landed at Ostend, and at once marched up to Brussels, where we remained until the middle of June, having been assigned to the 5th (Picton's) Division of the Reserve. For some reason the Highland regiments had been massed into the Reserve, and were billeted about the capital, our own quarters lying between the 92nd (Gordons) and General Kruse's Nassauers, whose lodgings stretched out along the Louvain road; and although I could have wished some harder and more responsible service to get the Morays into training, I felt what advantage they derived from rubbing shoulders with the fine fellows of the 42nd, 79th, and 92nd, all First Battalions toughened by Peninsular work. The gaieties of life in Brussels during these two months have been described often enough; but among the military they were chiefly confined to those officers whose means allowed them to keep the pace set by rich civilians, and the Morays played the part of amused spectators. Yet the work and the few gaieties which fell to our share, while adding to our experiences, broke up to some degree the old domestic habits of the battalion. Excepting on duty I saw less of Mr. Mackenzie and thought less about him; he might be left now to be shaped by active service. But I was glad to find him often in company with Mr. Urquhart.

I come now to the memorable night of June 15th, concerning which and the end it brought upon the festivities of Brussels so much has been written. All the world has heard of the Duchess of Richmond's ball, and seems to conspire in decking it out with pretty romantic fables. To contradict the most of these were waste of time; but I may point out (1) that the ball was over and, I believe, all the company dispersed, before the actual alarm awoke the capital; and (2) that all responsible officers gathered there shared the knowledge that such an alarm was impending, might arrive at any moment, and would almost certainly arrive within a few hours. News of the French advance across the frontier and attack on General Zieten's outposts had reached Wellington

at three o'clock that afternoon. It should have
been brought five hours earlier; but he gave his
orders at once, and quietly, and already our troops
were massing for defence upon Nivelles. We of
the Reserve had secret orders to hold ourselves
prepared. Obedient to a hint from their Commander-in-chief, the generals of division and brigade who attended the Duchess' ball withdrew
themselves early on various pleas. Her Grace had
honoured me with an invitation, probably because
I represented a Highland regiment; and Highlanders (especially the Gordons, her brother's
regiment) were much to the fore that night with
reels, flings, and strathspeys. The many with-
drawals warned me that something was in the
wind, and after remaining just so long as seemed
respectful, I took leave of my hostess and walked
homewards across the city as the clocks were striking eleven.

We of the Morays had our headquarters in a
fairly large building—the Hôtel de Liège—in time
of peace a resort of *commis-voyageurs* of the better
class. It boasted a roomy hall, out of which
opened two coffee-rooms, converted by us into
guard- and mess-room. A large drawing-room on
the first floor overlooking the street served me for
sleeping as well as working quarters, and to reach

it I must pass the *entresol*, where a small apartment had been set aside for occasional uses. We made it, for instance, our ante-room, and assembled there before mess; a few would retire there for smoking or card-playing; during the day it served as a waiting-room for messengers or any one whose business could not be for the moment attended to.

I had paused at the entrance to put some small question to the sentry, when I heard the crash of a chair in this room, and two voices broke out in fierce altercation. An instant after, the mess-room door opened, and Captain Murray, without observing me, ran past me and up the stairs. As he reached the *entresol*, a voice—my brother's—called down from an upper landing, and demanded, "What's wrong there?"

"I don't know, Major," Captain Murray answered, and at the same moment flung the door open. I was quick on his heels, and he wheeled round in some surprise at my voice, and to see me interposed between him and my brother, who had come running downstairs, and now stood behind my shoulder in the entrance.

"Shut the door," I commanded quickly. "Shut the door, and send away any one you may hear outside. Now, gentlemen, explain yourselves, please."

32

THE LAIRD'S LUCK

Mr. Urquhart and Mr. Mackenzie faced each other across a small table, from which the cloth had been dragged and lay on the floor with a scattered pack of cards. The elder lad held a couple of cards in his hand; he was white in the face.

"He cheated!" He swung round upon me in a kind of indignant fury, and tapped the cards with his forefinger.

I looked from him to the accused. Mackenzie's face was dark, almost purple, rather with rage (as it struck me) than with shame.

"It's a lie." He let out the words slowly, as if holding rein on his passion. "Twice he's said so, and twice I've called him a liar." He drew back for an instant, and then lost control of himself. "If that's not enough——." He leapt forward, and almost before Captain Murray could interpose had hurled himself upon Urquhart. The table between them went down with a crash, and Urquhart went staggering back from a blow which just missed his face and took him on the collarbone before Murray threw both arms around the assailant.

"Mr. Mackenzie," said I, "you will consider yourself under arrest. Mr. Urquhart, you will hold yourself ready to give me a full explanation.

33

Whichever of you may be in the right, this is a disgraceful business, and dishonouring to your regiment and the cloth you wear: so disgraceful, that I hesitate to call up the guard and expose it to more eyes than ours. If Mr. Mackenzie "—I turned to him again—" can behave himself like a gentleman, and accept the fact of his arrest without further trouble, the scandal can at least be postponed until I discover how much it is necessary to face. For the moment, sir, you are in charge of Captain Murray. Do you understand? "

He bent his head sullenly. "He shall fight me, whatever happens," he muttered.

I found it wise to pay no heed to this. "It will be best," I said to Murray, "to remain here with Mr. Mackenzie until I am ready for him. Mr. Urquhart may retire to his quarters, if he will—I advise it, indeed—but I shall require his attendance in a few minutes. You understand," I added significantly, "that for the present this affair remains strictly between ourselves." I knew well enough that, for all the King's regulations, a meeting would inevitably follow sooner or later, and will own I looked upon it as the proper outcome, between gentlemen, of such a quarrel. But it was not for me, their Colonel, to betray this knowledge or my feelings, and by imposing

secrecy I put off for the time all the business of
a formal challenge with seconds. So I left them,
and requesting my brother to follow me, mounted
to my own room. The door was no sooner shut
than I turned on him.

" Surely," I said, " this is a bad mistake of
Urquhart's? It's an incredible charge. From all
I've seen of him, the lad would never be
guilty . . ." I paused, expecting his ascent. To
my surprise he did not give it, but stood fingering
his chin and looking serious.

" I don't know," he answered unwillingly.
" There are stories against him."

" What stories? "

" Nothing definite." My brother hesitated.
" It doesn't seem fair to him to repeat mere whispers. But the others don't like him."

" Hence the whispers, perhaps. They have not
reached me."

" They would not. He is known to be a fa-
vourite of yours. But they don't care to play
with him." My brother stopped, met my look,
and answered it with a shrug of the shoulders,
adding, " He wins pretty constantly."

" Any definite charge before to-night's? "

" No: at least, I think not. But Urquhart may
have been put up to watch."

"Fetch him up, please," said I promptly; and seating myself at the writing-table I lit candles (for the lamp was dim), made ready the writing materials and prepared to take notes of the evidence.

Mr. Urquhart presently entered, and I wheeled round in my chair to confront him. He was still exceedingly pale—paler, I thought, than I had left him. He seemed decidedly ill at ease, though not on his own account. His answer to my first question made me fairly leap in my chair.

"I wish," he said, "to qualify my accusation of Mr. Mackenzie. That he cheated I have the evidence of my own eyes; but I am not sure how far he knew he was cheating."

"Good heavens, sir!" I cried. "Do you know you have accused that young man of a villainy which must damn him for life? And now you tell me——" I broke off in sheer indignation.

"I know," he answered quietly. "The noise fetched you in upon us on the instant, and the mischief was done."

"Indeed, sir," I could not avoid sneering, "to most of us it would seem that the mischief was done when you accused a brother-officer of fraud to his face."

He seemed to reflect. "Yes, sir," he assented

36

slowly; " it is done. I saw him cheat: that I must persist in; but I cannot say how far he was conscious of it. And since I cannot, I must take the consequences."

" Will you kindly inform us how it is possible for a player to cheat and not know that he is cheating?"

He bent his eyes on the carpet as if seeking an answer. It was long in coming. " No," he said at last, in a slow, dragging tone, " I cannot."

" Then you will at least tell us exactly what Mr. Mackenzie did."

Again there was a long pause. He looked at me straight, but with hopelessness in his eyes. " I fear you would not believe me. It would not be worth while. If you can grant it, sir, I would ask time to decide."

" Mr. Urquhart," said I sternly, " are you aware you have brought against Mr. Mackenzie a charge under which no man of honour can live easily for a moment? You ask me without a word of evidence in substantiation to keep *him* in torture while I give *you* time. It is monstrous, and I beg to remind you that, unless your charge is proved, you can—and will—be broken for making it."

" I know it, sir," he answered firmly enough; " and because I knew it, I asked—perhaps selfishly

—for time. If you refuse, I will at least ask permission to see a priest before telling a story which I can scarcely expect you to believe." Mr. Urquhart too was a Roman Catholic.

But my temper for the moment was gone. " I see little chance," said I, " of keeping this scandal secret, and regret it the less if the consequences are to fall on a rash accuser. But just now I will have no meddling priest share the secret. For the present, one word more. Had you heard before this evening of any hints against Mr. Mackenzie's play?"

He answered reluctantly, " Yes."

" And you set yourself to lay a trap for him?"

" No, sir; I did not. Unconsciously I may have been set on the watch: no, that is wrong— I *did* watch. But I swear it was in every hope and expectation of clearing him. He was my friend. Even when I *saw*, I had at first no intention to expose him until——"

" That is enough, sir," I broke in, and turned to my brother. " I have no option but to put Mr. Urquhart too under arrest. Kindly convey him back to his room, and send Captain Murray to me. He may leave Mr. Mackenzie in the *entresol*."

My brother led Urquhart out, and in a minute

38

Captain Murray tapped at my door. He was an honest Scot, not too sharp-witted, but straight as a die. I am to show him this description, and he will cheerfully agree with it.

"This is a hideous business, Murray," said I as he entered. "There's something wrong with Urquhart's story. Indeed, between ourselves it has the fatal weakness that he won't tell it."

Murray took a minute to digest this, then he answered, "I don't know anything about Urquhart's story, sir. But there's something wrong about Urquhart." Here he hesitated.

"Speak out, man," said I: "in confidence. That's understood."

"Well, sir," said he, "Urquhart won't fight."

"Ah! so that question came up, did it?" I asked, looking at him sharply.

He was not abashed, but answered, with a twinkle in his eye, "I believe, sir, you gave me no orders to stop their talking, and in a case like this—between youngsters—some question of a meeting would naturally come up. You see, I know both the lads. Urquhart I really like; but he didn't show up well, I must own—to be fair to the other, who is in the worse fix."

"I am not so sure of that," I commented; "but go on."

He seemed surprised. "Indeed, Colonel?
Well," he resumed, "I being the sort of fellow
they could talk before, a meeting *was* discussed.
The question was how to arrange it without seconds
—that is, without breaking your orders and dragging in outsiders. For Mackenzie wanted blood
at once, and for awhile Urquhart seemed just as
eager. All of a sudden, when . . . ." here he
broke off suddenly, not wishing to commit himself.

"Tell me only what you think necessary," said I.

He thanked me. "That is what I wanted," he
said. "Well, all of a sudden, when we had found
out a way and Urquhart was discussing it, he
pulled himself up in the middle of a sentence, and
with his eyes fixed on the other—a most curious
look it was—he waited while you could count ten,
and, 'No,' says he, 'I'll not fight you at once'—
for we had been arranging something of the sort—
'not to-night, anyway, nor to-morrow,' he says.
'I'll fight you; but I won't have your blood on
my head *in that way.*' Those were his words. I
have no notion what he meant; but he kept
repeating them, and would not explain, though
Mackenzie tried him hard and was for shooting
across the table. He was repeating them when
the Major interrupted us and called him up."

"He has behaved ill from the first," said I.

" To me the whole affair begins to look like an abominable plot against Mackenzie. Certainly I cannot entertain a suspicion of his guilt upon a bare assertion which Urquhart declines to back with a tittle of evidence."

" The devil he does! " mused Captain Murray. " That looks bad for him. And yet, sir, I'd sooner trust Urquhart than Mackenzie, and if the case lies against Urquhart——"

" It will assuredly break him," I put in, " unless he can prove the charge, or that he was honestly mistaken."

" Then, sir," said the Captain, " I'll have to show you this. It's ugly, but it's only justice."

He pulled a sovereign from his pocket and pushed it on the writing-table under my nose.

" What does this mean? "

" It is a marked one," said he.

" So I perceive." I had picked up the coin and was examining it.

" I found it just now," he continued, " in the room below. The upsetting of the table had scattered Mackenzie's stakes about the floor."

" You seem to have a pretty notion of evidence," I observed sharply. " I don't know what accusation this coin may carry; but why need it be Mackenzie's? He might have won it from Urquhart."

41

"I thought of that," was the answer. "But no money had changed hands. I enquired. The quarrel arose over the second deal, and as a matter of fact Urquhart had laid no money on the table, but made a pencil-note of a few shillings he lost by the first hand. You may remember, sir, how the table stood when you entered."

I reflected. "Yes, my recollection bears you out. Do I gather that you have confronted Mackenzie with this?"

"No. I found it and slipped it quietly into my pocket. I thought we had trouble enough on hand for the moment."

"Who marked this coin?"

"Young Fraser, sir, in my presence. He has been losing small sums, he declares, by pilfering. We suspected one of the orderlies."

"In this connection you had no suspicion of Mr. Mackenzie?"

"None, sir." He considered for a moment, and added: "There was a curious thing happened three weeks ago over my watch. It found its way one night to Mr. Mackenzie's quarters. He brought it to me in the morning; said it was lying, when he awoke, on the table beside his bed. He seemed utterly puzzled. He had been to one or two already to discover the owner. We joked him about

it, the more by token that his own watch had
broken down the day before and was away at the
mender's.   The whole thing was queer, and has
not been explained.   Of course in that instance
he was innocent: everything proves it.   It just occurred to me as worth mentioning, because in both
instances the lad may have been the victim of a
trick."

"I am glad you did so," I said; "though just
now it does not throw any light that I can see."
I rose and paced the room.   "Mr. Mackenzie had
better be confronted with this, too, and hear your
evidence.   It's best he should know the worst
against him; and if he be guilty it may move him
to confession."

"Certainly, sir," Captain Murray assented.
"Shall I fetch him?"

"No, remain where you are," I said; "I will
go for him myself."

I understood that Mr. Urquhart had retired to
his own quarters or to my brother's, and that Mr.
Mackenzie had been left in the *entresol* alone.   But
as I descended the stairs quietly I heard within that
room a voice which at first persuaded me he had
company, and next that, left to himself, he had
broken down and given way to the most childish
wailing.   The voice was so unlike his, or any

grown man's, that it arrested me on the lowermost stair against my will. It resembled rather the sobbing of an infant mingled with short strangled cries of contrition and despair.

"What shall I do? What shall I do? I didn't mean it—I meant to do good! What shall I do?"

So much I heard (as I say) against my will, before my astonishment gave room to a sense of shame at playing, even for a moment, the eavesdropper upon the lad I was to judge. I stepped quickly to the door, and with a warning rattle (to give him time to recover himself) turned the handle and entered.

He was alone, lying back in an easy chair—not writhing there in anguish of mind, as I had fully expected, but sunk rather in a state of dull and hopeless apathy. To reconcile his attitude with the sounds I had just heard was merely impossible; and it bewildered me worse than any in the long chain of bewildering incidents. For five seconds or so he appeared not to see me; but when he grew aware his look changed suddenly to one of utter terror, and his eyes, shifting from me, shot a glance about the room as if he expected some new accusation to dart at him from the corners. His indignation and passionate defiance were gone: his eyes seemed to ask me, "How much do you know?"

before he dropped them and stood before me, sullenly submissive.

"I want you upstairs," said I: "not to hear your defence on this charge, for Mr. Urquhart has not yet specified it. But there is another matter."

"Another?" he echoed dully, and, I observed, without surprise.

I led the way back to the room where Captain Murray waited. "Can you tell me anything about this?" I asked, pointing to the sovereign on the writing-table.

He shook his head, clearly puzzled, but anticipating mischief.

"The coin is marked, you see. I have reason to know that it was marked by its owner in order to detect a thief. Captain Murray found it just now among your stakes."

Somehow—for I liked the lad—I had not the heart to watch his face as I delivered this. I kept my eyes upon the coin, and waited, expecting an explosion—a furious denial, or at least a cry that he was the victim of a conspiracy. None came. I heard him breathing hard. After a long and very dreadful pause some words broke from him, so lowly uttered that my ears only just caught them.

"This too? O my God!"

45

I seated myself, the lad before me, and Captain Murray erect and rigid at the end of the table. "Listen, my lad," said I. "This wears an ugly look, but that a stolen coin has been found in your possession does not prove that you've stolen it."

"I did not. Sir, I swear to you on my honour, and before Heaven, that I did not."

"Very well," said I: "Captain Murray asserts that he found this among the moneys you had been staking at cards. Do you question that assertion?"

He answered almost without pondering. "No, sir. Captain Murray is a gentleman, and incapable of falsehood. If he says so, it was so."

"Very well again. Now, can you explain how this coin came into your possession?"

At this he seemed to hesitate; but answered at length, "No, I cannot explain."

"Have you any idea? Or can you form any guess?"

Again there was a long pause before the answer came in low and strained tones: "I can guess."

"What is your guess?"

He lifted a hand and dropped it hopelessly. "You would not believe," he said.

I will own a suspicion flashed across my mind on hearing these words—the very excuse given a

46

while ago by Mr. Urquhart—that the whole affair was a hoax and the two young men were in conspiracy to fool me. I dismissed it at once: the sight of Mr. Mackenzie's face was convincing. But my temper was gone.

"Believe you?" I exclaimed. "You seem to think the one thing I can swallow as creditable, even probable, is that an officer in the Morays has been pilfering and cheating at cards. Oddly enough, it's the last thing I'm going to believe without proof, and the last charge I shall pass without clearing it up to my satisfaction. Captain Murray, will you go and bring me Mr. Urquhart and the Major?"

As Captain Murray closed the door I rose, and with my hands behind me took a turn across the room to the fireplace, then back to the writing-table.

"Mr. Mackenzie," I said, "before we go any further I wish you to believe that I am your friend as well as your Colonel. I did something to start you upon your career, and I take a warm interest in it. To believe you guilty of these charges will give me the keenest grief. However unlikely your defence may sound—and you seem to fear it—I will give it the best consideration I can. If you are innocent, you shall not find me prejudiced because many are against you and you are alone. Now, this coin——" I turned to the table.

The coin was gone.

I stared at the place where it had lain; then at the young man. He had not moved. My back had been turned for less than two seconds, and I could have sworn he had not budged from the square of carpet on which he had first taken his stand, and on which his feet were still planted. On the other hand, I was equally positive the incriminating coin had lain on the table at the moment I turned my back.

" It is gone! " cried I.

" Gone? " he echoed, staring at the spot to which my finger pointed. In the silence our glances were still crossing when my brother tapped at the door and brought in Mr. Urquhart, Captain Murray following.

Dismissing for a moment this latest mystery, I addressed Mr. Urquhart. " I have sent for you, sir, to request in the first place that here in Mr. Mackenzie's presence and in colder blood you will either withdraw or repeat and at least attempt to substantiate the charge you brought against him."

" I adhere to it, sir, that there was cheating. To withdraw would be to utter a lie. Does he deny it? "

I glanced at Mr. Mackenzie. "I deny that I cheated," said he sullenly.

"Further," pursued Mr. Urquhart, "I repeat what I told you, sir. He *may*, while profiting by it, have been unaware of the cheat. At the moment I thought it impossible; but I am willing to believe——"

"*You* are willing!" I broke in. "And pray, sir, what about me, his Colonel, and the rest of his brother officers? Have you the coolness to suggest——"

But the full question was never put, and in this world it will never be answered. A bugle call, distant but clear, cut my sentence in half. It came from the direction of the Place d'Armes. A second bugle echoed it from the height of the Montagne du Parc, and within a minute its note was taken up and answered across the darkness from quarter after quarter.

We looked at one another in silence. "Business," said my brother at length, curtly and quietly.

Already the rooms above us were astir. I heard windows thrown open, voices calling questions, feet running.

"Yes," said I, "it is business at length, and for the while this inquiry must end. Captain Mur-

ray, look to your company. You, Major, see that
the lads tumble out quick to the alarm-post. One
moment!"—and Captain Murray halted with his
hand on the door—"It is understood that for the
present no word of to-night's affair passes our lips."
I turned to Mr. Mackenzie and answered the question I read in the lad's eyes. "Yes, sir; for the
present I take off your arrest. Get your sword.
It shall be your good fortune to answer the enemy
before answering me."

To my amazement Mr. Urquhart interposed.
He was, if possible, paler and more deeply agitated
than before. "Sir, I entreat you not to allow Mr.
Mackenzie to go. I have reasons—I was mistaken
just now——"

"Mistaken, sir?"

"Not in what I saw. I refused to fight him—
under a mistake. I thought——"

But I cut his stammering short. "As for
you," I said, "the most charitable construction I
can put on your behaviour is to believe you mad.
For the present you, too, are free to go and do your
duty. Now leave me. Business presses, and I
am sick and angry at the sight of you."

It was just two in the morning when I reached
the alarm-post. Brussels by this time was full of

the rolling of drums and screaming of pipes; and
the regiment formed up in darkness rendered ten-
fold more confusing by a mob of citizens, some
wildly excited, others paralysed by terror, and all
intractable. We had, moreover, no small trouble
to disengage from our ranks the wives and families
who had most unwisely followed many officers
abroad, and now clung to their dear ones bidding
them farewell. To end this most distressing scene
I had in some instances to use a roughness which
it still afflicts me to remember. Yet in actual time
it was soon over, and dawn scarcely breaking when
the Morays with the other regiments of Pack's
brigade filed out of the park and fell into stride on
the road which leads southward to Charleroi.

In this record it would be immaterial to describe
either our march or the since-famous engagement
which terminated it. Very early we began to
hear the sound of heavy guns far ahead and to
make guesses at their distance; but it was close
upon two in the afternoon before we reached the
high ground above Quatre Bras, and saw the battle
spread below us like a picture. The Prince of
Orange had been fighting his ground stubbornly
since seven in the morning. Ney's superior artillery and far superior cavalry had forced him back,
it is true; but he still covered the cross-roads which

were the key of his defence, and his position remained sound, though it was fast becoming critical.
Just as we arrived, the French, who had already
mastered the farm of Piermont, on the left of the
Charleroi road, began to push their skirmishers
into a thicket below it and commanding the road
running east to Namur.   Indeed, for a short space
they had this road at their mercy, and the chance
within grasp of doubling up our left by means of it.

This happened, I say, just as we arrived; and
Wellington, who had reached Quatre Bras a short
while ahead of us (having fetched a circuit from
Brussels through Ligny, where he paused to inspect Field-Marshal Blücher's dispositions for
battle), at once saw the danger, and detached one
of our regiments, the 95th Rifles, to drive back the
tirailleurs from the thicket; which, albeit scarcely
breathed after their march, they did with a will,
and so regained the Allies' hold upon the Namur
road.   The rest of us meanwhile defiled down this
same road, formed line in front of it, and under a
brisk cannonade from the French heights waited
for the next move.

It was not long in coming.   Ney, finding that
our artillery made poor play against his, prepared
to launch a column against us.   Warned by a
cloud of skirmishers, our light companies leapt for-

ward, chose their shelter, and began a very pretty exchange of musketry. But this was preliminary work only, and soon the head of a large French column appeared on the slope to our right, driving the Brunswickers slowly before it. It descended a little way, and suddenly broke into three or four columns of attack. The mischief no sooner threatened than Picton came galloping along our line and roaring that our division would advance and engage with all speed. For a raw regiment like the Morays this was no light test; but, supported by a veteran regiment on either hand, they bore it admirably. Dropping the Gordons to protect the road in case of mishap, the two brigades swung forward in the prettiest style, their skirmishers running in and forming on either flank as they advanced. Then for a while the work was hot; but, as will always happen when column is boldly met by line, the French quickly had enough of our enveloping fire, and wavered. A short charge with the bayonet finished it, and drove them in confusion up the slope: nor had I an easy task to resume a hold on my youngsters and restrain them from pursuing too far. The brush had been sharp, but I had the satisfaction of knowing that the Morays had behaved well. They also knew it, and fell to jesting in high good-humour as General Pack withdrew the brigade from the ground of its exploit and posted us in line with the 42nd and 44th regiments on the left of the main road to Charleroi.

To the right of the Charleroi road, and some way in advance of our position, the Brunswickers were holding ground as best they could under a hot and accurate artillery fire. Except for this, the battle had come to a lull, when a second mass of the enemy began to move down the slopes: a battalion in line heading two columns of infantry direct upon the Brunswickers, while squadron after squadron of lancers crowded down along the road into which by weight of numbers they must be driven. The Duke of Brunswick, perceiving his peril, headed a charge of his lancers upon the advancing infantry, but without the least effect. His horsemen broke. He rode back and called on his infantry to retire in good order. They also broke, and in the attempt to rally them he fell mortally wounded.

The line taken by these flying Brunswickers would have brought them diagonally across the Charleroi road into our arms, had not the French lancers seized this moment to charge straight down it in a body. They encountered, and the indiscriminate mass was hurled on to us, choking and overflowing the causeway. In a minute we were swamped—the two Highland regiments. and the 44th bending against a sheer weight of French horsemen. So suddenly came the shock that the 42nd had no time to form square, until two companies were cut off and well-nigh destroyed; *then* that noble regiment formed around the horsemen who could boast of having broken it, and left not one to bear back the tale. The 44th behaved more cleverly, but not more intrepidly: it did not attempt to form square, but faced its rear rank round and gave the Frenchmen a volley; before they could check their impetus the front rank poured in a second; and the light company, which had held its fire, delivered a third, breaking the crowd in two, and driving the hinder-part back in disorder and up the Charleroi road. But already the fore-part had fallen upon the Morays, fortunately the last of the three regiments to receive the shock. Though most fortunate, they had least experience, and were consequently slow in answering my shout. A wedge of lancers broke through us as we formed around the two standards, and I saw Mr. Urquhart with the King's colours hurled back in the rush. The pole fell with him, after swaying within a yard of a French lancer, who thrust out an arm to grasp it. And with that I saw Mackenzie divide the rush and stand—it may have been for five seconds—erect, with his foot upon the standard. Then three lancers pierced him, and he fell. But the lateral pressure of their own troopers broke the wedge which the French had pushed into us. Their leading squadrons were pressed down the road and afterwards accounted for by the Gordons. Of the seven-and-twenty assailants around whom the Morays now closed, not one survived.

Towards nightfall, as Ney weakened and the Allies were reinforced, our troops pushed forward and recaptured every important position taken by the French that morning. The Morays, with the rest of Picton's division, bivouacked for the night in and around the farmstead of Gemiancourt.

So obstinately had the field been contested that darkness fell before the wounded could be collected with any thoroughness; and the comfort of the men around many a camp-fire was disturbed by groans (often quite near at hand) of some poor comrade or enemy lying helpless and undiscovered, or exerting his shattered limbs to crawl towards the blaze. And these interruptions at length became so distressing to the Morays, that two or three officers sought me and demanded leave to form a fatigue party of volunteers and explore the hedges and thickets with lanterns. Among them was

Mr. Urquhart: and having readily given leave and accompanied them some little way on their search, I was bidding them good-night and good-speed when I found him standing at my elbow.

"May I have a word with you, Colonel?" he asked.

His voice was low and serious. Of course I knew what subject filled his thoughts. "Is it worth while, sir?" I answered. "I have lost to-day a brave lad for whom I had a great affection. For him the account is closed; but not for those who liked him and are still concerned in his good name. If you have anything further against him, or if you have any confession to make, I warn you that this is a bad moment to choose."

"I have only to ask," said he, "that you will grant me the first convenient hour for explaining; and to remind you that when I besought you not to send him into action to-day, I had no time to give you reasons."

"This is extraordinary talk, sir. I am not used to command the Morays under advice from my subalterns. And in this instance I had reasons for not even listening to you." He was silent. "Moreover," I continued, "you may as well know, though I am under no obligation to tell you, that I do most certainly not regret having given that permission to one who justified it by a signal service to his king and country."

"But would you have sent him *knowing* that he must die? Colonel," he went on rapidly, before I could interrupt, "I beseech you to listen. I *knew* he had only a few hours to live. I saw his wraith last night. It stood behind his shoulder in the room when in Captain Murray's presence he challenged me to fight him. You are a Highlander, sir: you may be sceptical about the second sight; but at least you must have heard many claim it. I swear positively that I saw Mr. Mackenzie's wraith last night, and for that reason, and no other, tried to defer the meeting. To fight him, knowing he must die, seemed to me as bad as murder. Afterwards, when the alarm sounded and you took off his arrest, I knew that his fate must overtake him—that my refusal had done no good. I tried to interfere again, and you would not hear. Naturally you would not hear; and very likely, if you had, his fate would have found him in some other way. That is what I try to believe. I hope it is not selfish, sir; but the doubt tortures me."

"Mr. Urquhart," I asked, "is this the only occasion on which you have possessed the second sight, or had reason to think so?"

"No, sir."

" Was it the first or only time last night you believed you were granted it? "

" It was the *second* time last night," he said
steadily.

We had been walking back to my bivouac fire,
and in the light of it I turned and said: " I will
hear your story at the first opportunity. I will
not promise to believe, but I will hear and weigh
it. Go now and join the others in their search."

He saluted, and strode away into the darkness.
The opportunity I promised him never came. At
eleven o'clock next morning we began our with-
drawal, and within twenty-four hours the battle
of Waterloo had begun. In one of the most heroic
feats of that day—the famous resistance of Pack's
brigade—Mr. Urquhart was among the first to
fall.

III

THUS it happened that an affair which so nearly
touched the honour of the Morays, and which had
been agitating me at the very moment when the
bugle sounded in the Place d'Armes, became a
secret shared by three only. The regiment joined
in the occupation of Paris, and did not return to
Scotland until the middle of December.

I had ceased to mourn for Mr. Mackenzie, but

neither to regret him nor to speculate on the mystery which closed his career, and which, now that death had sealed Mr. Urquhart's lips, I could no longer hope to penetrate, when, on the day of my return to Inverness, I was reminded of him by finding, among the letters and papers awaiting me, a visiting-card neatly indited with the name of the Reverend Samuel Saul. On inquiry I learnt that the minister had paid at least three visits to Inverness during the past fortnight, and had, on each occasion, shown much anxiety to learn when the battalion might be expected. He had also left word that he wished to see me on a matter of much importance.

Sure enough, at ten o'clock next morning the little man presented himself. He was clearly bursting to disclose his business, and our salutations were scarce over when he ran to the door and called to some one in the passage outside.

"Elspeth! Step inside, woman. The housekeeper, sir, to the late Mr. Mackenzie of Ardlaugh," he explained, as he held the door to admit her.

She was dressed in ragged mourning, and wore a grotesque and fearful bonnet. As she saluted me respectfully I saw that her eyes indeed were dry and even hard, but her features set in an expression of quiet and hopeless misery. She did not speak, but left explanation to the minister.

"You will guess, sir," began Mr. Saul, "that we have called to learn more of the poor lad." And he paused.

"He died most gallantly," said I: "died in the act of saving the colours. No soldier could have wished for a better end."

"To be sure, to be sure. So it was reported to us. He died, as one might say, without a stain on his character?" said Mr. Saul, with a sort of question in his tone.

"He died," I answered, "in a way which could only do credit to his name."

A somewhat constrained silence followed. The woman broke it. "You are not telling us all," she said, in a slow, harsh voice.

It took me aback. "I am telling all that needs to be known," I assured her.

"No doubt, sir, no doubt," Mr. Saul interjected. "Hold your tongue, woman. I am going to tell Colonel Ross a tale which may or may not bear upon anything he knows. If not, he will interrupt me before I go far; but if he says nothing I shall take it I have his leave to continue. Now, sir, on the 16th day of June last, and at six in the morning—that would be the day of Quatre Bras——"

He paused for me to nod assent, and continued. "At six in the morning or a little earlier, this woman, Elspeth Mackenzie, came to me at the Manse in great perturbation. She had walked all the way from Ardlaugh. It had come to her (she said) that the young Laird abroad was in great trouble since the previous evening. I asked, 'What trouble? Was it danger of life, for instance?'—asking it not seriously, but rather to compose her; for at first I set down her fears to an old woman's whimsies. Not that I would call Elspeth *old* precisely——"

Here he broke off and glanced at her; but, perceiving she paid little attention, went on again at a gallop. "She answered that it was worse—that the young Laird stood very near disgrace, and (the worst of all was) at a distance she could not help him. Now, sir, for reasons I shall hereafter tell you, Mr. Mackenzie's being in disgrace would have little surprised me; but that she should know of it, he being in Belgium, was incredible. So I pressed her, and she being distraught and (I verily believe) in something like anguish, came out with a most extraordinary story: to wit, that the Laird of Ardlaugh had in his service, unbeknown to him (but, as she protested, well known to her), a familiar spirit—or, as we should say commonly, a 'brownie'—which in general served him most faithfully but at times erratically, having no conscience nor any Christian principle to direct him. I cautioned her, but she persisted, in a kind of wild terror, and added that at times the spirit would, in all good faith, do things which no Christian allowed to be permissible, and further, that she had profited by such actions. I asked her, ' Was thieving one of them? ' She answered that it was, and indeed the chief.

"Now, this was an admission which gave me some eagerness to hear more. For to my knowledge there were charges lying against young Mr. Mackenzie—though not pronounced—which pointed to a thief in his employment and presumably in his confidence. You will remember, sir, that when I had the honour of meeting you at Mr. Mackenzie's table, I took my leave with much abruptness. You remarked upon it, no doubt. But you will no longer think it strange when I tell you that there—under my nose—were a dozen apples of a sort which grows nowhere within twenty miles of Ardlaugh but in my own Manse garden. The tree was a new one, obtained from Herefordshire, and planted three seasons before as

an experiment. I had watched it, therefore, particularly; and on that very morning had counted
the fruit, and been dismayed to find twelve apples
missing. Further, I am a pretty good judge of
wine (though I taste it rarely), and could there and
then have taken my oath that the claret our host
set before us was the very wine I had tasted at the
table of his neighbour Mr. Gillespie. As for the
venison—I had already heard whispers that deer
and all game were not safe within a mile or two of
Ardlaugh. These were injurious tales, sir, which
I had no mind to believe; for, bating his religion,
I saw everything in Mr. Mackenzie which disposed
me to like him. But I knew (as neighbours must)
of the shortness of his purse; and the multiplied
evidence (particularly my own Goodrich pippins
staring me in the face) overwhelmed me for a
moment.

"So then, I listened to this woman's tale with
more patience—or, let me say, more curiosity—
than you, sir, might have given it. She persisted,
I say, that her master was in trouble; and that the
trouble had something to do with a game of cards,
but that Mr. Mackenzie had been innocent of
deceit, and the real culprit was this spirit I tell
of——"

Here the woman herself broke in upon Mr.

Saul. " He had nae conscience—he had nae conscience. He was just a poor luck-child, born by
mischance and put away without baptism. He had
nae conscience. How should he? "

I looked from her to Mr. Saul in perplexity.

" Whist! " said he; " we'll talk of that anon."

" We will not," said she. " We will talk of it
now. He was my own child, sir, by the young
Laird's own father. That was before he was
married upon the wife he took later——"

Here Mr. Saul nudged me, and whispered:
" The old Laird had her married to that daun-
derin' old half-wit Duncan, to cover things up.
This part of the tale is true enough, to my knowledge."

" My bairn was overlaid, sir," the woman went
on; " not by purpose, I will swear before you and
God. They buried his poor body without baptism; but not his poor soul. Only when the young
Laird came, and my own bairn clave to him as
Mackenzie to Mackenzie, and wrought and hunted
and mended for him—it was not to be thought that
the poor innocent, without knowledge of God's
ways——"

She ran on incoherently, while my thoughts
harked back to the voice I had heard wailing
behind the door of the *entresol* at Brussels; to

the young Laird's face, his furious indignation, followed by hopeless apathy, as of one who in the interval had learnt what he could never explain; to the marked coin so mysteriously spirited from sight; to Mr. Urquhart's words before he left me on the night of Quatre Bras.

"But he was sorry," the woman ran on; "he was sorry—sorry. He came wailing to me that night; yes, and sobbing. He meant no wrong; it was just that he loved his own father's son, and knew no better. There was no priest living within thirty miles; so I dressed, and ran to the minister here. He gave me no rest until I started."

I addressed Mr. Saul. "Is there reason to suppose that, besides this woman and (let us say) her accomplice, any one shared the secret of these pilferings?"

"Ardlaugh never knew," put in the woman quickly. "He may have guessed we were helping him; but the lad knew nothing, and may the saints in heaven love him as they ought! He trusted me with his purse, and slight it was to maintain him. But until too late, he never knew —no, never, sir!"

I thought again of that voice behind the door of the *entresol*.

"Elspeth Mackenzie," I said, "I and two other

living men alone know of what your master was accused. It cannot affect him; but these two shall hear your exculpation of him. And I will write the whole story down, so that the world, if it ever hears the charge, may also hear your testimony, which of the two (though both are strange) I believe to be not the less credible."

THREE MEN OF BADAJOS

I

You enter the village of Gantick between two round-houses set one on each side of the high road where it dips steeply towards the valley bottom. On the west of the opposite hill the road passes out between another pair of round-houses. And down in the heart of the village among the elms facing the churchyard lych-gate stands a fifth, alone.

The five, therefore, form an elongated St. Andrew's cross; but nobody can tell for certain who built them, or why. They are all alike; each built of cob, circular, whitewashed, having pointed windows and a conical roof of thatch with a wooden cross on the apex. When I was a boy these thatched roofs used to be pointed out to me as masterpieces; and they still endure. But the race of skilled thatchers, once the peculiar pride of Gantick, has come to an end. What time has eaten modern and clumsy hands have tried to repair; yet a glance will tell you that the old sound work means to outwear the patches.

THREE MEN OF BADAJOS

The last of these famous thatchers lived in the round-house on your right as you leave Gantick by the seaward road. His name was old Nat Ellery, or Thatcher Ellery, and his age (as I remember him) between seventy or eighty. Yet he clung to his work, being one of those lean men upon whom age, exposure, and even drink take a long while to tell. For he drank; not socially at the Ring of Bells, but at home in solitude with a black bottle at his elbow. He lived there alone; his neighbours, even of the round-house across the road, shunned him and were shunned by him: children would run rather than meet him on the road as he came along, striding swiftly for his age (the drink never affected his legs), ready greaved and sometimes gauntleted as if in haste for his job, always muttering to himself; and when he passed us with just a side-glance from his red eyes, we observed that his pale face did not cease to twitch nor his lips to work. We felt something like awe for the courage of Archie Passmore, who followed twenty paces behind with his tools and a bundle of spars or straw-rope, or perhaps at the end of a ladder which the two carried between them. Archie (aged sixteen) used to boast to us that he did not fear the old man a ha'penny; and the old man treated Archie as a Gibeonite, a hewer of wood, a drawer

of water, never as an apprentice. Of his craft, except what he picked up by watching, the lad
learned nothing.

What made him so vaguely terrible to us was
the common rumour in the village that Thatcher
Ellery had served once under his Majesty's colours,
but had deserted and was still liable to be taken
and shot for it. Now this was true and everyone
knew it, though why and how he had deserted were
questions answered among us only by dark and
frightful guesses. He had outlived all risk of the
law's revenge; no one, it was certain, would take
the trouble to seize and execute justice upon a
drunkard of seventy. But we children never
thought of this, and for us as we watched him
down the road there was always the thrilling
chance that over the hedge or around the next corner would pop up a squad of redcoats. Some of
us had even seen it, in dreams.

II

This is the story of Thatcher Ellery as it was
told to me after his death, which happened one
night a few weeks before I came home from school
on my first summer holidays.

His father, in the early years of the century,
had kept the mill up at Trethake Water, two miles

above Gantick. There were two sons, of whom Reub, the elder, succeeded to the mill. Nat had been apprenticed to the thatching. Accident of birth assigned to the two these different walks of life, but by taking thought their parents could not have chosen more wisely, for Nat was born clever, with an ambition to cut a figure in man's eyes and just that sense of finish and the need of it which makes the good workman. Whereas his brother went the daily round at home as contentedly as a horse at a cider press. But Nat made the mistake of lodging under his father's roof, and his mother made the worse mistake of liking her first-born the better and openly showing it. Nat, jealous and sensitive by nature, came to imagine the whole world against him, and Reub, who had no vice beyond a large thick-witted selfishness, seemed to make a habit of treading on his corns. At length came the explosion: a sudden furious assault which sent Reub souse into the paternal mill-leat.

The mother cursed Nat forth from the door, and no doubt said a great deal more than she meant. The boy—he was just seventeen—carried his box down to the Ring of Bells. Next morning as he sat viciously driving in spars astride on a rick ridge, whence he could see far over the Channel, there came into sight round Derryman's Point a ship-of-war, running before the strong easterly breeze with piled canvas, white stun-sails bellying, and a fine froth of white water running off her bluff bows. Another ship followed, and another—at length a squadron of six. Nat watched them from time to time until they trimmed sails and stood in for Falmouth. Then he climbed down from the rick and put on his coat.

Two years later he landed at Portsmouth, heartily sick of the sea and all belonging to it. He drank himself silly that night and for ten nights following, and one morning found himself in the streets without a penny. Portsmouth just then (July, 1808) was filled with troops embarking under Sir John Moore for Portugal. One regiment especially took Nat's eye—the 4th or King's Own, and indeed the whole service contained no finer body of men. He sidled up to a corporal and gave a false name. Varcoe had been his mother's maiden name, and it came handy. The corporal took him to a recruiting sergeant and handed him over with a wink. The recruiting sergeant asked a few convenient questions, and within the hour Nat was a soldier of King George. To his disgust, however, they did not embark him for Portugal, but marched him up the length of England to Lancaster, to learn his drill with the second battalion.

Seventeen months later they marched him back through the length of England—outwardly a made soldier—and shipped him on a transport for Gibraltar. In the meanwhile he had found two friends, the only two real ones he ever found in his life. They were Dave McInnes and Teddy Butson, privates of the 4th Regiment of Foot, 2nd Battalion, C Company. Dave McInnes came from somewhere to the west of Perth and drank like a fish when he had the chance. Teddy Butson came from the Lord knew where, with a tongue that wagged about everything except his own past. It did indeed wag about that, but told nothing but lies which were understood and accepted for lies and by consequence didn't count. These two had christened Nat Ellery " Spuds." He had no secret from them but one.

He was the cleverest of the three, and they admired him for it. He admired them in return for possessing something he lacked. It seemed to him the most important, almost the only important, thing in the world.

For (this was his secret) he believed himself to be a coward. He was not really a coward, though he carried about in his heart the liveliest fear of death and wounds. He was always asking himself how he would behave under fire, and somehow

73

he found the odds heavy against his behaving well.
He put roundabout questions to Dave and Teddy
with the aim of discovering what they felt about
it. They answered in a careless, matter-of-fact
way, as men to whom it had never occurred to
have any doubt about themselves. Nat was desperately afraid they might guess his reason for
asking. Just here, when their friendship might
have been helpful, it failed altogether. He felt
angry with them for not understanding, while he
prayed that they might not understand. He took
to observing other men in the regiment, and found
them equally cheerful, concerned only with the
moment. He became secretly religious after a
fashion. He felt that he was the one and only
coward in the King's Own, and prayed and planned
his behaviour day and night to avoid being found
out.

In this state of mind he landed at Gibraltar.
When the order came for the 4th to move up to
the front, he cheered with the rest, watching their
faces.

III

At ten o'clock on the night of April 6th, 1812, our troops were to assault Badajos. It was now a few minutes past nine.

The night had closed in without rain, but cloudy and thick, with river fog. The moon would not rise for another hour or more. After the day's furious bombardment silence had fallen on besieged and besiegers; but now and then a light flitted upon the ramparts, and at intervals the British in the trenches could hear the call of a sentinel proclaiming that all was well in Badajos.

In the trenches a low continuous murmur mingled with the voices of running water. On the right by the Guadiana waited Picton's Third Division, breathing hard as the time drew nearer. Kempt commanded these for the moment. Picton was in camp attending to a hurt, but his men knew that before ten o'clock he would arrive to lead across the Rivillas by the narrow bridge and up to the walls of the Castle frowning over the river at the city's north-east corner.

In the centre and over against the wall to the left of the Castle were assembled Colville's and Barnard's men of the Fourth and Light Divisions. Theirs, according to the General's plan, was to be

the main business to-night—to carry the breaches
hammered in the Trinidad and Santa Maria bastions and the curtain between; the Fourth told off
for the Trinidad and the curtain, the Light Bobs
for the Santa Maria—heroes these of Moore's
famous rear-guard, tried men of the 52nd Foot and
the 95th Rifles, with the 43rd beside them, and
destined to pay the heaviest price of all to-night
for the glory of such comradeship. But, indeed,
Ciudad Rodrigo had given the 43rd a title to stand
among the best.

And far away to the left, on the lower slopes of
the hills, Leigh's Fifth Division was halted in deep
columns. A knoll separated his two brigades, and
across the interval of darkness they could hear
each other's movements. They were to operate
independently; and concerning the task before the
brigade on the right there could be no doubt: a
dash across the gorge at their feet, and an assault
upon the outlying Pardaleras, on the opposite slope.
But the business before Walker's brigade, on the
left, was by no means so simple. The storming
party had been marching light, with two companies of Portuguese to carry their ladders, and
stood discussing prospects: for as yet they were
well out of earshot of the walls, and the moment
for strict silence had not arrived.

" The Vincenty," grumbled Teddy Butson; " and by shot to me if I even know what it's like."

" Like!" McInnes' jaws shut on the word like a steel trap. " The scarp's thirty feet high, and the ditch accordin'. The last on the west side it will be—over by the river. I know it like your face, and its uglier, if that's possible."

" Dick Webster was saying it's mined," put in Nat, commanding a firm voice.

" Eh? The glacis? I shouldn't wonder. Walker will know."

" But what'll he do?"

" Well, now "—Dave seemed to be considering —" it will not be for the likes of me to be telling the brigadier-general. But if Walker comes to me and says, ' Dave, there's a mine hereabouts. What will I be doing?' it's like enough I shall say: ' Your honour knows best; but the usual course is to walk round it.' "

Teddy Butson chuckled, and rubbed the back of his axe approvingly. Nat held his tongue for a minute almost, and then broke out irritably: " To hell with this waiting!"

His nerves were raw. Two minutes later a man on his right kicked awkwardly against his foot. It startled him, and he cursed furiously.

" Hold hard, Spuds, my boy," said the man

cheerfully; " you ain't Lord Wellington, nor his next-of-kin, to be makin' all the noise."

Teddy Butson wagged his head solemnly at a light which showed foggily for a moment on the distant ramparts.

" All right," said he, " you——town! Little you know 'tis Teddy's birthday."

" There will be wine," said Dave, dreamily.

" Lashins of it; wine and women, and loot things. I wonder how our boys are feeling on the right? What's that?"—as a light shot up over the ridge to the eastward. " Wish I could see what's doing over there. My belief we're only put up for a feint."

" O hush it, you royal mill-clappers! " This came from the darkness behind—from some man of the 30th, no doubt.

The voice was tense, with a note of nervousness in it, which Nat recognised at once. He turned with a sudden desire to see the speaker's face. Here was one who felt as he did, one who could understand him, but his eyes sought in vain among the lines of glimmering black shakos.

" Silence in the ranks! " Two officers came forward, talking together and pausing to watch the curious light now rising and sinking and rising again in the sky over the eastern ridges. " They

must have caught sight of our fellows—listen,
wasn't that a cheer? What time is it?" The
officer was Captain Hopkins commanding Nat's
Company, but now in charge of the stormers. A
voice hailed him, and he ran back. "Yes, sir, I
think so decidedly," Nat heard him saying, and he
came running clutching his sword sheath. "Silence men—the brigade will advance."

The Portuguese picked up and shouldered their
ladders: the orders were given, and the columns
began to move down the slope. For a while they
could hear the tramp of the other brigade moving
parallel with them on the other side of the knoll,
then fainter and fainter as it wheeled aside and
down the gorge to the right. At the foot of the
slope they opened a view up the gorge lit for a moment by a flare burning on the ramparts of the
Pardaleras, and saw their comrades moving down
and across the bottom like a stream of red lava
pouring towards the foot. The flare died down
and our brigade struck away to the left over the
level country. On this side Badajos remained dark
and silent.

They were marching quickly, yet the pace did
not satisfy Nat. He wanted to be through with it,
to come face to face with the worst and know it.
And yet he feared it abominably. For two years

he had contrived to hide his secret. He had marched, counter-marched, fed, slept, and fought with his comrades; had dodged with them behind cover, loaded, fired, charged with them; had behaved outwardly like a decent soldier, but almost always with a sickening void in the pit of the stomach. Once or twice in particularly bad moments he had caught himself blubbering, and with a deadly shame. He had not an idea that at least a dozen of his comrades—among them Dave and Teddy—had seen it, and thought nothing of it; still less did he imagine that those had been his most courageous moments. Soldiers fight differently. Teddy Butson, for instance, talked all the time until his tongue swelled, and then he barked like a dog. Dave shut his teeth and groaned. But these symptoms escaped Nat, whose habit was to think all the while of himself. Of one thing he felt sure, that he had never yet been anything but glad to hear the recall sounded.

Well, so far he had escaped. Heaven knew how he had managed it; he only knew that the last two years had been as long as fifty, and he seemed to have been living since the beginning of the world. But here he was, and actually keeping step with a storming party. He kept his eyes on Dave's long lean back immediately in front and trudged on, divided between an insane desire to know of what Dave was thinking, and an equally insane wonder what Dave's body might be worth to him as cover.

What was the silly word capering in his head? " Mill-clappers." Why on earth " Mill-clappers? " It put him in mind of home: but he had no silly tender thoughts to waste on home, or the folks there. He had never written to them. If they should happen on the copy of the *Gazette*—and the chances were hundred to one against it—the name of Nathaniel Varcoe among the killed or wounded would mean nothing to them. He tramped on, chewing his fancy, and extracted this from it: " A man with never a friend at home hasn't even an excuse to be a coward, curse it! "

Suddenly the column halted, in a bank of fog through which his ear caught the lazy ripple of water. He woke up with a start. The fog was all about them.

" What's this? " he demanded aloud; then, with a catch of his breath, " Mines? "

" Eh, be quiet," said Teddy Butson at his elbow; " listen to yonder." And the word was hardly out when an explosion split the sky and was followed by peal after peal of musketry. Nat had a swift vision of a high black wall against a background

of flame, and then night came down again as you
might close a shutter. But the musketry continued. "That will be at the breaches," Dave flung
the words over his left shoulder. Then followed
another flash and another explosion. This time,
however, the light, though less vivid than the first
flash, did not vanish. While he wondered at this
Nat saw first of all the rim of the moon through
the slant of an embrasure, and then Teddy's pale
but cheerful face.

The head of the column had been halted a few
yards only from a breastwork, with a stockade above
it and a *chevaux de frise* on top of all. As far as
knowledge of his whereabouts went, Nat might
have been east, west, north or south of Badajos,
or somewhere in another planet. But the past two
years had somehow taught him to divine that behind this ugly obstruction lay a covered way with
a guard house. And sure enough the men, keeping dead silence now, could hear the French soldiers chatting in that unseen guard house and
laughing.

"Now's the time." Nat heard the word passed
back by the young engineer officer who had crept
forward to reconnoitre: and then an order given
in Portuguese.

"Ay, bring up the ladders, you greasers, and

let's put it through." This from Teddy Butson chafing by Nat's side.

The two Portuguese companies came forward with the ladders as the storming party moved up to the gateway. And just at that moment there the sentry let off his alarm shot. It set all within the San Vincente bastion moving and whirring like the works of a mechanical toy; feet came running along the covered way; muskets clinked on the stone parapet; tongues of fire spat forth from the embrasures; and then, as the musketry quickened, a flash and a roar lifted the glacis away behind, to the right of our column, so near that the wind of it drove our men sideways.

" All right, Johnny," Dave grunted, recovering himself as the clods of earth began to fall: " Blaze away, my silly ducks—we're not there! "

But the Portuguese companies as the mine exploded cast down the ladders and ran. Half a dozen came charging back along the column's right flank, and our soldiers cursed and struck at them as they fled. But the curses were as nothing beside those of the Portuguese officers striving to rally their men.

" My word," said Teddy. " Hear them scandalous greasers! It's poor talk, is English."

" On with you, lads "—it was Walker himself

who shouted. " Pick up the ladders, and on with you! "

They hardly waited for the word, but, shouldering the ladders, ran forward through the dropping bullets to the gate, cheering and cheered by the rear ranks.

But they flung themselves in vain on the gate. On its iron-bound and iron-studded framework their axes made no impression. A dozen men charged it, using a ladder as a battering ram. " Aisy with that, ye blind ijjits! " yelled an Irish sergeant. " Ye'll be needin' them ladders prisintly! " Our three privates found themselves in the crowd surging towards the breastwork to the right of the gate. " Nip on my shoulders, Teddy lad," grunted McInnes, and Teddy nipped up and began hacking at the *chevaux de frise* with his axe. " That's av ut, bhoys," yelled the Irish sergeant again. " Lave them spoikes an' go for the stockade. Good for you, little man—whirro! " Nat by this time was on a comrade's back, and using his axe for dear life; one of twenty men hacking, ripping, tearing down the wooden stakes. But it was Teddy who wriggled through first with Dave at his heels. The man beneath Nat gave a heave with his shoulders and shot him through his gap, a splinter tearing his cheek open. He fell head foremost, sprawling down the slippery slope of the ditch.

While he picked himself up and stretched out a hand to recover his axe a bullet struck the blade of it—ping! He caught up the axe and ran his finger over it stupidly. Phut—another bullet spat into the soft earth behind his shoulder. Then he understood. A fellow came tumbling through the gap, pitched exactly where Nat had been sprawling a moment before, rose to his knees, and then with a quiet bubbling sound lay down again.

"Ugh! he would be killed—he must get out of this!" But there was no cover unless he found it across the ditch and close under the high stone curtain. They would be dropping stones, beams, fire barrels; but at least he would be out of the reach of the bullets. He forgot the chance—the certainty—of an enfilading fire from the two bastions. His one desire was to get across and pick some place of shelter.

But by this time the men were pouring in behind and fast filling the ditch. A fire-ball came crashing over the rampart, rolled down the grass slope and lay sputtering, and in the infernal glare he saw all his comrades' faces—every detail of their dress down to the moulded pattern on their buttons. "Fourth! Fourth!" some one shouted, and then

voice and vision were caught up and drowned together in a hell of musketry. He must win across
or be carried he knew not where by the brute pressure of the crowd. A cry broke from him and he
ran, waving his axe, plunged down the slope and
across. On the further slope an officer caught him
up and scrambled beside him. " Whirro, Spuds!
After him, boys! " sang out Teddy Butson. But
Spuds did not hear.

He and the officer were at the top of the turf—
at the foot of the curtain. " Ladders! Ladders! "
He caught hold of the first as it was pushed up and
helped—now the centre of a small crowd—to plant
it against the wall. Then he fell back, mopping
his forehead, and feeling his torn cheek. What
the devil were they groaning at? Short? The
ladder too short? He stared up foolishly. The
wall was thirty feet high perhaps and the ladder
ten feet short of that or more. " Heads! " A heavy
beam crashed down, snapping the foot of the ladder
like a cabbage stump. Away to the left a group
of men were planting another. Half a dozen
dropped while he watched them. Why in the
world were they dropping like that? He stared
beyond and saw the reason. The French marks-
men in the bastion were sweeping the face of the
curtain with their cross fire—those cursed bullets

again! And the ladder did not reach, after all. O, it was foolishness—flinging away men like this for no earthly good! Why not throw up the business and go home? Why didn't somebody stop those silly bugles sounding the Advance?

There they went again! It was enough to drive a man mad!

He turned and ran down the slope a short way. For the moment he held a grip on himself, but it was slackening, and in another half-minute he would have lost it and run in mere blind horror. But in the first group he blundered upon were Dave and Teddy, and a score of the King's Own, with a couple of ladders between them; and better still, they were listening to Captain Hopkins, who waved an arm and pointed to an embrasure to the left. Nat, pulling himself up and staring with the rest, saw that no gun stood in this embrasure, only a gabion. In a moment he was climbing the slope again; if a man must die, there's comfort at least in company. He bore a hand in planting the two ladders; a third was fetched—heaven knew whence or how—and planted beside them, and up the men swarmed, three abreast, Dave leading on the right-hand one, at the foot of which Nat hung back and swayed. He heard Dave's long sigh, the sigh, the sob almost, of desire answered at last. He watched him as he mounted. The ladders were still too short, and the leader on each must climb on the second man's shoulders to get hand-hold on the coping. In that moment he might be clubbed on the head, defenceless. On the middle ladder a young officer of the 30th mounted by Dave's side. Nat turned his head away, and as he did so a rush of men, galled by the fire from the bastion to the right, came on him like a wave, and swept him up the first four rungs.

He was in for it now. Go back he could not, and he followed the tall Royal ahead, whose heels scraped against his breast buttons, and once or twice bruised him in the face; followed up, wondering what face of death would meet him at the top, where men were yelling and jabbering in three languages—French, English, and that tongue which belongs equally to men and brutes at close quarters and killing.

Something came sliding down the ladder. The man in front of Nat ducked his head; Nat ducked too; but the body slid sideways before it reached them and dropped plumb—the inert lump which had been Dave McInnes. His shako, spinning straight down the ladder, struck Nat on the shoulder and leaped off it down into darkness.

He saw other men drop; he saw Teddy Butson

parallel with him on the far ladder, and mounting with him step for step—now earlier, now later, but level with him most of the time. They would meet at the embrasure; find together whatever waited for them there. Nat was sobbing by this time—sweat and tears together running down the caked blood on his cheek—but he did not know it.

He had almost reached the top when a sudden pressure above forced his feet off the rung and his body over the ladder's side; and there he dangled, hooked by his armpit. Someone grabbed his leg, and, pulling him into place, thrust him up over the shoulders of the tall Royal in front. He saw the leader on the middle ladder go down under a clubbed blow which burst through his japanned shako-cover, and then a hand came down to help him.

" Spuds, O Spuds! "

It was Teddy reaching down from the coping to help him, and he paid for it with his life. The two wriggled into the embrasure together, Nat's head and shoulders under Teddy's right arm. Nat did not see the bayonet thrust given, but heard a low grunt, as he and his friend's corpse toppled over the coping together and into Badajos.

He rose on his knees, caught a man by the leg, flung him, and as the fellow clutched his musket, wrenched the bayonet from it and plunged it into his body. While the Frenchman heaved, he pulled out the weapon for another stab, dropped sprawling on his enemy's chest, and the first wave of the storming party broke over him, beating the breath out of him, and passed on.

Yet he managed to wriggle his body from under this rush of feet, and, by-and-bye, to raise himself, still grasping the sidearm. Men of the 4th were pouring thick and fast through the embrasure, and turning to the right in pursuit of the enemy now running along the curve of the ramparts. A few only pressed straight forward to silence the musketry jetting and crackling from the upper windows of two houses facing on the fortifications.

Nat staggered down after them, but turned as soon as he gained the roadway, and, passing to the right, plunged down a black side street. An insane notion possessed him of taking the two houses in the rear, and as he went he shouted to the 4th to follow him. No one paid him the smallest attention, and presently he was alone in the darkness, rolling like a drunkard, shaken by his sobs, but still shouting and brandishing his sidearm. He clattered against a high blank wall.

Still he lurched forward over uneven cobbles. He had forgotten his design upon the two houses, but a light shone at the end of this dark lane, and he made for it, gained it, and found himself in a wider street. And there the enchantment fell on him.

For the street was empty, utterly empty, yet brilliantly illuminated. Not a soul could he see: yet in house after house as he passed lights shone from every window, in the lower floors behind blinds or curtains which hid the inmates. It was as if Badajos had arrayed itself for a fête; and still, as he staggered forward a low buzz, a whisper of voices surrounded him, and now and again at the sound of his footstep on the cobbles a lattice would open gently and be as gently re-shut. Hundreds of eyes were peering at him, the one British soldier in a bewitched city; hundreds of unseen eyes, stealthy, expectant. And always ahead of him, faint and distant, sounded the bugles and the yells around the Trinidad and the breaches.

He stood alone in the great square. While he paused at the corner, his eyes following the rows of mysterious lights from house to house, from storey to storey, the regular tramp of feet fell on his ears and a company of Foot marched down into the moonlight patch facing him and grounded arms with a clatter. They were men of his own regiment, and they formed up in the moonlight like a company of ghosts. One or two shots were fired at them, low down, from the sills of a line of door-ways to his right; but no citizen showed himself and no one appeared to be hit. And ever from the direction of the Trinidad came the low roar of combat and the high notes of the bugles.

He was creeping along the side of the square towards an outlet at its north-east corner, when the company got into motion again and came towards him. Then he turned up a narrow lane to the left and fled. He was sobbing no longer; the passion had died out of him, and he knew himself to be mad. In the darkness the silent streets began to fill; random shots whistled at every street corner; but he blundered on, taking no account of them. Once he ran against a body of Picton's men—half a score of the 74th Regiment let loose at length from the captured Castle, and burning for loot. One man thrust the muzzle of his musket against his breast before he was recognized. Then two or three shook hands with him.

He was back in the square again and fighting—Heaven knew why—with an officer of the Bruns-wickers over a birdcage. Whence the birdcage came he had no clear idea, but there was a canary-bird inside, and he wanted it. A random shot smashed his left hand as he gripped the cage, and he dropped it as something with which he had no further concern. As he turned away, hugging his hand, and cursing the marksman, a second shot from another direction took the Brunswicker between the shoulders.

At dawn he found himself on the ramparts by the Trinidad breach, peering curiously among the slain. Across the top of the breach stretched a heavy beam studded with sword blades, and all the bodies on this side of it were French. Right beneath it lay one red-coat whose skull had been battered out of shape as he attempted to wriggle through. All the upper blades were stained, and on one fluttered a strip of flannel shirt. Powder blackened every inch of the rampart hereabouts, and as Nat passed over he saw the bodies piled in scores on the glacis below—some hideously scorched —among beams, gabions, burnt out fire-pots, and the wreckage of ladders. A horrible smell of singed flesh rose on the morning air; and, beyond the stench and the sullen smoke, birds sang in dewy fields, and the Guadiana flowed between grey olives and green promise of harvest.

Below, a single British officer, wrapped in a dark cape, picked his way among the corpses. Behind, intermittent shots and outcries told of the sack in progress. Save for Nat and the dead, the Trinidad was a desert. Yet he talked incessantly, and, stooping to pat the shoulder of the red-coat beneath the *chevaux de frise,* spoke to Dave McInnes and Teddy Butson to come and look. He never doubted they were beside him. " Pretty mess they've made of this chap." He touched the man's collar: " 48th, a corporal! Ugh, let's get out of this! " In imagination he linked arms with two men already stiffening, one at the foot and the other on the summit of the San Vincent's bastion. " King's Own— all friends in the King's Own! " he babbled as he retraced his way into the town.

He had a firelock in his hands . . . he was fumbling with it, very clumsily, by reason of his shattered fingers. He had wandered down a narrow street, and was groping at an iron-studded door. " Won't open," he told the ghosts beside him. " Must try the patent key." He put the muzzle against the lock and fired, flung himself against the door, and as it broke before him, stood swaying, staring across a whisp of smoke into a mean room, where a priest knelt in one corner by a straw pallet, and a girl rose from beside him and slowly confronted the intruder. As she rose she caught at the edge of a deal table, and across the smoke she too seemed to be swaying.

IV

SEVENTEEN years later Nat Ellery walked down
the hill into Gantick village, and entered the Ring
of the Bells.

" I've come," said he, " to inquire about a chest
I left here, one time back along." And he told his
name and the date.

The landlord, Joshua Martin—son of old Joshua,
who had kept the inn in 1806—rubbed his double
chin. " So you be Nat Ellery? I can just mind'ee
as a lad. As for the chest—come to think, father
sent it back to Trethake Water. Reckon it went
in the sale."

" What sale? "

" Why, don't 'ee know? When Reub sold up.
That would be about five years after the old folks
died. The mill didn' pay after the war, so Reub
sold up and emigrated."

" Ah! What became of him? "

" I did hear he was dead too," said Joshua Martin, " out in Canady somewhere. But that may
be lies," he added cheerfully.

Nat made no further comment, but paid for his
gin-and-water, picked up his carpet bag, and went
out to seek for a cottage. On his way he eyed the
thatched roofs critically. " Old Thatcher Hock-

aday will be dead," he told himself. "There's work for me here." He felt certain of it in Farmer Sprague's rick-yard. Farmer Sprague owned the two round-houses at the seaward end of the village, and wanted a tenant for one of them. Nat applied for it, and declared his calling.

"Us can't afford to pay the old prices these times," said the farmer.

Nat's eyes had wandered off to the ricks. "You'll find you can when you've seen my work," he answered.

Thus he became tenant of the round-house, and lived in it to the day of his death. No one in my day knew when or how the story first spread that he had been in the army and deserted. Perhaps he let slip the secret in his cups; for at first he spent his Saturday evenings at the Ring of Bells, dropping this habit when he found that every soul there disliked him. Perhaps some discharged veteran of the 4th, tramping through Gantick in search of work, had recognised him and let fall a damning hint. Long before I can remember the story had grown up uncontradicted, believed in by everyone. Beneath it the man lived on and deteriorated; but his workmanship never deteriorated, and no man challenged its excellence.

About a month before his death (I have this from

the postmistress) he sat down and wrote a letter, and ten days later a visitor arrived at the round-house. This visitor the Jago family (who lived across the road) declare to have been Satan himself; they have assured me so again and again, and I cannot shake their belief. But that is nonsense. The man was a grizzled artizan looking fellow well over fifty; extraordinarily like the old Thatcher, though darker of skin—yellow as a guinea, said Gantick; in fact and beyond doubt, the old man's son. He made no friends, no acquaintances ever, but confined himself to nursing the Thatcher, now tied to his chair by rheumatism. One thing alone gives colour to the Jagos' belief; the Thatcher who had sent for him could not abide the sight of him. The Jago children, who snatched a fearful joy by stealing after dark into the unkempt garden and peering through the uncurtained lattice windows, reported that as the pair sat at table with the black bottle between them, the Thatcher's eyes would be drawn to fix themselves on the other's with a stealthy shrinking terror—or, as they put it, " vicious when he wasna' lookin' and afeared when he was."

They would sit (so the children reported) half an hour, or maybe an hour, at a time, without a word spoken between them; but, indeed, the yellow

97

stranger troubled few with his speech. His only visits were paid to the postmistress, who kept a small grocery store, where he bought arrowroot and other spoon-food for the invalid, and the Ring of Bells, where he went nightly to. have the black bottle refilled with rum. On the doctor he never called.

It was on July 12th that the end came. The fine weather, after lasting for six weeks, had broken up two days before into light thunderstorms, which did not clear the air as usual. Ky Jago (short for Caiaphas), across the way, prophesied a big thunderstorm to come, but allowed he might be mistaken when on the morning of the 12th the rain came down in sheets. This torrential rain lasted until two in the afternoon, when the sky cleared and a pleasant northwesterly draught played up the valley. At six o'clock Ky Jago, who, in default of the Thatcher, was making shift to cover up Farmer Sprague's ricks, observed dense clouds massing themselves over the sea and rolling up slowly against the wind, and decided that the big storm would happen after all. At nine in the evening it broke.

It broke with such fury that the Stranger, with the black bottle under his arm, paused on the threshold as much as to ask his father, " Shall I go?" But the old man was clamouring for drink, and he went. He was half-way down the hill when with a crack the heavens opened and the white jagged lightning fairly hissed by him. Crack followed crack, flash and peal together, or so quick on each other, that no mortal could distinguish the rattle of one discharge from the bursting explosion of the other. No such tempest, he decided, could last for long, and he fled down to the Ring of Bells for shelter until the worst should be over. He waited there perhaps twenty minutes, and still the infernal din grew worse instead of better, until his anxiety for the old man forced him out in the teeth of it and up the hill, where the gutters had over-flowed upon the roadway, and the waters raced over his ankles. The first thing he saw at the top in one lurid instant was the entire Jago family gathered by their garden gate—six of them—and all bareheaded under the deluge.

The next flash revealed why they were there. Against the round-house opposite a ladder rested, and above it on the steep roof clung a man—his father. He had clamped his small ladder into the thatch, and as the heaven opened and shut, now silhouetting the round-house, now wrapping it in white flames—they saw him climbing up, and still up, towards the cross at the top.

"Help, there!" shouted the Stranger. "Come down! O help, you!—we must get him down!" The women and children screamed. A fresh explosion drowned shout and screams.

Jago and the Stranger reached the ladder together. The Stranger mounted first; but as he did so, the watchers in one blinding moment saw the old Thatcher's hand go up and grip the cross. The shutters of darkness came to with a roar, but above it rose a shrill, a terribly human cry.

"*Dave!*" cried the voice. "*Ted!*"

Silence followed, and then a heavy thud. They waited for the next flash. It came. There was no one on the roof of the round-house, but a broken stump where the cross had been.

V

This was the story the yellow Stranger told to the Coroner. And the Coroner listened and asked:

"Can you account for conduct of deceased? Had he been drinking that evening?"

"He had," answered the witness, and for a moment, while the Coroner took a note, it seemed he had said all. Then he seemed to think better of it, and added "My father suffered from delusions, sir."

"Hey? What sort of delusions?" The Coroner glanced at the jury, who sat impassive.

"Well, sir, my father in his young days had served as a soldier."

Here the jurymen began to show interest suddenly. One or two leaned forward. "He belonged to the 4th Regiment, and was at the siege of Badajos. During the sack of the city he broke into a house, and—and—after that he was missing."

"Go on," said the Coroner, for the witness had paused.

"That was where he first met my mother, sir. It was her house, and she and a priest kept him hidden till the English had left. After that he married her. There were three children—all boys. My brothers came first: they were twins. I was born two years later."

"All born in Badajos?"

"All in Badajos, sir. My brothers will be there still, if they're living."

"But these delusions——"

"I'm coming to them. My father must have been hurt, somehow hurt in his head. He would have it that my two brothers—twins, sir, if you'll be pleased to mark it—were no sons of his, but of two friends of his, soldiers of the 4th Regiment who had been killed, the both, that evening by the San

101

Vincente bastion. So you see he must have been wrong in his head."

" And you?"

" O, there couldn't be any mistake about me. I was his very image, and—perhaps I ought to say, sir—he hated me for it. When my mother died —she had been a fruit-seller—he handed the business over to my brothers, taking only enough to carry him back to England and me with him. The day after we landed in London he apprenticed me to a brassworker. I was just turned fifteen, and from that day until last Wednesday three weeks we never set eyes on each other."

" Let me see," said the Coroner, turning back a page or two. " At the last moment just before he fell, you say—and the other witnesses confirm it— that he called out twice—uttered two names, I think."

" They were the names by which he used to call my brothers, sir—the names of his two mates in the storming party."

THE TWO SCOUTS

Chapters from the Memoirs of Manuel (or Manus) McNeill, an agent in the Secret Service of Great Britain during the campaigns of the Peninsula (1808–1813). A Spanish subject by birth, and a Spaniard in all his upbringing, he traces in the first chapter of his Memoirs his descent from an old Highland family through one Manus McNeill, a Jacobite agent in the Court of Madrid at the time of the War of Succession, who married and settled at Aranjuez. The authenticity of these Memoirs has been doubted, and according to Napier the name of the two scouts whom Marmont confused together (as will appear in a subsequent chapter) was not McNeill, but Grant: which is probable enough, but not sufficient to stamp the Memoirs as forgeries. Their author may have chosen McNeill as a nom de guerre, and been at pains to deceive his readers on this point while adhering to strictest truth in his relation of events. And this I conceive to be the real explanation of a narrative which itself clears up, and credibly, certain obscurities in Napier.—Q.]

THE TWO SCOUTS

I

THE FORD OF THE TORMES

In the following chapters I shall leave speaking of my own adventures and say something of a man whose exploits during the campaigns of 1811–1812 fell but a little short of mine. I do so the more readily because he bore my own patronymic, and was after a fashion my kinsman; and I make bold to say that in our calling Captain Alan Mc-Neill and I had no rival but each other. The reader may ascribe what virtue he will to the parent blood of a family which could produce at one time in two distinct branches two men so eminent in a service requiring the rarest conjunction of courage and address.

I had often heard of Captain McNeill, and doubtless he had as often heard of me. At least thrice in attempting a *coup d'espionage* upon ground he had previously covered—albeit long before and on a quite different mission—I had been forced to take into my calculations the fame left behind by " the Great McNeill," and a wariness in our adversaries whom he had taught to lock the stable door after the horse had been stolen. For while with the Allies the first question on hearing of some peculiarly daring feat would be "Which McNeill?" the French supposed us to be one and the same person; which, if possible, heightened their grudging admiration.

Yet the ambiguity of our friends upon these occasions was scarcely more intelligent than our foes' complete bewilderment; since to anyone who studied even the theory of our business the Captain's method and mine could have presented but the most superficial resemblance. Each was original, and each carried even into details the unmistakable stamp of its author. My combinations, I do not hesitate to say, were the subtler. From choice I worked alone; while the Captain relied for help on his servant José (I never heard his surname), a Spanish peasant of remarkable quickness of sight, and as full of resource as of devotion. Moreover I habitually used disguises, and prided myself in their invention, whereas it was the Captain's vanity to wear his conspicuous scarlet uniform upon all occasions, or at most to cover it with his short dark-blue riding cloak. This, while to be sure it enhanced the showiness of his exploits, obliged him to carry them through with a suddenness and dash foreign to the whole spirit of my patient work. I must always maintain that mine were the sounder methods; yet if I had no other reason for my admiration I could not withhold it from a man who, when I first met him, had been wearing a British uniform for three days and nights within the circuit of the French camp. I myself had been living within it in a constant twitter for hard upon three weeks.

It happened in March, 1812, when Marmont was concentrating his forces in the Salamanca district, with the intent (it was rumoured) of marching and retaking Ciudad Rodrigo, which the Allies had carried by assault in January. This stroke, if delivered with energy, Lord Wellington could parry; but only at the cost of renouncing a success on which he had set his heart, the capture of Badajos. Already he had sent forward the bulk of his troops with his siege-train on the march to that town, while he kept his headquarters to the last moment in Ciudad Rodrigo as a blind. He felt confident of smashing Badajos before Soult with the army of the south could arrive to relieve it; but to do this he must leave both Almeida and Ciudad Rodrigo exposed to Marmont, the latter with its breaches scarcely healed and its garrison disaffected. He did not fear actual disaster to these fortresses; he could hurry back in time to defeat that, for he knew that Marmont had no siege guns, and could only obtain them by successfully storming Almeida and capturing the battering train which lay there protected by 3,000 militia. Nevertheless, a serious effort by Marmont would force him to abandon his scheme.

All depended therefore (1) on how much Marmont knew and (2) on his readiness to strike boldly. Consequently, when that General began to draw his scattered forces together and mass them on the Tormes before Salamanca, Wellington grew anxious; and it was to relieve that anxiety or confirm it that I found myself serving as tapster of the Posada del Rio in the village of Huerta, just above a ford of the river, and six miles from Salamanca. Neither the pay it afforded nor the leisure had attracted me to the Posada del Rio. Pay there was little, and leisure there was none, since Marmont's lines came down to the river here, and we had a battalion of infantry quartered about the village—sixteen under our roof—and all extraordinarily thirsty fellows for Frenchmen; besides a squadron of cavalry, vedettes of which constantly patrolled the farther bank of the Tormes. The cavalry officers kept their chargers—six in all—in the ramshackle stable in the court-yard facing the inn; and since (as my master explained to me the first morning) it was a tradition of the posada to combine the duties of tapster and ostler in one person, I found all the exercise I needed in running between the cellar and the great kitchen, and between the kitchen and the stable, where the troopers had always a job for me, and allowed me in return to join in their talk. They seemed to think this an adequate reward, and I did not grumble.

Now, beside the stable, and divided from it by a midden-heap, there stood at the back of the inn a small outhouse with a loft. This in more prosperous days had accommodated the master's own mule, but now was stored with empty barrels, strings of onions, and trusses of hay—which last had been hastily removed from the larger stable when the troopers took possession. Here I slept by night, for lack of room indoors, and also to guard the fodder—an arrangement which suited me admirably, since it left me my own master for six or seven hours of the twenty-four. My bedroom furniture consisted of a truss of hay, a lantern, a tinder-box, and a rusty fowling piece. For my toilet I went to the bucket in the stable yard.

On the fifth night, having some particular information to send to headquarters, I made a cautious expedition to the place agreed upon with my messenger — a fairly intelligent muleteer, and honest, but new to the business. We met in the garden at the rear of his cottage, conveniently approached by way of the ill-kept cemetery which stood at the end of the village. If surprised, I was to act the nocturnal lover, and he the angry defender of his sister's reputation—a foolish but not ill-looking girl, to whom I had confided nothing beyond a few amorous glances, so that her evidence (if unluckily needed) might carry all the weight of an obvious incapacity to invent or deceive.

These precautions proved unnecessary. But my muleteer, though plucky, was nervous, and I had to repeat my instructions at least thrice in detail before I felt easy. Also he brought news of a fresh movement of battalions behind Huerta, and of a sentence in the latest General Order affecting my own movements, and this obliged me to make some slight alteration in my original message. So that, what with one thing and another, it wanted but an hour of dawn when I regained the yard of the Posada del Rio and cautiously re-entered the little granary.

Rain had fallen during the night—two or three short but heavy showers. Creeping on one's belly between the damp graves of a cemetery is not the pleasantest work in the world, and I was shivering with wet and cold and an instant want of sleep. But as I closed the door behind me and turned to grope for the ladder to my sleeping loft, I came to a halt, suddenly and painfully wide awake. There was someone in the granary. In the pitch darkness my ear caught the sound of breathing—of someone standing absolutely still and checking his breath within a few paces of me—perhaps six, perhaps less.

I, too, stood absolutely still, and lifted my hand towards the hasp of the door. And as I did so—in all my career I cannot recall a nastier moment—as my hand went up, it encountered another. I felt the fingers closing on my wrist, and wrenched loose. For a moment our two hands wrestled confusedly; but while mine tugged at the latch the other found the key and twisted it round with a click. (I had oiled the lock three nights before.) With that I flung myself on him, but again my adversary was too quick, for as I groped for his throat my chest struck against his uplifted knee, and I dropped on the floor and rolled there in intolerable pain.

No one spoke. As I struggled to raise myself on hands and knees, I heard the chipping of steel on flint, and caught a glimpse of a face. As its lips blew on the tinder this face vanished and reappeared, and at length grew steady in the blue light of the sulphur match. It was not the face, however, on which my eyes rested in a stupid wonder,

110

but the collar below it—the scarlet collar and tunic of a British officr.

And yet the face may have had something to do with my bewilderment. I like, at any rate, to think so; because I have been in corners quite as awkward, yet have never known myself so pitifully demoralised. The uniform might be that of a British officer, but the face was that of Don Quixote de la Mancha, and shone at me in that blue light straight out of my childhood and the story-book. High brow, high cheek-bone, long pointed jaw, lined and patient face—I saw him as I had known him all my life, and I turned up at the other man, who stooped over me, a look of absurd surmise.

He was a Spanish peasant, short, thick-set and muscular, but assuredly no Sancho: a quiet quick-eyed man, with a curious neat grace in his movements. Our tussle had not heated him in the least. His right fist rested on my back, and I knew he had a knife in it; and while I gasped for breath he watched me, his left hand hovering in front of my mouth to stop the first outcry. Through his spread fingers I saw Don Quixote light the lantern and raise it for a good look at me. And with that in a flash my wits came back, and with them the one bit of Gaelic known to me.

" *Latha math leat*," I gasped, and caught my

111

breath again as the fingers closed softly on my jaw, " *O Alan mhic Neill!* "

The officer took a step and swung the lantern close to my eyes—so close that I blinked.

" Gently, José." He let out a soft pleased laugh while he studied my face. Then he spoke a word or two in Gaelic—some question which I did not understand.

" My name is McNeill," said I; " but that's the end of my mother tongue."

The Captain laughed again. " We've caught the other one, José," said he. And José helped me to my feet—respectfully, I thought. " Now this," his master went on, as if talking to himself, " this explains a good deal."

I guessed. " You mean that my presence has made the neighbourhood a trifle hot for you! "

" Exactly; there is a General Order issued which concerns one or both of us."

I nodded. " In effect it concerns us both; but, merely as a matter of history, it was directed against me. Pardon the question, Captain, but how long have you been within the French lines? "

" Three days," he answered simply; " and this is the third night."

" What? In that uniform? "

112

"I never use disguises," said he—a little too stiffly for my taste.

"Well, I do. And I have been within Marmont's cantonments for close on three weeks. However, there's no denying you're a champion. But did you happen to notice the date on the General Order?"

"I did; and I own it puzzled me. I concluded that Marmont must have been warned beforehand of my coming."

"Not a bit of it. The order is eight days old. I secured a copy on the morning it was issued; and the next day, having learnt all that was necessary in Salamanca, I allowed myself to be hired in the market-place of that city by the landlord of this damnable inn."

"I disapprove of swearing," put in Captain McNeill, very sharp and curt.

"As well as of disguises? You seem to carry a number of scruples into this line of business. I suppose," said I, nettled, "when you read in the General Order that the notorious McNeill was lurking disguised within the circle of cantonments, you took it that Marmont was putting a wanton affront on your character, just for the fun of the thing?"

"My dear sir," said the Captain, "if I have expressed myself rudely, pray pardon me: I have heard too much of you to doubt your courage, and I have envied your exploits too often to speak slightingly of your methods. As a matter of fact, disguise would do nothing, and worse than nothing, for a man who speaks Spanish with my Highland accent. I may, perhaps, take a foolish pride in my disadvantage, but," and here he smiled, " so, you remember, did the fox without a tail."

"And that's very handsomely spoken," said I; " but unless I'm mistaken, you will have to break your rule for once, if you wish to cross the Tormes this morning."

" It's a case of *must*. Barring the certainty of capture if I don't, I have important news to carry —Marmont starts within forty-eight hours."

" Since it seems that for once we are both engaged on the same business, let me say at once, Captain, and without offence, that my news is as fresh as yours. Marmont certainly starts within forty-eight hours to assault Ciudad Rodrigo, and my messenger is already two hours on his way to Lord Wellington."

I said this without parade, not wishing to hurt his feelings. Looking up I found his mild eyes fixed on me with a queer expression, almost with a twinkle of fun.

" To assault Ciudad Rodrigo? I think not."

114

" Almeida, then, and Ciudad Rodrigo next. So far as we are concerned the question is not important."

" My opinion is that Marmont intends to assault neither."

" But, my good sir," I cried, " I have seen and counted the scaling-ladders! "

" And so have I. I spent six hours in Salamanca itself," said the Captain quietly.

" Well, but doesn't that prove it? What other place on earth can he want to assault? He certainly is not marching south to join Soult." I turned to José, who had been listening with an impassive face.

" The Captain will be right. He always is," said José, perceiving that I appealed to him.

" I will wager a month's pay——"

" I never bet," Captain McNeill interrupted, as stiffly as before. " As you say, Marmont will march upon the Agueda, but in my opinion he will not assault Ciudad Rodrigo."

" Then he will be a fool."

" H'm! As to that I think we are agreed. But the question just now is how am I to get across the Tormes? The ford, I suppose, is watched on both sides." I nodded. " And I suppose it will be absolutely fatal to remain here long after daybreak? "

"Huerta swarms with soldiers," said I, "we have sixteen in the posada and a cavalry picket just behind. A whole battalion has eaten the village bare, and is foraging in all kinds of unlikely places. To be sure you might have a chance in the loft above us, under the hay."

"Even so, you cannot hide our horses."

"Your horses?"

"Yes, they're outside at the back. I didn't know there was a cavalry picket so close, and José must have missed it in the darkness."

José looked handsomely ashamed of himself.

"They are well-behaved horses," added the Captain. "Still, if they cannot be stowed somewhere, it is unlikely they can be explained away, and of course it will start a search."

"Our stable is full."

"Of course it is. Therefore you see we have no choice—apart from our earnest wish—but to cross the ford before daybreak. How is it patrolled on the far side?"

"Cavalry," said I; "two vedettes."

"Meeting, I suppose, just opposite the ford? How far do they patrol?"

"Three hundred yards maybe: certainly not more."

The Captain pursed up his lips as if whistling.

116

"Is there good cover on the other side? My map shows a wood of fair size."

"About half a mile off; open country between. Once there, you ought to be all right; I mean that a man clever enough to win there ought to make child's-play of the rest."

He mused for half a minute. "The stream is two wide for me to hear the movements of the patrols opposite. José has a wonderful ear."

"Yes, Captain, I can hear the water from where we stand," José put in.

"He is right," said I, "it's not a question of distance, but of the noise of the water. The ford itself will not be more than twenty yards across."

"What depth?"

"Three feet in the middle, as near as can be. I have rubbed down too many horses these last three days not to know. The river may have fallen an inch since yesterday. They have cleared the bottom of the ford, but just above and below there are rocks, and slippery ones."

"My horse is roughed. Of course the bank is watched on this side?"

"Two sentries by the ford, two a little up the road, and the guard-house not twenty yards beyond. Captain, I think you'll have to put on a disguise for once in your life."

" Not if I can help it."

" Then, excuse me, but how the devil do you propose to manage? "

He frowned at the oath, recovered himself, and looked at me again with something like a twinkle of fun in his solemn eyes.

" Do you know," said he, " it has just occurred to me to pay you a tremendous compliment—Mc-Neill to McNeill, you understand? I propose to place myself entirely in your hands."

" Oh, thank you! " I pulled a wry face. " Well, it's a compliment if ever there was one—an infernally handsome compliment. Your man, I suppose, can look after himself? " But before he could reply I added, " No; he shall go with me: for if you *do* happen to get across, I shall have to follow, and look sharp about it." Then, as he seemed inclined to protest, " No inconvenience at all—my work here is done, and you are pretty sure to have picked up any news I may have missed. You had best be getting your horse at once; the dawn will be on us in half an hour. Bring him round to the door here. José will find straw—hay—anything —to deaden his footsteps. Meanwhile I'll ask you to excuse me for five minutes."

The Spaniard eyed me suspiciously.

" Of course," said I, reading his thoughts, " if your master doubts me——"

" I think, Señor McNeill, I have given you no cause to suspect it," the Captain gravely interrupted. " There is, however, one question I should like to ask, if I may do so without offence. Is it your intention that I should cross in the darkness or wait for daylight?"

" We must wait for daylight; because although it increases some obvious dangers——"

" Excuse me; your reasons are bound to be good ones. I will fetch around my horse at once, and we shall expect you back here in five minutes."

In five minutes time I returned to find them standing in the darkness outside the granary door. José had strewn a space round about with hay; but at my command he fetched more and spread it carefully, step by step, as Captain McNeill led his horse forward. My own arms were full; for I had spent the five minutes in collecting a score of French blankets and shirts off the hedges, where the regimental washermen had spread them the day before to dry.

The sketch on the following page will explain my plan and our movements better than a page of explanation:—

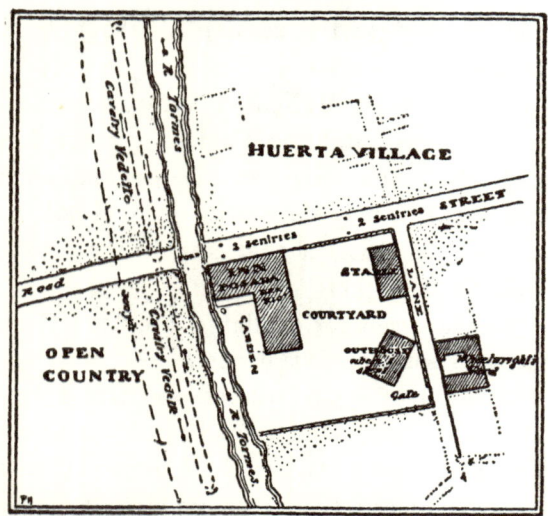

The reader will observe that the Posada del Rio, which faces inwards upon its own courtyard, thrusts out upon the river at its rear a gable which overhangs the stream and flanks its small waterside garden from view of the village street. Into this garden, where the soldiers were used to sit and drink their wine of an evening, I led the Captain, whispering him to keep silence, for eight of the Frenchmen slept behind the windows above. In the corner by the gable was an awning, sufficient, when cleared of stools and tables, to screen him and his horse from any eyes looking down from these windows, though not tall enough to allow him to mount. And

120

at daybreak, when the battalion assembled at its
alarm-post above the ford, the gable itself would
hide him. But of course the open front of the garden—where in two places the bank shelved easily
down to the water—would leave him in full view
of the troopers across the river. It was for this
that I had brought the blankets. Across the angle
by the gable there ran a clothes line on which the
house-servant, Mercedes, hung her dish-clouts to
dry. Unfastening the inner end, I brought it forward and lashed it to a post supporting a dovecote
on the river wall. To fasten it high enough I had
to climb the post, and this set the birds moving
uneasily in the box overhead. But before their
alarm grew serious I had slipped down to earth
again, and now it took José and me but a couple
of minutes to fling the blankets over the line and
provide the Captain with a curtain, behind which,
when day broke, he could watch the troopers and
his opportunity. Already, in the village behind us,
a cock was crowing. In twenty minutes the sun
would be up and the bugles sounding the réveille.
" Down the bank by the gable," I whispered. " It
runs shallow there, and six or seven yards to the
right you strike the ford. When the vedettes are
separated—just before they turn to come back—
that's your time."

121

I took José by the arm. "We may as well be there to see. How were you planning to cross?"

"Oh," said he, "a marketer—with a raw-boned Galician horse and two panniers of eggs — for Arapiles——"

"That will do; but you must enter the village at the farther end and come down the road to the ford. Get your horse "—we crept back to the granary together—" but wait a moment, and I will show you the way round."

When I rejoined him at the back of the granary he had his horse ready, and we started to work around the village. But I had miscalculated the time. The sky was growing lighter, and scarcely were we in the lane behind the courtyard before the bugles began to sound.

"Well," said I, "that may save us some trouble after all."

Across the lane was an archway leading into a wheelwright's yard. It had a tall door of solid oak studded with iron nails; but this was unlocked and unbolted, and I knew the yard to be vacant, for the French farriers had requisitioned all the wheelwright's tools three days before, and the honest man had taken to his bed and proposed to stay there pending compensation.

To this archway we hastily crossed, and had

barely time to close the door behind us before the soldiers, whose billets lay farther up the lane, came running by in twos and threes for the alarm-post, the later ones buckling their accoutrements as they ran, halting now and then, and muttering as they fumbled with a strap or a button. José at my instruction had loosened his horse's off hind shoe just sufficiently to allow it to clap; and as soon as he was ready I opened the door boldly, and we stepped out into the lane among the soldiers, cursing the dog's son of a smith who would not arise from his lazy bed to attend to two poor marketers pressed for time.

Now it had been dim within the archway, but out in the lane there was plenty of light, and it did me good to see José start when his eyes fell on me. For a couple of seconds I am sure he believed himself betrayed: and yet, as I explained to him afterwards, it was perhaps the simplest of all my disguises and—barring the wig—depended more upon speech and gait than upon any alteration of the face. (For a particular account of it I must refer the reader back to my adventure in Villafranca. On this occasion, having proved it once, I felt more confident; and since it deceived José, I felt I could challenge scrutiny as an aged peasant travelling with his son to market.)

A couple of soldiers passed us and flung jests behind them as we hobbled down the lane, the loose
shoe clacking on the cobbles, José tugging at his
bridle, and I limping behind and swearing volubly,
with bent back and head low by the horse's rump,
and on the near side, which would be the unex-
posed one when we gained the ford. And so we
reached the main street and the river, José turning to point with wonder at the troops as we hustled
past. One or two made a feint to steal an egg
from our panniers. José protested, halting and
calling in Spanish for protection. A sergeant inter-
fered; whereupon the men began to bait us, calling
after us in scraps of camp Spanish. José lost his
temper admirably; for me, I shuffled along as an
old man dazed with the scene; and when we came
to the water's edge felt secure enough to attempt
a trifle of comedy business as José hoisted my old
limbs on to the horse's back behind the panniers.
It fetched a shout of laughter. And then, having
slipped off boots and stockings deliberately, José
took hold of the bridle again and waded into the
stream. We were safe.

I had found time for a glance at the farther bank,
and saw that the troopers were leisurely riding to
and fro. They met and parted just as we entered
the ford. Before we were half-way across they had

come near to the end of their beat, with about three hundred yards between them, and I was thinking this a fair opportunity for the Captain when José whispered, " There he goes," very low and quick, and, with a souse, horse and rider struck the water behind us by the gable of the inn. As the stream splashed up around them we saw the horse slip on the stony bottom and fall back, almost burying his haunches, but with two short heaves he had gained the good gravel and was plunging after us. The infantry spied him first—the two vedettes were in the act of wheeling about and heard the warning before they saw. Before they could put their charges to the gallop Captain McNeill was past us and climbing the bank between them. A bullet or two sang over us from the Huerta shore. Not knowing of what his horse was capable, I feared he might yet be headed off; but the troopers in their flurry had lost their heads and their only chance unless they could drop him by a fluking shot. They galloped straight for the ford-head, while the Captain slipped between, and were almost charging each other before they could pull up and wheel at right angles in pursuit.

" Good," said José simply. A shot had struck one of our panniers, smashing a dozen eggs (by the smell he must have bought them cheap), and he halted and gesticulated in wrath like a man in two minds about returning and demanding compensation. Then he seemed to think better of it, and we moved forward; but twice again before we reached dry land he turned and addressed the soldiers in furious Spanish across the babble of the ford. José had gifts.

For my part I was eager to watch the chase which the rise of the bank hid from us, though we could hear a few stray shots. But José's confidence proved well grounded, for when we struck the high road there was the Captain half a mile away within easy reach of the wood, and a full two hundred yards ahead of the foremost trooper.

" Good! " said José again. " Now we can eat! " and he pulled out a loaf of coarse bread from the injured pannier, and trimming off an end where the evil-smelling eggs had soaked it, divided it in two. On this and a sprig of garlic we broke our fast, and were munching and jogging along contentedly when we met the returning vedettes. They were not in the best of humours, you may be sure, and although we drew aside and paused with crusts half lifted to our open mouths to stare at them with true yokel admiration, they cursed us for taking up too much of the roadway, and one

126

of them even made a cut with his sabre at the near pannier of eggs.

" It's well he broke none," said I as we watched them down the road. " I don't deny you and your master any reasonable credit, but for my taste you leave a little too much to luck."

Our road now began to skirt the wood into which the Captain had escaped, and we followed it for a mile and more, José all the while whistling a gipsy air which I guessed to carry a covert message; and sure enough, after an hour of it, the same air was taken up in the wood to our right, where we found the Captain dismounted and seated comfortably at the foot of a cork tree.

He was good enough to pay me some pretty compliments, and, after comparing notes, we agreed that—my messenger being a good seven hours on his way with all the information Lord Wellington could need for the moment—we would keep company for a day or two, and a watch on the force and disposition of the French advance. We had yet to discover Marmont's objective. For though in Salamanca the French officers had openly talked of the assault on Ciudad Rodrigo, there was still a chance (though neither of us believed in it) that their general meant to turn aside and strike southward for the Tagus. Our plan, therefore, was to make for Tammames where the roads divided, where the hills afforded good cover, and to wait.

So towards Tammames (which lay some thirty miles off) we turned our faces, and arriving there on the 27th, encamped for two days among the hills. Marmont had learnt on the 14th that none of Wellington's divisions were on the Algueda, and we agreed, having watched his preparations, that on the 27th he would be ready to start. These two days, therefore, we spent at ease, and I found the Captain, in spite of his narrow and hide-bound religion, an agreeable companion. He had the McNeills' genealogy at his finger ends, and I picked up more information from him concerning our ancestral home in Ross and our ancestral habits than I have ever been able to verify. Certainly our grandfathers, Manus of Aranjuez and Angus (slain at Sheriff-muir), had been first cousins. But this discovery had no sooner raised me to a claim on his regard than I found his cordiality chilled by the thought that I believed in the Pope or (as he preferred to put it) Antichrist. My eminence as a genuine McNeill made the shadow of my error the taller. In these two days of inactivity I felt his solicitude growing until, next to the immediate movements of Marmont, my conversion became for him the most important question in the Peninsula, and I saw that, unless I allowed him at least to attempt it, another forty-eight hours would wear him to fiddle-strings.

Thus it happened that mid-day of the 30th found us on the wooded hill above the cross-roads; found me stretched at full length on my back and smoking, and the Captain (who did not smoke) seated beside me with his pocket Testament, earnestly sapping the fundamental errors of Rome, when José, who had been absent all the morning reconnoitring, brought news that Marmont's van (which he had been watching, and ahead of which he had been dodging since ten o'clock) was barely two miles away. The Captain pulled out his watch, allowed them thirty-five minutes, and quietly proceeded with his exposition. As the head of the leading column swung into sight around the base of the foot-hills, he sought in his haversack and drew out a small volume—the *Pilgrim's Progress* —and having dog's-eared a page of it inscribed my name on the fly-leaf, " from his kinsman, Alan McNeill."

" It is a question," said he, as I thanked him, " and one often debated, if it be not better that a whole army, such as we see approaching, should perish bodily in every circumstance of horror than that one soul, such as yours or mine, should fail

to find the true light. For my part "—and here
he seemed to deprecate a weakness—" I have never
been able to go quite so far; I hope not from any
lack of intellectual courage. Will you take notes
while I dictate?"

So on the last leaf of the *Pilgrim's Progress* I
entered the strength of each battalion, and noted
each gun as the great army wound its way into
Tammames below us, and through it for the cross-
roads beyond, but not in one body, for two of
the battalions enjoyed an hour's halt there before
setting forward after their comrades, by this
time out of sight. They had taken the northern
road.

" Ciudad Rodrigo!" said I. " And there goes
Wellington's chance of Badajos."

The Captain beckoned to José and whispered in
his ear, then opened his Testament again as the
sturdy little Spaniard set off down the hill with his
leisurely, lopping gait, so much faster than it
seemed. The sun was setting when he returned
with his report.

" I thought so," said the Captain. " Marmont
has left three-fourths of his scaling ladders behind
in Tammames. Ciudad Rodrigo he will not attempt; I doubt if he means business with Almeida.
If you please," he added, " José and I will push

after and discover his real business, while you carry to Lord Wellington a piece of news it will do him good to hear."

II

THE BARBER-SURGEON OF SABUGAL

So, leaving my two comrades to follow up and detect the true object of Marmont's compaign, I headed south for Badajos. The roads were heavy, the mountain torrents in flood, the only procurable horses and mules such as by age or debility had escaped the strictest requisitioning. Nevertheless, on the 4th of April I was able to present myself at Lord Wellington's headquarters before Badajos, and that same evening started northwards again with his particular instructions. I understood (not, of course, by direct word of mouth) that disquieting messages had poured in ahead of me from the allied commanders scattered in the north, who reported Ciudad Rodrigo in imminent peril; that my news brought great relief of mind; but that in any case our army now stood committed to reduce Badajos before Soult came to its relief. Our iron guns had worked fast and well, and already three breaches on the eastern side of the town were nearly practicable. Badajos once secured, Wellington would press northward again to teach Marmont

131

manners; but for the moment our weak troops opposing him must even do the best they could to gain time and protect the magazines and stores.

At six o'clock then in the evening of the 4th, on a fresh mount, I turned my back on the doomed fortress, and crossing the Guadiana by the horse ferry above Elvas, struck into the Alemtejo.

On the 6th I reached Castello Branco and found the position of the Allies sufficiently serious. Victor Alten's German cavalry were in the town—600 of them—having fallen back before Marmont without striking a blow, and leaving the whole country four good marches from Rodrigo exposed to the French marauders. They reported that Rodrigo itself had fallen (which I knew to be false, and, as it turned out, Marmont had left but one division to blockade the place); they spoke openly of a further retreat upon Vilha Velha. But I regarded them not. They had done mischief enough already by scampering southward and allowing Marmont to push in between them and the weak militias on whom it now depended to save Almeida with its battering train, Celorico and Pinhel with their magazines, and even Ciudad Rodrigo itself; and while I listened I tasted to myself the sarcastic compliments they were likely to receive from Lord Wellington when he heard their tale.

132

THE TWO SCOUTS

Clearly there was no good to be done in Castello Branco, and the next morning I pushed on. I had no intention of rejoining Captain McNeill; for, as he had observed on parting—quoting some old Greek for his authority—" three of us are not enough for an army, and for any other purpose we are too many," and although pleased enough to have a kinsman's company he had allowed me to see that he preferred to work alone with José, who understood his methods, whereas mine (in spite of his compliments) were unfamiliar and puzzling. I knew him to be watching Marmont, and even speculated on the chances of our meeting, but my own purpose was to strike the Coa, note the French force there and its disposition, and so make with all serviceable news for the north, where Generals Trant and Wilson with their Portuguese militia were endeavouring to cover the magazines.

Travelling on mule-back now as a Portuguese drover out of work, I dodged a couple of marauding parties below Penamacor, found Marmont in force in Sabugal at the bend of the Coa, on the 9th reached Guarda, a town on the top of a steep mountain, and there found General Trant in position with about 6,000 raw militiamen. To him I presented myself with my report—little of which was new to him except my reason for believing Ciudad

Rodrigo safe for the present; and this he heard with real pleasure, chiefly because it confirmed his own belief and gave it a good reason which it had hitherto lacked.

And here I must say a word on General Trant. He was a gallant soldier and a clever one, but inclined (and here lay his weakness) to be on occasion too clever by half. In fact, he had a leaning towards my own line of business, and naturally it was just here that I found him out. I am not denying that during the past fortnight his cleverness had served him well. He had with a handful of untrained troops to do his best for a group of small towns and magazines, each valuable and each in itself impossible of defence. His one advantage was that he knew his weakness and the enemy did not, and he had used this knowledge with almost ludicrous success.

For an instance; immediately on discovering the true line of Marmont's advance he had hurried to take up a position on the lower Coa, but had been met on his march by an urgent message from Governor Le Mesurier that Almeida was in danger and could not resist a resolute assault. Without hesitation Trant turned and pushed hastily with one brigade to the Cabeça Negro mountain behind the bridge of Almeida, and reached it just as the French drew near, driving 200 Spaniards before them across the plain. Trant, seeing that the enemy had no cavalry at hand, with the utmost effrontery and quite as if he had an army behind him, threw out a cloud of skirmishers beyond the bridge, dressed up a dozen guides in scarlet coats to resemble British troopers, galloped with these to the glacis of Almeida, spoke the governor, drew off a score of invalid troopers from the hospital in the town, and at dusk made his way back up the mountain, which in three hours he had covered with sham bivouac fires.

These were scarcely lit when the governor, taking his cue, made a determined sortie and drove back the French light troops, who in the darkness had no sort of notion of the numbers attacking them. So completely hoaxed, indeed, was their commander that he, who had come with two divisions to take Almeida, and held it in the hollow of his hand, decamped early next morning and marched away to report the fortress so strongly protected as to be unassailable.

Well this, as I say, showed talent. Artistically conceived as a *ruse de guerre*, in effect it saved Almeida. But a success of the kind too often tempts a man to try again and overshoot his mark. Now Marmont, with all his defects of vanity, was no fool. He had a strong army moderately well concentrated; he had, indeed, used it to little purpose, but he was not likely, with his knowledge of the total force available by the Allies in the north, to be seriously daunted or for long by a game of mere impudence. In my opinion Trant, after brazening him away from Almeida, should have thanked Heaven and walked humbly for a while. To me even his occupation of Guarda smelt of dangerous bravado, for Guarda is an eminently treacherous position, strong in itself, and admirable for a force sufficient to hold the ridges behind it, but capable of being turned on either hand, affording bad retreat, and, therefore, to a small force as perilous as it is attractive. But I was to find that Trant's enterprise reached farther yet.

To my description of Marmont's forces he listened (it seemed to me) impatiently, asking few questions and checking off each statement with " Yes, yes," or " Quite so." All the while his fingers were drumming on the camp table, and I had no sooner come to an end than he began to question me about the French marshal's headquarters in Sabugal. The town itself and its position he knew as well as I did, perhaps better. I had not entered it on my way, but kept to the left bank of the Coa. I knew Marmont to be quartered there, but in what house or what part of the town I was ignorant. "And what the deuce can it matter?" I wondered.

"But could you not return and discover?" the general asked at length.

"Oh, as for that," I answered, "it's just as you choose to order."

"It's risky of course," said he.

"It's risky to be sure," I agreed; "but if the risk comes in the day's work I take it I shall have been in tighter corners."

"Excuse me," he said with a sort of deprecatory smile, "but I was not thinking of you; at least not altogether." And I saw by his face that he held something in reserve and was in two minds about confiding it.

"I beg that you won't think of me," I said simply, for I have always made it a rule to let a general speak for himself and ask no questions which his words may not fairly cover. Outside of my own business (the limits of which are well defined) I seek no responsibility, least of all should I seek it in serving one whom I suspect of over-cleverness.

"Look here," he said at length, "the Duke of Ragusa is a fine figure of a man."

"Notoriously," said I. "All Europe knows it, and he certainly knows it himself."

137

"I have heard that his troops take him at his own valuation."

"Well," I answered, "he sits his horse gallantly; he has courage. At present he is only beginning to make his mistakes; and soldiers, like women, have a great idea of what a warrior ought to look like."

"In fact," said General Trant, "the loss of him would make an almighty difference."

Now he had asked me to be seated and had poured me out a glass of wine from his decanter. But at these words I leapt up suddenly, jolting the table so that the glass danced and spilled half its contents.

"What the dickens is wrong?" asked the general, snatching a map out of the way of the liquor. "Good Lord, man! You don't suppose I was asking you to assassinate Marmont!"

"I beg your pardon," said I, recovering myself. "Of course not; but it sounded——"

"Oh, did it?" He mopped the map with his pocket handkerchief and looked at me as who should say "Guess again."

I cast about wildly. "This man cannot be wanting to kidnap him!" thought I to myself.

"You tell me his divisions are scattered after supplies. I hear that the bulk of his troops are in camp above Penamacor; that at the outside he has in Sabugal under his hand but 5,000. Now Silveira should be here in a couple of days; that will make us roughly 12,000.

"Ah!" said I, "a surprise?" He nodded. "Night?" He nodded again. "And your cavalry?" I pursued.

"I could, perhaps, force General Bacellar to spare his squadron of dragoons from Celorico. Come, what do you think of it?"

"I do as you order," said I, "and that I suppose is to return to Sabugal and report the lie of the land. But since, general, you ask my opinion, and speaking without local knowledge, I should say——"

"Yes?"

"Excuse me, but I will send you my opinion in four days' time." And I rose to depart.

"Very good, but keep your seat. Drink another glass of wine."

"Sabugal is twenty miles off, and when I arrive I have yet to discover how to get into it," I protested.

"That is just what am going to tell you."

"Ah," said I, "so you have already been making arrangements?"

He nodded while he poured out the wine. "You come opportunely, for I was about to rely on a far less *rusé* hand. The plan, which is my own, I submit to your judgment, but I think you will allow some merit in it."

Well, I was not well-disposed to approve of any plan of his. In truth he had managed to offend me seriously. Had an English gentleman committed my recent error of supposing him to hint at assassination, General Trant (who can doubt it?) would have flamed out in wrath; but me he had set right with a curt carelessness which said as plain as words that the dishonouring suspicion no doubt came natural enough to a Spaniard. He had entertained me with a familiarity which I had not asked for, and which became insulting the moment he allowed me to see that it came from cold condescension. I have known a dozen combinations spoilt by English commanders who in this way have combined extreme offensiveness with conscious affability; and I have watched their allies—Spaniards and Portuguese of the first nobility—raging inwardly, while ludicrously impotent to discover a peg on which to hang their resentment.

I listened coldly, therefore, leaving the general's wine untasted and ignoring his complimentary deference to my judgment. Yet the neatness and originality of his scheme surprised me. He certainly had talent.

He had found (it seemed) an old vine-dresser at Bellomonte, whose brother kept a small shop in Sabugal, where he shaved chins, sold drugs, drew teeth, and on occasion practised a little bone-setting. This barber-surgeon or apothecary had shut up his shop on the approach of the French and escaped out of the town to his brother's roof. As a matter of fact he would have been safer in Sabugal, for the excesses of the French army were all committed by the marauding parties scattered up and down the country-side and out of the reach of discipline, whereas Marmont (to his credit) sternly discouraged looting, paid the inhabitants fairly for what he took, and altogether treated them with uncommon humanity.

It was likely enough, therefore, that the barber-surgeon's shop stood as he had left it. And General Trant proposed no less than that I should boldly enter the town, take down the shutters, and open business, either personating the old man or (if I could persuade him to return) going with him as his assistant. In either case the danger of detection was more apparent than real, for so violently did the Portuguese hate their invaders that scarcely an instance of treachery occurred during the whole of this campaign. The chance of the neighbours betraying me was small enough, at any rate, to justify

141

the risk, and I told the General promptly that I would take it.

Accordingly I left Guarda that night, and reaching Bellomonte a little after daybreak, found the vine-dresser and presented Trant's letter.

He was on the point of starting for Sabugal, whither he had perforce to carry a dozen skins of wine, and with some little trouble I persuaded the old barber-surgeon to accompany us, bearing a petition to Marmont to be allowed peaceable possession of his shop. We arrived and were allowed to enter the town, where I assisted the vine-dresser in handling the heavy wine skins, while his brother posted off to headquarters and returned after an hour with the marshal's protection. Armed with this, he led me off to the shop, found it undamaged, helped me to take down the shutters, showed me his cupboards, tools, and stock in trade, and answered my rudimentary questions in the art of compounding drugs—in a twitter all the while to be gone. Nor did I seek to delay him (for if my plans miscarried, Sabugal would assuredly be no place for him). Late in the afternoon he left me and went off in search of his brother, and I fell to stropping my razors with what cheerfulness I could assume.

Before nightfall my neighbours on either hand had looked in and given me good evening. They asked few questions when I told them I was taking over old Diego's business for the time, and kept their speculations to themselves. I lay down to sleep that night with a lighter heart.

The adventure itself tickled my humour, though I had no opinion at all of the design—Trant's design—which lay at the end of it. This, however, did not damp my zeal in using eyes and ears; and on the third afternoon, when the old vine-dresser rode over with more wine skins, and dropped in to inquire about business and take home a pint of rhubarb for the stomach-ache, I had the satisfaction of making up for him, under the eyes of two soldiers waiting to be shaved, a packet containing a compendious account of Marmont's dispositions with a description of his headquarters. My report concluded with these words:—

"*With regard to the enterprise on which I have had the honour to be consulted I offer my opinion with humility. It is, however, a fixed one. You will lose two divisions; and even a third, should you bring it.*"

On the whole I had weathered through these three days with eminent success. The shaving I managed with something like credit (for a Portuguese). My pharmaceutics had been (it was vain to deny) in the highest degree empirical, but if my patients had not been cured they even more certainly had not died—or at least their bodies had not been found. What gravelled me was the phlebotomy. Somehow the chance of being called upon to let blood had not occurred to me, and on the second morning when a varicose sergeant of the line dropped into my operating chair and demanded to have a vein opened, I bitterly regretted that I had asked my employer neither where to insert the lancet nor how to stop the bleeding. I eyed the brawn in the chair, so full of animal life and rude health —no, strike at random I could not! I took his arm and asked insinuatingly, " Now, where do you usually have it done?" "Sometimes here, sometimes there," he answered. Joy! I remembered a bottle of leeches on the shelf. I felt the man's pulse and lifted his eyelids with trembling fingers. " In your state," said I, " it would be a crime to bleed you. What you want is leeches." " You think so?" he asked—" how many?" " Oh, half-a-dozen—to begin with." In my sweating hurry I forgot (if I had ever known) that the bottle contained but three. " No," said I, " we'll start with a couple and work up by degrees." He took them on his palm and turned them over with a stubby forefinger. " Funny little beasts!" said he and marched out of the shop into the sunshine. To this day when recounting his Peninsular exploits he omits his narrowest escape.

I can hardly describe the effect of this ridiculous adventure upon my nerves. My heart sank whenever a plethoric customer entered the shop, and I caught fright or snatched relief even from the weight of a footfall or the size of a shadow in my doorway. A dozen times in intervals of leisure I reached down the bottle from its shelf and studied my one remaining leech. A horrible suspicion possessed me that the little brute was dead. He remained at any rate completely torpid, though I coaxed him almost in agony to show some sign of life. Obviously the bottle contained nothing to nourish him; to offer him my own blood would be to disable him for another patient. On the fourth afternoon I went so far as to try him on the back of my hand. I waited five minutes; he gave no sign. Then, startled by a footstep outside, I popped him hurriedly back in his bottle.

A scraggy, hawk-nosed trooper of hussars entered and flung himself into my chair demanding a shave. In my confusion I had lathered his chin and set to work before giving his face any particular attention. He had started a grumble at being overworked (he was just off duty and smelt potently of the stable), but sat silent as men usually do at the

145

first scrape of the razor. On looking down I saw in a flash that this was not the reason. He was one of the troopers whose odd jobs I had done at the Posada del Rio in Huerta, an ill-conditioned Norman called Michu—Pierre Michu. Since our meeting, with the help of a little walnut juice, I had given myself a fine Portuguese complexion with other small touches sufficient to deceive a cleverer man. But by ill-luck (or to give it a true name, by careless folly) I had knotted under my collar that morning a yellow-patterned handkerchief which I had worn every day at the Posada del Rio, and as his eyes travelled from this to my face I saw that the man recognised me.

There was no time for hesitating. If I kept silence, no doubt he would do the same; but if I let him go, it would be to make straight for head-quarters with his tale. I scraped away for a second or two in dead silence, and then holding my razor point I said, sharp and low, " I am going to kill you."

He turned white as a sheet, opened his mouth, and I could feel him gathering his muscles together to heave himself out of the chair; no easy matter. I laid the flat of the razor against his flesh, and he sank back helpless. My hand was over his mouth. " Yes, I shall have plenty of time before they find you." A sound in his throat was the only answer, something between a grunt and a sob. "To be sure," I went on, "I bear you no grudge. But there is no other way, unless——"

"No, no," he gasped. "I promise. The grave shall not be more secret."

"Ah," said I, "but how am I to believe that?"

"Parole d'honneur."

"I must have even a little more than that." I made him swear by the faith of a soldier and half-a-dozen other oaths which occurred to me as likely to bind him if, lacking honour and religion, he might still have room in his lean body for a little superstition. He took every oath eagerly, and with a pensive frown I resumed my shaving. At the first scrape he winced and tried to push me back.

"Indeed no," said I; "business is business," and I finished the job methodically, relentlessly. It still consoles me to think upon what he must have suffered.

When at length I let him up he forced an uneasy laugh. "Well, comrade, you had the better of me I must say. Eh! but you're a clever one—and at Huerta, eh?" He held out his hand. "No rancour though—a fair trick of war, and I am not the man to bear a grudge for it. After all war's war, as they say. Some use one weapon, some another. You know," he went on confidentially, " it isn't as if you had learnt anything out of me. In that case—well, of course, it would have made all the difference."

I fell to stropping my razor. " Since I have your oath——" I began.

" That's understood. My word, though, it is hard to believe! "

" You had best believe it, anyway," said I; and with a sort of shamefaced swagger he lurched out of the shop.

Well, I did not like it. I walked to the door and watched him down the street. Though it wanted an hour of sunset I determined to put up my shutters and take a stroll by the river. I had done the most necessary part of my work in Sabugal; to-morrow I would make my way back to Bellomonte, but in case of hindrance it might be as well to know how the river bank was guarded. At this point a really happy inspiration seized me. There were many pools in the marsh land by the river—pools left by the recent floods. Possibly by hunting among these and stirring up the mud I might replenish my stock of leeches. I had the vaguest notion how leeches were gathered, but the pursuit would at the worst give me an excuse for dawdling and spying out the land.

THE TWO SCOUTS

I closed the shop at once, hunted out a tin box, and with this and my bottle (to serve as evidence, if necessary, of my good faith) made my way down to the river side north of the town. The bank here was well guarded by patrols, between whom a number of peaceful citizens sat a-fishing. Seen thus in line and with their backs turned to me they bore a ludicrous resemblance to a row of spectators at a play; and gazing beyond them, though dazzled for a moment by the full level rays of the sun, I presently became aware of a spectacle worth looking at.

On the road across the river a squadron of lancers was moving northward.

"Hallo!" thought I, "here's a reconnaissance of some importance." But deciding that any show of inquisitiveness would be out of place under the eyes of the patrols, I kept my course parallel with the river's, at perhaps 300 yards distance from it. This brought me to the first pool, and there I had no sooner deposited my bottle and tin box on the brink than beyond the screen of the town wall came pushing the head of a column of infantry.

Decidedly here was something to think over. The column unwound itself in clouds of yellow dust —a whole brigade; then an interval, then another dusty column—two brigades! Could Marmont be planning against Trant the very *coup* which Trant had planned against him? Twenty miles—it could be done before daybreak; and the infantry (I had seen at the first glance) were marching light.

I do not know to this day if any leeches inhabit the pools outside Sabugal. It is very certain that I discovered none. About a quarter of a mile ahead of me and about the same distance back from the river there stood a ruinous house which had been fired, but whether recently or by the French I could not tell; once no doubt the country villa of some well-to-do townsman, but now roofless, and showing smears of black where the flames had licked its white outer walls. Towards this I steered my way cautiously, that behind the shelter of an out-building I might study the receding brigades at my leisure.

The form of the building was roughly a hollow square enclosing a fair-sized patio, the entrance of which I had to cross to gain the rearward premises and slip out of sight of the patrols. The gate of this entrance had been torn off its hinges and now lay jammed aslant across the passage; beyond it the patio lay heaped with bricks and rubble, tiles, and charred beams. I paused for a moment and craned in for a better look at the *débris.*

And then the sound of voices arrested me—a

moment too late. I was face to face with two French officers, one with a horse beside him. They saw me, and on the instant ceased talking and stared; but without changing their attitudes, which were clearly those of two disputants. They stood perhaps four paces apart. Both were young men, and the one whose attitude most suggested menace I recognised as a young lieutenant of a line regiment (the 102nd) whom I had shaved that morning. The other wore the uniform of a staff officer, and at the first glance I read a touch of superciliousness in his indignant face. His left hand held his horse's bridle, his other he still kept tightly clenched while he stared at me.

" What the devil do *you* want here? " demanded the lieutenant roughly in bad Portuguese. " But, hallo! " he added, recognising me, and turned a curious glance on the other.

" Who is it? " the staff officer asked.

" It's a barber; and I believe something of a surgeon. That's so, eh? " He appealed to me.

" In a small way," I answered apologetically.

The lieutenant turned again to his companion. " He might do for us; the sooner the better, unless——"

" Unless," interrupted the staff officer with cold politeness, " you prefer the apology you owe me."

The lieutenant swung round again with a brusque laugh. " Look here, have you your instruments about you?"

For answer I held up my bottle with the one absurd leech dormant at the bottom. He laughed again just as harshly.

" That is about the last thing to suit our purpose. Listen "—he glanced out through the passage— " the gates won't be shut for an hour yet. It will take you perhaps twenty minutes to fetch what is necessary. You understand? Return here, and don't keep us waiting. Afterwards, should the gates be shut, one of us will see you back to the town."

I bowed without a word and hurried back across the water meadow. Along the river bank between the patrols the anglers still sat in their patient row. And on the road to the north-west the tail of the second brigade was winding slowly out of sight.

Once past the gate and through the streets, I walked more briskly, paused at my shop door to fit the key in the lock, and was astonished when the door fell open at the push of my hand.

Then in an instant I understood. The shop had been ransacked — by that treacherous scoundrel Michu, of course. Bottles, herbs, shaving appa-

152

ratus, all was topsy-turvy. Drawers stood half-
open; the floor was in a litter.

I had two consolations: the first that there were
no incriminating papers in the house; the second
that Michu had clearly paid me a private visit before carrying his tale to headquarters. Otherwise
the door would have been sealed and the house
under guard. I reflected that the idiot would
catch it hot for this unauthorised piece of work.
Stay! he might still be in the house rummaging
the upper rooms. I crept upstairs.

No, he was gone. He had left my case of instruments, too, after breaking the lock and scattering them about the floor. I gathered them together
in haste, descended again, snatched up a roll of lint,
and pausing only at the door for a glance up and
down the street, made my escape post haste for the
water meadow.

In the patio I found the two disputants standing
much as I had left them, the staff officer gently
and methodically smoothing his horse's crupper, the
lieutenant with a watch in his hand.

" Good," said he, closing it with a snap, " seventeen minutes only. By the way, do you happen
to understand French? "

" A very little," said I.

" Because, as you alone are the witness of this

our little difference, it will be in order if I explain that I insulted this gentleman."

"Somewhat grossly," put in the staff officer.

"Somewhat grossly, in return for an insult put upon me—somewhat grossly—in the presence of my company, two days ago, in the camp above Penamacor, when I took the liberty to resent a message conveyed by him to my colonel—as he alleges upon the authority of the marshal, the Duke of Ragusa."

"An assertion," commented the staff officer, "which I am able to prove on the marshal's return and with his permission, provided always that the request be decently made."

They had been speaking in French and meanwhile removing their tunics. The staff officer had even drawn off his riding boots. "Do you understand?" asked the lieutenant.

"A little," said I; "enough to serve the occasion."

"Excellent barber-surgeon! Would that all your nation were no more inquisitive!" He turned to the staff officer. "Ready? On guard, then, monsieur!"

The combat was really not worth describing. The young staff officer had indeed as much training as his opponent (and that was little), but no wrist

at all.   He had scarcely engaged before he attempted a blind cut over the scalp.   The lieutenant,
parrying clumsily, but just in time, forced blade
and arm upward until the two pointed almost verti-
cally to heaven, and their forearms almost rubbed
as the pair stood close and chest to chest.   For an
instant the staff officer's sword was actually driven
back behind his head; and then with a rearward
spring the lieutenant disengaged and brought his
edge clean down on his adversary's left shoulder
and breast, narrowly missing his ear.   The cut itself, delivered almost in the recoil, had no great
weight behind it, but the blood spurted at once,
and the wounded man, stepping back for a fresh
guard, swayed foolishly for a moment and then
toppled into my arms.

" Is it serious? " asked the lieutenant, wiping his
sword and looking, it seemed to me, more than a
little scared.

" Wait a moment," said I, and eased the body to
the ground.   " Yes, it looks nasty.   And keep
back, if you please; he has fainted."

Being off my guard I said it in very good
French, which in his agitation he luckily failed to
remark.

" I had best fetch help," said he.

" Assuredly."

"I'll run for one of the patrols; we'll carry him back to the town."

But this would not suit me at all. "No," I objected, "you must fetch one of your surgeons. Meanwhile I will try to stop the bleeding; but I certainly won't answer for it if you attempt to move him at once."

I showed him the wound as he hurried into his tunic. It was a long and ugly gash, but (as I had guessed) neither deep nor dangerous. It ran from the point of the collar-bone aslant across the chest, and had the lieutenant put a little more drag into the stroke it must infallibly have snicked open the artery inside the upper arm. As it was, my immediate business lay in frightening him off before the bleeding slackened, and my heart gave a leap when he turned and ran out of the patio, buttoning his tunic as he went.

It took me ten minutes perhaps to dress the wound and tie a rude bandage; and perhaps another four to pull off coat and shoes and slip into the staff officer's tunic, pull on his riding boots over my blue canvas trousers—at a distance scarcely discernible in colour from his tight-fitting breeches—and buckle on his sword-belt. I had some difficulty in finding his cap, for he had tossed it carelessly behind one of the fallen beams, and by this time the light was bad within the patio. The horse gave me no trouble, being an old campaigner, no doubt, and used to surprises. I untethered him and led him gently across the yard, picking my way in a circuit which would take him as far as possible from his fallen master. But glancing back just before mounting, to my horror I saw that the wounded man had raised himself on his right elbow and was staring at me. Our eyes met; what he thought—whether he suspected the truth or accepted the sight as a part of his delirium—I shall never know. The next instant he fell back again and lay inert.

I passed out into the open. The warning gun must have sounded without my hearing it, for across the meadow the townspeople were retracing their way to the town gate, which closed at sunset. At any moment now the patrols might be upon me; so swinging myself into the saddle I set off at a brisk trot towards the gate.

My chief peril for the moment lay in the chance of meeting the lieutenant on his way back with the doctor; yet I must run this risk and ride through the town to the bridge gate, the river being unfordable for miles to the northward and trending farther and farther away from Guarda; and Guarda must be reached at all costs, or by to-morrow Trant's and Wilson's garrisons would have ceased to exist. My heart fairly sank when on reaching the gate I saw an officer in talk with the sentry there, and at least a score of men behind him. I drew aside; he stepped out and called an order to his company, which at once issued and spread itself in face of the scattered groups of citizens returning across the meadow.

" Yes, captain," said the sentry, answering the question in my look, " they are after a spy, it seems, who has been practising here as a barber. They say even the famous McNeill."

I rode through the gateway and spurred my horse to a trot again, heading him down a side street to the right. This took me some distance out of my way, but anything was preferable to the risk of meeting the lieutenant, and I believed that I had yet some minutes to spare before the second gun-fire.

In this I was mistaken. The gun boomed out just as I came in sight of the bridge gate, and the lieutenant of the guard appeared clanking out on the instant to close the heavy doors. I spurred my horse and dashed down at a canter, hailing loudly:—

" A spy!—a barber fellow; here, hold a minute! "

" Yes, we have had warning half an hour ago. Nobody has passed out since."

"At the gate below," I panted, "they sighted him; and he made for the river—tried to swim it. Run out your men and bring them along to search the bank!"

He began to shout orders. I galloped through the gate and hailed the sentry at the *tête du pont.* "A spy!" I shouted—"in the river. Keep your eyes open if he makes the bank!"

The fellow drew aside, and I clattered past him with a dozen soldiers at my heels fastening their belts and looking to their muskets as they ran. Once over the bridge I headed to the right again along the left bank of the river.

"This way! This way! Keep your eyes open!"

I was safe now. In the rapidly falling dusk, still increasing the distance between us, I led them down past the town and opposite the astonished patrols on the meadow bank. Even then, when I wheeled to the left and galloped for the high road, it did not occur to them to suspect me, nor shall I ever know when first it dawned on them that they had been fooled. Certainly not a shot was sent after me, and I settled down for a steady gallop northward, pleasantly assured of being at least twenty minutes ahead of any effective pursuit.

I was equally well assured of overtaking the brigades, but my business, of course, was to avoid and get ahead of them. And with this object, after an hour's brisk going, I struck a hill-track to the left which, as I remembered (having used it on my journey from Badajoz), at first ran parallel with the high road for two miles or more and then cut two considerable loops which the road followed along the valley bottom.

Recent rains had unloosed the springs on the mountain side and set them chattering so loudly that I must have reined up at least a score of times before I detected the tramp of the brigades in the darkness below me. Of the cavalry, though I rode on listening for at least another two miles, I could hear no sound. Yet, as I argued, they could not be far distant; and I pushed forward with heart elate at the prospect of trumping Marmont's card, for I remembered the staff officer's words, " on the marshal's return." I knew that Marmont had been in Sabugal no longer ago than mid-day; and irregular and almost derogatory as it might be thought for a marshal of France to be conducting a night surprise against a half-disciplined horde of militia, I would have wagered my month's pay that this was the fact.

And then, with a slip of my horse on the stony track, my good fortune suddenly ended, and smash went my basket of eggs while I counted the chickens. The poor brute with one false step came down heavily on his near side. Quick as I was in flinging my foot from the stirrup, I was just a moment too late; I fell without injury to bone, but his weight pinned me to earth by the boot, and when I extricated myself it was with a wrenched ankle. I managed to get him to his feet, but he had either dislocated or so severely wrung his near shoulder that he could scarcely walk a step. It went to my heart to leave him there on the mountain side, but it had to be done, for possibly the fate of the garrison at Guarda depended on it.

I left him, therefore, and limped forward along the track until it took an abrupt turn around a shoulder of the mountain. Immediately below me, unless I erred in my bearings, a desolate sheep farm stood but a short distance above the high road. Towards this I descended, and finding it with no great difficulty, knocked gently at the back door. To my surprise the shepherd opened it almost at once. He was fully dressed in spite of the lateness of the hour, and seemed greatly perturbed; nor, I can promise you, was he reassured when, after giving him the signal arranged between Trant and the peasantry, I followed him into his kitchen and his eyes fell on my French uniform.

But it was my turn to be perturbed when, satisfied with my explanation, he informed me that a body of cavalry had passed along the road towards Guarda a good twenty minutes before. It was this had awakened him. "No infantry?" I asked.

He shook his head positively. He had been on the watch ever since. And this, while it jumped with my own conviction that the infantry was at least a mile behind me, gave me new hope. I could not understand this straggling march, but it was at least reasonable to suppose that Marmont's horse would wait upon his foot before attempting such a position as Guarda.

"I must push on," said I, and instructed him where to seek for my unfortunate charger.

He walked down with me to the road. My ankle pained me cruelly.

"See here," said he, "the señor had best let me go with him. It is but six miles, and I can recover the horse in the morning."

He was in earnest, and I consented. It was fortunate that I did, or I might have dropped in the road and been found or trodden on by the French column behind us.

As it was I broke down after the second mile. The shepherd took me in his arms like a child and found cover for me below a bank to the left of the road beside the stream in the valley bottom. I gave him my instructions and he hurried on.

Lying there in the darkness half an hour later I heard the tramp of the brigade approaching, and lay and listened while they went by.

I have often, in writing these memoirs, wished I could be inventing instead of setting down facts. With a little invention only, how I could have rounded off this adventure! But that is the way with real events. All my surprising luck ended with the casual stumble of a horse, and it was not I who saved Guarda, nor even my messenger, but Marmont's own incredible folly.

When my shepherd reached the foot of the ascent to the fortress he heard a drum beaten suddenly in the darkness above. This single drum kept rattling (he told me) for at least a minute before a score of others took up the alarm. There had been no other warning, not so much as a single shot fired; and even after the drums began there was no considerable noise of musketry until the day broke and the shepherd saw the French cavalry retiring slowly down the hill scarcely 500 yards ahead of the Portuguese militia, now pouring forth from the gateway. These were at once checked and formed up in front of the town, the French still retiring slowly, with a few English dragoons hanging on their heels. A few shots only were exchanged, apparently without damage. The man assured me that the whole 400 or 500 troopers passed within a hundred yards of him and so down the slope and out of his sight.

What had happened was this: Marmont, impatient at the delay of his two brigades of infantry (which by some bungle in the starting did not reach the foot of the mountain before daylight), had pushed his horsemen up the hill and managed to cut off and silence the outposts without their firing a shot. Encouraged by this he pressed on to the very gates of the town, and had actually entered the street when the alarm was sounded—and by whom? By a single drummer whom General Trant, distrusting the watchfulness of his militia, had posted at his bedroom door! Trant's servant entering with his coffee at daybreak brought a report that the French were at the gates; the drummer plied his sticks like a madman; other drummers all over the town caught up their sticks and tattooed away without the least notion of what was happening; the militia ran helter-skelter to their alarm post; and the French marshal, who might have carried the town at a single rush and without losing a man, turned tail! Such are the absurdities of war.

But in fancy I sometimes complete the picture and see myself, in French staff officer's dress, boldly riding up to the head of the French infantry column and in the name of the Duke of Ragusa commanding its general to halt. True, I did not know the password—which might have been awkward. But a staff officer can swagger through some small difficulties, as I had already proved twice that night. But for the stumble of a horse—who knows? The possibility seems to me scarcely more fantastic than the accident which actually saved Guarda.

III

THE PAROLE

Marmont's night attack on Guarda, though immediately and even absurdly unsuccessful, did, in fact, convince Trant that the hill was untenable, and he at once attempted to fall back upon Celorico across the river Mondego, where lay Lord Wellington's magazines and very considerable stores, for the moment quite unprotected.

Marmont had from four to six thousand horsemen and two brigades of infantry. The horse could with the utmost ease have headed Trant off and trotted into Celorico while the infantry fell on him, and but for the grossest blundering the militia as a fighting force should have been wiped out of existence. But blunders dogged Marmont throughout this campaign. Trant and Wilson marched their men (with one day's provisions only) out of Guarda and down the long slopes toward the river. Good order was kept for three or four miles, and the head of the column was actually crossing by a pretty deep ford when some forty dragoons (which Trant had begged from Bacellar to help him in his proposed *coup* upon Sabugal, and which had arrived from Celorico but the day before) came galloping down through the woods with a squadron of French cavalry in pursuit, and charging in panic through the rearguard flung everything into confusion. The day was a rainy one, and the militia, finding their powder wet, ran for the ford like sheep. The officers, however, kept their heads and got the men over, though with the loss of two hundred prisoners. Even so, Marmont might have crossed the river on their flank and galloped into Celorico ahead of them. As it was, he halted and allowed the rabble to save themselves in the town. While blaming his head I must do justice to his heart and add that, finding what poor creatures he had to deal with, he forbade his horsemen to cut down the fugitives, and not a single man was killed.

Foreseeing that Trant must sooner or later retreat upon Celorico—though ignorant, of course, of
what was happening—I was actually crossing the
river at the time by a ford some four miles above,
not in the French staff officer's uniform which I
had worn out of Sabugal, but in an old jacket lent
me by my friend the shepherd. By the time I
reached the town Wilson had swept in his rabble
and was planting his outposts, intending to resist
and, if this became impossible, to blow up the magazines before retiring. Trant and Bacellar with the
bulk of the militia were continuing the retreat meanwhile towards Lamego.

I need only say here that Wilson's bold front
served its purpose. Once, when the French drove
in his outposts, he gave the order to fire the powder,
and a part of the magazine was actually destroyed
when Marmont (who above all things hated ridicule, and was severely taxing the respect of his
beautiful army by these serio-comic excursions after
a raw militia) withdrew his troops and retired in
an abominable temper to Sabugal.

How do I know that Marmont's temper was
abominable? By what follows.

On March 30th I had left my kinsman, Captain
Alan McNeill, with his servant José at Tammames.
They were to keep an eye on the French move-

ments while I rode south and reported to Lord Wellington at Badajoz. It was now April 16th, and in the meanwhile a great deal had happened; but of my kinsman's movements I had heard nothing. At first I felt sure he must be somewhere in the neighbourhood of Marmont's headquarters; but even in Sabugal itself no hint of him could I hear, and at length I concluded that having satisfied himself of the main lines of Marmont's campaign he had gone off to meet and receive fresh instructions from Wellington, now posting north to save the endangered magazines.

On the evening of the 16th General Wilson sent for me.

"Here is a nasty piece of news," said he. "Your namesake is a prisoner."

"Where?"

"In Sabugal; but it seems he was brought there from the main camp above Penamacor. Trant tells me that you are not only namesakes but kinsmen. Would you care to question the messenger?"

The messenger was brought in—a peasant from the Penamacor district. Out of his rambling tale one or two certainties emerged. McNeill—the celebrated McNeill—was a prisoner; he had been taken on the 14th somewhere in the pass above Penamacor, and conveyed to Sabugal to await the

French marshal's return. His servant was dead—
killed in trying to escape, or to help his master's
escape. So much I sifted out of the mass of inac-
curacies. For, as usual, the two McNeills had
managed to get mixed up in the story, a good half
of which spread itself into a highly coloured ver-
sion of my own escape from Sabugal on the evening
of the 13th; how I had been arrested by a French
officer in a back shop in the heart of the town;
how, as he overhauled my incriminating papers, I
had leapt on him with a knife and stabbed him to
the heart, while my servant did the same with his
orderly; how, having possessed ourselves of their
clothes and horses, we had ridden boldly through
the gate and southward to join Lord Wellington;
and a great deal more equally veracious. As I
listened I began to understand how legends grow
and demigods are made.

It was flattering; but without attempting to
show how I managed to disengage the facts, I will
here quote the plain account of them, sent to me
long afterwards by Captain Alan himself:—

Captain Alan McNeill's Statement.

" You wish, for use in your *Memoirs*, an account
of my capture in the month of April, 1811, and the
death of my faithful servant, José. I imagine this

does not include an account of all our movements from the time you left us at Tammames (though this, too, I shall be happy to send if desired), and so I come at once to the 14th, the actual date of the capture.

" The preceding night we had spent in the woods below the great French camp, and perhaps a mile above the mouth of the pass opening on Penamacor. All through the previous day there had been considerable stir in the camp, and I believed a general movement to be impending. I supposed Marmont himself to be either with the main army or behind in his headquarters at Sabugal, and within easy distance. It never occurred to me—nor could it have occurred to any reasonable man—to guess, upon no evidence, that a marshal of France had gone gallivanting with six thousand horse and two brigades of infantry in chase of a handful of undrilled militia.

" My impression was that his move, if he made one, would be a resolute descent through Penamacor and upon Castello Branco. As a matter of fact, although Victor Alten had abandoned that place to be held by Lecor and his two thousand five hundred militiamen, the French (constant to their policy of frittering away opportunities) merely sent down two detachments of cavalry to menace it, and

I believe that my capture was the only success which befel them.

"Early on the 14th, and about an hour before these troops (dragoons for the most part) began to descend the pass, I had posted myself with José on one of the lower ridges and (as I imagined) well under cover of the dwarf oaks which grew thickly there. They did indeed screen us admirably from the squadrons I was watching, and they passed unsuspecting within fifty yards of us. Believing them to be but an advance guard, and that we should soon hear the tramp of the main army, I kept my shelter for another ten minutes, and was prepared to keep it for another hour, when José —whose eyes missed nothing—caught me by the arm and pointed high up the hillside behind us.

" 'Scouts!' he whispered. 'They have seen us, sir!'

" I glanced up and saw a pair of horsemen about two gunshots away galloping down the uneven ridge towards us, with about a dozen in a cluster close behind. We leapt into saddle at once, made off through the oaks for perhaps a couple of hundred yards, and then wheeling sharply struck back across the hillside towards Sabugal. We were still in good cover, but the enemy had posted his men more thickly than we had guessed, and by-and-by

I crossed a small clearing and rode straight into the arms of a dragoon. Providentially I came on him with a suddenness which flurried his aim, and though he fired his pistol at me point-blank he wounded neither me nor my horse. But hearing shouts behind him in answer to the shot, we wheeled almost right-about and set off straight down the hill.

" This new direction did not help us, however; for almost at once a bugle was sounded above, obviously as a warning to the dragoons at the foot of the pass, who halted and spread themselves along the lower slopes to cut us off. Our one chance now lay in abandoning our horses and crawling deep into the covert of the low oaks where cavalry would have much ado to follow. This we promptly did, and for twenty minutes we managed to elude them, so that my hopes began to grow. But unhappily a knot of officers on the ridge above had watched this manœuvre through their telescopes, and now detached small parties of infantry down either side of the pass to beat the covers. Our hiding place quickly became too hot, and as we broke cover and dashed across another small clearing we were spied again by those on the ridge, who shouted to the soldiers and directed the chase by waving their caps. For another ten minutes we baffled them, and then crawling on hands and knees from a thicket where we could hear our enemies not a dozen yards away beating the bushes with the flat of their swords, we came face to face with a second party advancing straight upon us. I stood up straight and was on the point of making a last desperate run for it when I saw José sink on his face exhausted.

" ' Do not shoot! ' I called to the officer. ' We have hurt no man, monsieur.'—For it is, as you know, a fact that in our business I strongly disapprove of bloodshed, and in all our expeditions together José had never done physical injury to a living creature.

" But I was too late. The young officer fired, and though the ball entered my poor servant's skull and killed him on the instant, a hulking fellow beside him had the savagery to complete what was finished with a savage bayonet-thrust through the back.

" I stood still, fully expecting to be used no more humanely, but the officer lowered his pistol and curtly told me I was his prisoner. By this time the fellows had come up from beating the thicket behind and surrounded me. I therefore surrendered, and was marched up the hill to the camp with poor José's body at my heels borne by a couple of soldiers.

" In all the hurry and heat of this chase I had
found time to wonder how our pursuers happened
to be so well posted. For a good fortnight and more
—in fact, since my escape across the ford at Huerta
—I could remember nothing that we had done to
give the French the slightest inkling that we were
watching them or, indeed, were anywhere near.
And yet the affair suggested no casual piece of
scouting, but a deliberate plan to entrap somebody
of whose neighbourhood they were aware.

" Nor was this perplexity at all unravelled by
the general officer to whose tent they at once conveyed me—a little round white-headed man, Ducrôt by name. He addressed me at once as Captain McNeill, and seemed vastly elated at my
capture.

" ' So we have you at last! ' he said, regarding
me with a jocular smile and a head cocked on one
side, pretty much after the fashion of a thrush eyeing a worm. ' But, excuse me, after so much
finesse it was a blunder—hein? '

" Now *finesse* is not a word which I should
have claimed at any time for my methods,* and I

* NOTE BY MANUEL MCNEILL.—Here the captain, in his hurry
to pay me a compliment, does himself some injustice. *Finesse*,
to be sure, was not generally characteristic of his methods, but
he used it at times with amazing dexterity, as, for instance, the

cast about in my memory for the exploit to which he could be alluding.

" ' It is the mistake of clever men,' continued General Ducrôt sagely, ' to undervalue their opponents; but surely after yesterday the commonest prudence might have warned you to put the greatest possible distance between yourself and Sabugal.'

" ' Sabugal?' I echoed.

" ' Oh, my dear sir, *we* know. It was amusing —eh!—the barber's shop? I assure you I laughed. It was time for you to be taken; for really, you know, you could never have bettered it, and it is not for an artist to wind up by repeating inferior successes.'

" For a moment I thought the man daft. What on earth (I asked myself) was this nonsense about Sabugal and a barber's shop? I had not been near Sabugal; as for the barber's shop it sounded to me like a piece out of the childish rigmarole about cutting a cabbage leaf to make an apple pie. Some fleeting suspicion I may have had that here was another affair in which you and I had again managed to get confused; but if so the suspicion

latter part of this very adventure will prove, if I can ever prevail on him to narrate it. On the whole I should say that he disapproved of *finesse* much as he disapproved of swearing, but had a natural aptitude for both.

occurred only to be dismissed. A fortnight before
you had left me on your way south to Badajoz,
and you will own that to connect you with something which apparently had happened yesterday in
a barber's shop in Sabugal was to overstrain guessing. Having nothing to say, I held my tongue; and
General Ducrôt put on a more magisterial air.
He resented this British phlegm in a prisoner with
whom he had been graciously jocose and fell back
on his national belief that we islanders, though oc-
casionally funny, are so by force of eccentricity
rather than by humour.

"'I do not propose to deal with you myself,' he
announced. 'At one time and another, sir, you
have done our cause an infinity of mischief, and I
prefer that the Duke of Ragusa should decide your
fate. I shall send you therefore to Sabugal to await
his return.'

"This gave me my first intimation that Marmont was neither in Sabugal nor with his main
army. That same afternoon they marched me off
to the town and set me under guard in a house
next door to his headquarters.

"Marmont returned from Celorico (if my memory serves me) on the afternoon of the 17th. I
was taken before him at once. He treated me with
the greatest apparent kindness, hoped I had suffered

no ill-usage, and wound up by inviting me to dinner. A couple of hours later I was escorted to headquarters, where, on entering the room where he received his guests, I found him in conversation with a young staff officer who wore his arm in a sling.

"The marshal turned to me at once, and very gaily. 'I understand,' said he with a smile, 'that I have no need to introduce you to Captain de Brissac.'

"I looked from him to the young officer in some bewilderment, and saw in a moment that Captain de Brissac was certainly not less bewildered than I.

"'But Monsieur le Maréchal—but this is not the man!'

"'Not the man?'

"'Most decidedly not. The man of whom I spoke was dark and not above middle height. He spoke Portuguese like a native, and belonged to a class altogether different. It would be impossible for this gentleman to disguise himself so.'

"For a moment Marmont seemed no less puzzled than we. Then he broke out laughing again.

"'Ah! of course; that will have been Captain McNeill's servant—the poor fellow who was killed,' he added more gravely. 'I am told, sir, that this servant shared and furthered most of your adventures?'

" ' He did indeed, M. le Maréchal,' said I; ' but excuse me if I am at a loss——'

" The Duke interrupted me by laughing again and laying a hand on my shoulder as an orderly announced dinner. ' Rest easy, my friend, we know of all your little tricks.' And at table he amused himself and more and more befogged me by a precise account of my haunts and movements. How I had kept a barber's shop in Sabugal under his very nose; what disguises I used (and you know that I never used a disguise in my life); how my servant had assisted M. de Brissac in a duel and afterwards escaped in his uniform—with much more, and all of it news to me. My astonished face merely excited his laughter; he set it down to my eccentricity. But after dinner, when M. de Brissac had taken his departure, Marmont crossed his handsome legs and came to business.

" ' Sir,' said he, ' I am going to pay you a compliment. We have suffered heavily through your cleverness; and although Lord Wellington may choose to call you a scouting officer, you must be aware (and will forgive me for reminding you) that I might well be excused for calling you by an uglier name.'

" You may be sure I did not like this. You may also remember how at Huerta on the occasion of

178

our first meeting the question of *disguise* came up
between us, and how I assured you that to me, with
my Scottish face and accent, a disguise would be
worse than useless. Well, that was true enough
so far as it went; but I fear that in my anxiety not
to offend your feelings I spoke less than the whole
truth, for I have always held that in our business
as soon as a man resorts to disguise his work ceases
to be legitimate *scouting*. It may be no less justi-
fiable and even more useful, but it is no longer
scouting. I admit the distinction to be a nice one; *
and I have sometimes asked myself, when covering
my uniform with my dark riding cloak, ' What,
after all, is a disguise?' Nevertheless, I had always observed it, and standing before Marmont now
in His Majesty's scarlet, which (as I might have
told him) I had never discarded either to further
a plan or to avoid a danger, I put some constraint
on myself to listen in silence on the merest off-
chance that my silence might help an affair with
which the marshal assumed my perfect acquaintance, while I could only surmise that somehow you
were mixed up in it, and therefore presumably it
aimed at some advantage to our arms. I *did* keep

* NOTE BY MANUEL McNEILL.—I should think so indeed! To
me the moral difference, say, between hiding in a truss of hay
and hiding under a wig is not worth discussing outside a seminary.

silence, however, though without so much as a bow to signify that I assented.

" ' But you are a gentleman,' Marmont con tinued, ' and I propose to treat you as one. You will be sent in safe custody to France, and beyond this I propose to take no revenge on you—but upon one condition.'

" I waited.

" ' The condition is you give me your parole that on your journey through Spain to France you not only make no effort to escape, but will not consent to be rescued should the attempt be made by any of the *partidas* in hope of reward.'

" I considered this for a moment. ' That is not a small thing to require, since Wellington may be reasonably expected to offer a round price for my recapture.'

" The marshal laughed not too pleasantly. ' Truly,' said he, ' I have heard that Scotsmen are hard bargainers. But considering that I could have you shot out of hand for a spy, I believed I was offering you generous terms.'

" Well, that was unfortunately true; so after a few seconds' pause I answered, ' Monsieur le Duc, by imposing these terms on me you at any rate pay me a handsome compliment. I accept it and give you my word.'

THE TWO SCOUTS

" Upon this parole, then, on the 19th I began my journey towards France and captivity, escorted only by M. Gérard, a young lieutenant of dragoons, and one trooper. The rest you know."

(Conclusion of Captain McNeill's Statement.)

As I have said, the bare news of my kinsman's capture and of poor José's death reached me at Celorico on the 16th, late in the evening. Knowing that Lord Wellington was by this time well on his way northward, and believing that for more than one reason the captain's fate would concern him deeply—feeling, moreover, some compunction at the toils I had all innocently helped to wind about an honest man—I at once sought and obtained leave from General Wilson to ride southward to meet the Commander-in-Chief with the tidings, and if necessary solicit his help in a rescue. The captain (on this point the messenger was precise) had been taken to Sabugal to await Marmont's return. I did not know that Marmont was actually at that moment on his way thither, but I thought him at least likely to be returning very soon. To be sure he might decide to shoot Captain Alan out of hand. My recent performances gave him a colourable excuse, unless the prisoner could disassociate himself from these and prove an *alibi*, which under the circumstances and without the help of José's evidence he could scarcely hope to do. I built, however, some faith on Marmont's known humanity, of which in his pursuit of the militia he had just given striking proof. The longer I weighed the chances the more certain I became that Marmont would treat him as an ordinary prisoner of war and send him up to France under escort.

Why, then (the reader may ask), did I lose time in seeking Lord Wellington instead of making my way at once to the north and doing my best to incite the *partidas* to attempt a rescue somewhere on the road north of Burgos, or even between Valladolid and Burgos? My answer is that such an affair would certainly turn on the question of money. The French held the road right away to the Pyrenees, not so strongly perhaps as to forbid hope, but strongly enough to make an attempt upon it risky in the extreme. The bands of Mendizabal, Mina, and Merino were kept busy by Generals Bonnet and Abbé; for a big convoy they might be counted on to exert themselves, but for a single prisoner they as certainly had no time to spare without the incitement of such a reward as only the Commander-in-Chief could offer.

Accordingly I made my way south to Castello Branco and reached it on the 18th, to find Lord

Wellington arrived there and making ready to push on as soon as overtaken by the bulk of his troops. I had always supposed him to cherish a peculiar liking for my kinsman, but was fairly astonished by the emotion he showed.

"Rescued? Of course he must be rescued!" He broke off to use (I must confess) some very strong words upon Trant's design against Marmont and the tomfoolery, as he called it, which had taken me into Sabugal, and left a cloud of suspicion hanging over "the best scouting officer in my service; the only man of the lot, sir, who knows his business." Lord Wellington could, when he lost his temper, be singularly unjust. I strove to point out that my "tomfoolery" in Sabugal had as a matter of fact put a stop to the very scheme of General Trant's which he condemned. He cut me short by asking if I proposed to argue with him.

"Ride back, sir. Choose the particular blackguard who can effect your purpose, and inform him that on the day he rescues Captain McNeill I am his debtor for twelve thousand francs."

The speech was ungracious enough, but the price more than I had dared to hope for. Feeling pretty sure that in his lordship's temper a word of thanks would merely invite him to consign my several members to perdition, I bowed and left him.

183

Twenty minutes later I was on the road and galloping north again.

Before starting from Celorico I had sent the peasant who brought news of Captain Alan's plight back to Sabugal with instructions to discover what more he could, and bring his report to Bellomonte on my northward road not later than the 20th. On the afternoon of the 19th when I rode into that place I could hear no news of him. But late in the evening he arrived with word that " the great McNeill " had been sent off under escort towards Salamanca. Of the strength of that escort he could tell me nothing, and had very wisely not stayed to inquire; he had picked up the news from camp gossip and brought it at once, rightly judging that time was more valuable to me just now than detailed information.

His news was doubly cheering; it assured me that my kinsman still lived, and also that by riding to secure Lord Wellington's help I had not missed my opportunity. Yet there was need to hurry, for I had not only to fetch a long circuit by difficult paths before striking the road to the Pyrenees,—I had to find the *partidas*, persuade them, and get them on to the road ahead of their quarry.

I need not describe my journey at length. I rode by Guarda, Almeida, Ledesma, keeping to the north of the main road, and travelling, not by day only, but through the better part of each night. Beyond the ford of Tordesillas, left for the while unguarded, I was in country where at any moment I might stumble on the guerilla bands, or at least get news of them. The chiefs most likely for my purpose were " the three M's "—the curate Merino, Mina, and Mendizabal. Of these, the curate was about the biggest scoundrel in Spain. I learned on my way that having lately taken about a hundred prisoners near Aranda, he had hanged the lot, sixty to avenge three members of the local junta put to death by the French, and the rest in proportion of ten for every soldier of his lost in the action. From dealing with such a blackguard I prayed to be spared. And by all accounts Mina ran him close for brutal ferocity. I hoped, therefore, for Mendizabal, but at Sedano I heard that Bonnet, after foiling an attack by him on a convoy above Burgos, had beaten him into the Asturias, where his scattered bands were now shifting as best they could among the hills. Merino was in no better case, and my only hope rested on Mina, who after a series of really brilliant operations, helped out by some lucky escapes, had on the 7th with five thousand men planted himself in ambush behind Vittoria, cut up a Polish regiment, and mastered the same enor-

mous convoy which had escaped the curate and
Mendizabal at Burgos, releasing no less than four
hundred Spanish prisoners and enriching himself
to the tune of a million francs, not to speak of
carriages, arms, stores, and a quantity of church
plate.

This was no cheerful hearing, since so much in
his pocket must needs lessen the attractiveness of
my offer of twelve thousand francs. And, indeed,
when I found him in his camp above the road a little to the east of Salvatierra his first answer was to
bid me go to the devil. Although for months he
had only supported his troops on English money
conveyed through Sir Howard Douglas, this ignorant fellow snapped his dirty fingers at the mention
of Wellington and, flushed with a casual triumph,
had nothing but contempt for the allied troops who
were saving his country while he and his like wasted
themselves on futile raids. I can see him now as
he sat smoking and dangling his legs on a rock in
the midst of his unwashed staff officers.

" For an Englishman," he scoffed, " I won't say
but twelve thousand francs is a high price to pay.
Unfortunately, it is no price for my troops to earn.
Here am I expecting at any moment a convoy
which is due from the Valencia side, and Lord
Wellington asks me to waste my men and miss my

chance for the sake of a single redcoat. He must be a fool."

Said I, nettled, "For a Spaniard you have certainly acquired a rare suit of manners. But may I suggest that their rarity will scarcely prove worth the cost when your answer comes to Lord Wellington's ears."

He glared at me for a moment, during which no doubt he weighed the temptation of shooting me against the probable risk. Then his features relaxed into a grin, and withdrawing the chewed cigarette from his teeth he spat very deliberately on the ground. "The interview," he announced, "is ended."

I took my way down the hillside in no gay mood. I had travelled far; my nerves were raw with lack of sleep. I judged myself at least a day ahead of any convoy with which the captain could be travelling, even though it had moved with the minimum of delay. But where in the next two days was I to find the help which Mina had refused? To be sure I had caught up at Sedano a flying rumour that the curate Merino had eluded Bonnet, broken out of the Asturias, and was again menacing the road above Burgos. I had come across no sign of him on my way, yet could hit on no more hopeful course than to hark back along the road on the chance of striking the trail of a man who as likely as not was a hundred miles away.

It was about nine in the morning when Mina gave me his answer, and at three in the afternoon I was scanning the road towards Miranda de Ebro from a hill about a mile beyond Arinez (the same hill, in fact, where General Gazan's centre lay little more than a year afterwards on the morning of the battle of Vittoria). I had been scanning the road perhaps for ten minutes when my heart gave a jump and my hand, I am not ashamed to confess, shook on the small telescope. To the south-west, between me and Nanclares three horsemen were advancing at a walk, and the rider in the middle wore a scarlet jacket.

It took me some seconds to get my telescope steady enough for a second look, and with that I wheeled my horse, struck spur and posted back towards Salvatierra as fast as the brute would carry me through the afternoon heat.

I reached Mina's camp again at nightfall, and found the chief seated exactly as I had left him, still smoking and still dangling his legs. Were it not that he now wore a cloak against the night air I might have supposed him seated there all day without stirring, and the guard who led me to him promised with a grin that I was dangerously near one of those peculiar modes of death which his master passed his amiable leisure in inventing.

At the sight of me Mina's eyebrows went up and he chuckled. "Indeed," said he, "it has been a dull day, and I have been regretting that I let you off so easily this morning."

"This morning," I said, "I made you an offer of twelve thousand francs. You replied that you considered it too little for the services of your army. Perhaps it was; but you will admit it to be pretty fair pay for the services of a couple of men."

"Hullo!" He eyed me sharply. "What has happened?"

"That," I answered, "is my secret. Lend me a couple of men, say, for forty-eight hours. In return, on producing this paper, you receive twelve thousand francs; that is, as soon as Lord Wellington has assured himself on my report that you received the paper from me and did as I requested."

"Two men? This begins to look like business."

"It *is* business," said I curtly. "To your patriotism I should not have troubled to appeal a second time."

He warned me to keep a civil tongue in my head; but I knew my man, and within half-an-hour I rode out of his camp with two of his choicest ruffians, one beside me and one ahead to guide me through the darkness.

Now at Vittoria the road towards Irun and the frontier runs almost due north for some distance and then bends about in a rough arc towards the east. Another road runs almost due east from Vittoria to Pamplona. The first road would certainly be taken by my kinsman and his escort: Mina's camp lay above the second: but, a little way beyond, at Alsasua, a third road of about five leagues joins the two, and by this short cut I was certain of heading off our quarry.

There was no call to hurry. If, as I judged likely, the party meant to sleep the night at Vittoria, I had almost twenty-four hours in hand. So we rode warily, on the look-out for French vedettes, and reaching Beasain a little before two in the morning took up a comfortable position on the hillside above the junction of the roads.

At dawn we shifted into better shelter—a shepherd's hut, dilapidated and roofless—and eked out a long day with tobacco and a greasy pack of cards. A few bullock carts passed along the road below us, the most of them bound westward, and perhaps half-a-dozen peasants on mule-back. At about four in the afternoon a French patrol trotted by. As the evening drew on I began to feel anxious.

A little before sunset I sent off one of my ruffians
—Alonso something-or-other (I forget his magnificent surname)—to scout along the road. He had
been gone half-an-hour when his fellow, Juan Gal-
legos, flung down his cards in the dusk—the more
readily perhaps because he held a weak hand—and
pricked up his ears.

"Horses!" he whispered, and after a pause
nodded confidently. "Three horses!"

We picked up our muskets and crept down towards the road. Halfway down we met Alonso as-
cending with the news. Yes, there were three
horsemen on this side of Zumarraga and coming at
a trot. One of them wore a red coat.

"Be careful, then, how you pick them off. The
man in red must not be hurt; the money depends
on that."

They nodded. Night was now falling fast, yet
not so fast but that as the horsemen came up I could
distinguish Captain Alan. He was riding on the
left beside the young French officer, the orderly
about six yards behind. As they came abreast of
us Juan let fly, and the orderly's horse pitched forward at once and fell, flinging his man, who struck
the road and lay either stunned or dead. At the
noise of the report the other horses shied violently
and separated, thus giving us our chance without

191

danger to the prisoner. Alonso and I fired together, and rushed out upon the officer, who groaned in the act of wheeling upon us. One of the bullets had shattered his sword arm. Within the minute we had him prisoner, the captain not helping us at all.

"What is this?" he demanded in Spanish, peering at me out of the dusk and breaking off to quiet his frightened horse. "What is this, and who are you?"

"Well, it looks like a rescue," said I; "and I am your kinsman, Manus McNeill, and have been at some pains to effect it."

"You!" he peered at me. "I thank you," said he, "but you have done a bad evening's work. I am on parole, as a man so clever as you might have guessed by the size of my escort."

"We will talk of that later," I answered, and sent Juan and Alonso off to examine the fallen trooper. "Meanwhile the man here has fainted. Oblige me by helping him a little way up the hill, or by leading his horse while I carry him. The road here is not healthy."

Captain Alan followed in silence while I bore my burden up to the hut. Having tethered the horses outside, he entered and stood above me while I lit a lantern and examined the young officer's wound.

THE TWO SCOUTS

"Nothing serious," I announced, "a fracture of the forearm and maybe a splintered bone. I can fix this up in no time."

"You had better leave it to me and run," my kinsman answered. "This M. Gérard is an amiable young man and a friend of mine, and I charge myself to see him safe to Tolosa to-night. What are you doing?"

"Searching for his papers."

"I forbid it."

"*Alain mhic Neill*," said I, "you are not yet the head of our clan." And I broke the seal of a letter addressed to the Governor of Bayonne. "Ah! I thought as much," I added, having glanced over the missive. "It seems, my dear kinsman, that my knowledge of the Duke of Ragusa goes a bit deeper than yours. Listen to this: 'The prisoner I send you herewith is one Captain McNeill, a spy and a dangerous one, who has done infinite mischief to our arms. I have not executed him on the spot out of respect to something resembling an uniform which he wears. But I desire you to place him at once in irons and send him up to Paris, where he will doubtless suffer as he deserves' . . .."

Captain Alan took the paper from me and perused it slowly, biting his upper lip the while. "This is very black treachery," said he.

" It acquits you at any rate."

" Of my parole? " He pondered for a moment; then, " I cannot see that it does," he said. " If the Duke of Ragusa chooses to break an implied bond with me it does not follow that I can break an explicit promise to him."

" No? Well, I should have thought it did."

At once my kinsman put on that stiff pedantic tone which had irritated me at Huerta. " I venture to think," said he, " that no McNeill would say so unless he had been corrupted by traffic with the Scarlet Woman."

" Scarlet grandmother! " I broke out. " You seem to forget that I have ridden a hundred leagues to effect this rescue, for which, by the way, Lord Wellington offers twelve thousand francs. I have promised them to the biggest scoundrel in Spain; but because he happens to be even a bigger scoundrel than the Duke of Ragusa must I break my bond with him and let you go to be shot for the sake of your silly punctilio? "

I spoke with heat, and bent over the groaning officer. My kinsman rubbed his chin. " What you say," he replied, " demands a somewhat complicated answer, or rather a series of answers. In the first place, I thank you sincerely for what you have done, and not the less sincerely because I am

194

going to nullify it. I shall, perhaps, not cheat my-self by believing that a clansman's spirit went some way to help your zeal "—here I might well have blushed in truth, for it had not helped my zeal a peseta. " I thank Lord Wellington, too, for the extravagant price he has set upon my services, and I beg you to convey my gratitude to him. As for being shot, I might answer that my parole extends only to the Pyrenees; but I consider myself to have extended it tacitly to my young friend here, who has treated me with all possible consideration on the journey; and I shall go to Bayonne."

He spoke quietly and in the most matter-of-fact voice. But I have often thought since of his words; and often when I call up the figure of Marmont in exile at Venice, where, as he strode gloomily along the Riva dei Schiavoni, the very street urchins pointed and cried after him, " There goes the man who betrayed Napoleon! " I call up and contrast with it the figure of this humble gentleman of Scotland in the lonely hut declining simply and without parade to buy his life at the expense of a scruple of conscience.

" But," he continued, " I fancy I may persuade M. Gérard at least to delay the delivery of that letter, in which case I see my way at least to a chance of escape. For the rest, these *partidas* have been promised twelve thousand francs for a service which they have duly rendered. My patrimony is not a rich one, but I can promise that this sum, whether I escape or not, shall be as duly paid. Hush! " he ended as I sprang to my feet, and Juan and Alonso appeared in the doorway supporting the trooper, who had only been stunned after all.

" We did not care to kill him," Juan explained blandly, " until we had the señor's orders."

" You did rightly," I answered, and glanced at my kinsman. His jaw was set. I pulled out a couple of gold pieces for each. " An advance on your earnings," said I. " My orders are that you leave the trooper here with me, ride back instantly to your chief, report that your work has been well done and successfully, and the money for which he holds an order shall be forwarded as soon as I return and report to Lord Wellington in Beira."

MIDSUMMER FIRES

I

In the course of an eventful life John Penaluna did three very rash things.

To begin with, at seventeen, he ran away to sea.

He had asked his father's permission. But for fifty years the small estate had been going from bad to worse. John's grandfather in the piping days of agriculture had drunk the profits and mortgaged everything but the furniture. On his death, John's father (who had enlisted in a line regiment) came home with a broken knee-pan and a motherless boy, and turned market-gardener in a desperate attempt to rally the family fortunes. With capital he might have succeeded. But market-gardening required labour; and he could neither afford to hire it nor to spare the services of a growing lad who cost nothing but his keep. So John's request was not granted.

A week later, in the twilight of a May evening, John was digging potatoes on the slope above the harbour, when he heard—away up the first bend of the river—the crew of the *Hannah Hands* brigantine singing as they weighed anchor. He listened for a minute, stuck his visgy into the soil, slipped on his coat, and trudged down to the ferryslip.

Two years passed without word of him. Then on a blue and sunny day in October he emerged out of Atlantic fogs upon the Market Strand at Falmouth: a strapping fellow with a brown and somewhat heavy face, silver rings in his ears, and a suit of good sea-cloth on his back. He travelled by van to Truro, and thence by coach to St. Austell. It was Friday—market day; and in the market he found his father standing sentry, upright as his lame leg allowed, grasping a specimen apple-tree in either hand. John stepped up to him, took one of the apple-trees, and stood sentry beside him. Nothing was said—not a word until John found himself in the ramshackle market-cart, jogging homewards. His father held the reins.

" How's things at home? " John asked.

" Much as ever. Hester looks after me."

Hester was John's cousin, the only child of old Penaluna's only sister, and lately an orphan. John had never seen her.

" If I was you," said he, " I'd have a try with borrowed capital. You could raise a few hundreds easy. You'll never do anything as you 'm going."

" If I was you," answered his father, " I'd keep my opinions till they was asked for."

And so John did, for three years; in the course of which it is to be supposed he forgot them. When the old man died he inherited everything; including the debts, of course. " He knows what I would have him do by Hester," said the will. It went on: " Also I will not be buried in consicrated ground, but at the foot of the dufflin apple-tree in the waste piece under King's Walk, and the plainer the better. In the swet of thy face shalt thou eat bread, amen. P.S.—John knows the tree."

But since by an oversight the will was not read until after the funeral, this wish could not be carried out. John resolved to attend to the other all the more scrupulously; and went straight from the lawyer to the kitchen, where Hester stood by the window scouring a copper pan.

" Look here," he said, " the old man hasn' left you nothing."

" No? " said Hester. " Well, I didn't expect anything." And she went on with her scouring.

" But he 've a-left a pretty plain hint o' what he wants me to do."

He hesitated, searching the calm profile of her

199

face. Hester's face was always calm, but her eyes sometimes terrified him. Everyone allowed she had wonderful eyes, though no two people agreed about their colour. As a matter of fact their colour was that of the sea, and varied with the sea. And all her life through they were searching, unceasingly searching, for she knew not what—something she never had found, never would find. At times, when talking with you, she would break off as though words were of no use to her, and her eyes had to seek your soul on their own account. And in those silences your soul had to render up the truth to her, though it could never be the truth she sought. When at length her gaze relaxed and she remembered and begged pardon (perhaps with a deprecatory laugh), you sighed; but whether on her account or yours it was impossible to say.

John looked at her awkwardly, and drummed with one foot on the limeash floor.

" He wanted you to marry me," he blurted out. " I—I reckon I've wanted that, too . . . oh, yes, for a long time! "

She put both hands behind her—one of them still grasped the polishing-cloth—came over, and gazed long into his face.

" You mean it," she said at length. " You are a good man. I like you. I suppose I must."

She turned—still with her hands behind her—walked to the window, and stood pondering the harbour and the vessels at anchor and the rooks flying westward. John would have followed and kissed her, but divined that she wished nothing so little. So he backed towards the door, and said—

"There's nothing to wait for. 'Twouldn't do to be married from the same house, I expect. I was thinking—any time that's agreeable—if you was to lodge across the harbour for awhile, with the Mayows—Cherry Mayow's a friend of yours—we could put up the banns and all shipshape."

He found himself outside the door, mopping his forehead.

This was the second rash thing that John Penaluna did.

II

It was Midsummer Eve, and a Saturday, when Hester knocked at the Mayows' green door on the Town Quay. The Mayows' house hung over the tideway, and the *Touch-me-not* schooner, home that day from Florida with a cargo of pines, and warped alongside the quay, had her foreyard braced aslant to avoid knocking a hole in the Mayows' roof.

A Cheap Jack's caravan stood at the edge of the quay. The Cheap Jack was feasting inside on

fried ham rasher among his clocks and mirrors and
pewter ware; and though it wanted an hour of
dusk, his assistant was already lighting the naphtha-
lamps when Hester passed.

Steam issued from the Mayows' doorway, which
had a board across it to keep the younger Mayows
from straggling. A voice from the steam invited
her to come in. She climbed over the board, groped
along the dusky passage, pushed open a door and
looked in on the kitchen, where, amid clouds of
vapour, Mrs. Mayow and her daughter Cherry were
washing the children. Each had a tub and a child
in it; and three children, already washed, skipped
around the floor stark naked, one with a long
churchwarden pipe blowing bubbles which the
other two pursued. In the far corner, behind a deal
table, sat Mr. Mayow, and patiently tuned a fiddle
—a quite hopeless task in that atmosphere.

" My gracious! " Mrs. Mayow exclaimed, rising
from her knees; " if it isn't Hester already!
Amelia, get out and dry yourself while I make a
cup of tea."

Hester took a step forward, but paused at a sound
of dismal bumping on the staircase leading up from
the passage.

" That's Elizabeth Ann," said Mrs. Mayow com-
posedly, " or Heber, or both. We shall know when

they get to the bottom. My dear, you must be perishing for a cup of tea. Oh, it's Elizabeth Ann! Cherry, go and smack her, and tell her what I'll do if she falls downstairs again. It's all Matthew Henry's fault." Here she turned on the naked urchin with the churchwarden pipe. " If he'd only been home to his time——"

" I was listening to Zeke Penhaligon," said Matthew Henry (aged eight). " He's home to-day in the *Touch-me-not.*"

" He's no good to King nor country," said Mrs. Mayow.

" He was telling me about a man that got swallowed by a whale——"

" Go away with your Jonahses! " sneered one of his sisters.

" It wasn't Jonah. This man's name was Jones —*Captain* Jones, from Dundee. A whale swallowed him; but, as it happened, the whale had swallowed a cask just before, and the cask stuck in its stomach. So whatever the whale swallowed after that went into the cask, and did the whale no good. But Captain Jones had plenty to eat till he cut his way out with a clasp-knife——"

" How *could* he? "

" That's all you know. Zeke *says* he did. A whale always turns that way up when he's dying.

So Captain Jones cut his way into daylight, when, what does he see but a sail, not a mile away! He fell on his knees——"

" How *could* he, you silly? He'd have slipped."

But at this point Cherry swept the family off to bed. Mrs. Mayow, putting forth unexpected strength, carried the tubs out to the back-yard, and poured the soapy water into the harbour. Hester, having borrowed a touzer,* tucked up her sleeves and fell to tidying the kitchen. Mr. Mayow went on tuning his fiddle. It was against his principles to work on a Saturday night.

" Your wife seems very strong," observed Hester, with a shade of reproach in her voice.

" Strong as a horse," he assented cheerfully. " I call it wonnerful after what she 've a-gone through. 'Twouldn' surprise me, one o' these days, to hear she'd taken up a tub with the cheeld in it, and heaved cheeld and all over the quay-door. She 's terrible absent in her mind."

Mrs. Mayow came panting back with a kettleful of water, which she set to boil; and, Cherry now reappearing with the report that all the children were safe abed, the three women sat around the fire awaiting their supper, and listening to the voice of the Cheap Jack without.

* *Tout-serve*, apron.

"We'll step out and have a look at him by-and-by," said Cherry.

"For my part," Mrs. Mayow murmured, with her eyes on the fire, "I never hear one of those fellers without wishing I had a million of money. There's so many little shiny pots and pans you could go on buying for ever and ever, just like Heaven!"

She sighed as she poured the boiling water into the teapot. On Saturday nights, when the children were packed off, a deep peace always fell upon Mrs. Mayow, and she sighed until bed-time, building castles in the air.

Their supper finished, the two girls left her to her musings and stepped out to see the fun. The naphtha-lamps flared in Hester's face, and for a minute red wheels danced before her eyes, the din of a gong battered on her ears, and vision and hearing were indistinguishably blurred. A plank, like a diving-board, had been run out on trestles in front of the caravan, and along this the assistant darted forwards and backwards on a level with the shoulders of the good-humoured crowd, his arms full of clocks, saucepans, china ornaments, mirrors, feather brushes, teapots, sham jewellery. Sometimes he made pretence to slip, recovered himself with a grin on the very point of scattering his precious armfuls; and always when he did this the crowd laughed uproariously. And all the while the Cheap Jack shouted or beat his gong. Hester thought at first there were half-a-dozen Cheap Jacks at least—he made such a noise, and the mirrors around his glittering platform flashed forth so many reflections of him. Trade was always brisk on Saturday night, and he might have kept the auction going until eleven had he been minded. But he had come to stay for a fortnight (much to the disgust of credit-giving tradesmen), and cultivated eccentricity as a part of his charm. In the thickest of the bidding he suddenly closed his sale.

"I've a weak chest," he roared. "Even to make your fortunes—which is my constant joy and endeavour, as you know—I mustn't expose it too much to the night air. Now I've a pianner here, but it's not for sale. And I've an assistant here— a bit worn, but he's not for sale neither. I got him for nothing, to start with—from the work'us " (comic protest here from the assistant, and roars of laughter from the crowd)—" and I taught him a lot o' things, and among 'em to play the pianner. So as 'tis Midsummer's Eve, and I see some very nice-lookin' young women a tip-tapping their feet for it, and Mr. Mayow no further away than next door, and able to play the fiddle to the life—what I say is, ladies and gentlemen, let's light up a fire and see if, with all their reading and writing, the young folks have forgot how to dance!"

In the hubbub that followed, Cherry caught Hester by the arm and whispered—

"Why, I clean forgot 'twas Midsummer Eve! We'll try our fortun's afterwards. Aw, no need to look puzzled — I'll show 'ee. Here, feyther, feyther! . . ." Cherry ran down the passage and returned, haling forth Mr. Mayow with his fiddle.

And then—as it seemed to Hester, in less than a minute—empty packing-cases came flying from half-a-dozen doors—from the cooper's, the grocer's, the ship-chandler's, the china-shop, the fruit-shop, the " ready-made outfitter's," and the Cheap Jack's caravan; were seized upon, broken up, the splinters piled in a heap, anointed with naphtha and ignited almost before Mr. Mayow had time to mount an empty barrel, tune his " A " string by the piano, and dash into the opening bars of the Furry Dance. And almost before she knew it, Hester's hands were caught, and she found herself one of the ring swaying and leaping round the blaze. Cherry held her left hand and an old waterman her right. The swing of the crowd carried her off her feet, and she had to leap with the best. By-and-by, as her feet fell into time with the measure, she really began

to enjoy it all—the music, the rush of the cool night
air against her temples, even the smell of naphtha
and the heat of the flames on her face as the dancers
paused now and again, dashed upon the fire as if to
tread it out, and backed until the strain on their
arms grew tense again; and, just as it grew unbear-
able, the circular leaping was renewed. Always
in these pauses the same face confronted her across
the fire: the face of a young man in a blue jersey
and a peaked cap, a young man with crisp dark
hair and dark eyes, gay and challenging. In her
daze it seemed to Hester that, when they came face
to face, he was always on the side of the bonfire
nearest the water; and the moon rose above the
farther hill as they danced, and swam over his
shoulder, at each meeting higher and higher.

It was all new to her and strange. The music
ceased abruptly, the dancers unclasped their hands
and fell apart, laughing and panting. And then,
while yet she leaned against the Mayows' door-post,
the fiddle broke out again—broke into a polka tune;
and there, in front of her stood the young man in
the blue jersey and peaked cap.

He was speaking. She scarcely knew what she
answered; but, even while she wondered, she had
taken his arm submissively. And, next, his arm
was about her and she was dancing. She had never

danced before; but, after one or two broken paces, her will surrendered to his, her body and its movements answered him docilely. She felt that his eyes were fixed on her forehead, but dared not look up. She saw nothing of the crowd. Other dancers passed and re-passed like phantoms, neither jostling nor even touching — so well her partner steered. She grew giddy; her breath came short and fast. She would have begged for a rest, but the sense of his mastery weighed on her—held her dumb. Suddenly he laughed close to her ear, and his breath ruffled her hair.

"You dance fine," he said. "Shall us cross the fire?"

She did not understand. In her giddiness they seemed to be moving in a wide, empty space among many fires, nor had she an idea which was the real one. His arm tightened about her.

"Now!" he whispered. With a leap they whirled high and across the bonfire. Her feet had scarcely touched ground before they were off again to the music—or would have been; but, to her immense surprise, her partner had dropped on his knees before her and was clasping her about the ankles. She heard a shout. The fire had caught the edge of her skirt and her frock was burning.

It was over in a moment. His arms had stifled,

extinguished the flame before she knew of her danger. Still kneeling, holding her fast, he looked up,
and their eyes met. "Take me back," she murmured, swaying. He rose, took her arm, and she
found herself in the Mayows' doorway with Cherry
at her side. "Get away with you," said Cherry,
"and leave her to me!" And the young man
went.

Cherry fell to examining the damaged skirt.
"It's clean ruined," she reported; "but I reckon
that don't matter to a bride. John Penaluna 'll
not be grudging the outfit. I must say, though—
you quiet ones!"

"What have I done?"

"Done? Well, that's good. Only danced across
the bonfire with young Zeke Penhaligon. Why,
mother can mind when that was every bit so good
as a marriage before parson and clerk!—and not so
long ago neither."

III

"You go upstairs backwards," said Cherry an
hour later. "It don't matter our going together,
only you mustn't speak a word for ever so. You
undress in the dark, and turn each thing inside out
as you take it off. Prayers? Yes, you can say your
prayers if you like; but to yourself, mind. 'Twould

be best to say 'em backwards, I reckon; but I never
heard no instructions about prayers."

"And then?"

"Why, then you go to sleep and dream of your
sweetheart."

"Oh! is that all?"

"Plenty enough, *I* should think! I dessay it
don't mean much to you; but it means a lot to me,
who han't got a sweetheart yet an' don't know if
ever I shall have one."

So the two girls solemnly mounted the stairs
backwards, undressed in the dark, and crept into
bed. But Hester could not sleep. She lay for an
hour quite silent, motionless lest she should awake
Cherry, with eyes wide open, staring at a ray of
moonlight on the ceiling, and from that to the dimity window-curtains and the blind which waved ever
so gently in the night breeze. All the while she
was thinking of the dance; and by-and-by she
sighed.

"Bain't you asleep?" asked Cherry.

"No."

"Nor I. Can't sleep a wink. It's they children overhead: they 'm up to some devilment, I
know, because Matthew Henry isn't snoring. He
always snores when he's asleep, and it shakes the
house. I'll ha' gone to see, only I was afeard to

211

disturb 'ee. I'll war'n' they 'm up to some may-games on the roof."

" Let me come with you," said Hester.

They rose. Hester slipped on her dressing-gown, and Cherry an old macintosh, and they stole up the creaking stairs.

" Oh, you anointed limbs! " exclaimed Cherry, coming to a halt on the top.

The door of the children's garret stood ajar. On the landing outside a short ladder led up to a trap-door in the eaves, and through the open trapway a broad ray of moonlight streamed upon the stair-case.

" That's mother again! Now I know where Amelia got that cold in her head. I'll war'n' the door hasn't been locked since Tuesday! "

She climbed the ladder, with Hester at her heels. They emerged through the trap upon a flat roof, where on Mondays Mrs. Mayow spread her family " wash " to dry in the harbour breezes. Was that a part of the " wash " now hanging in a row along the parapet?

No; those dusky white objects were the younger members of the Mayow family leaning over the tideway, each with a stick and line—fishing for conger Matthew Henry explained, as Cherry took him by the ear; but Elizabeth Jane declared that, after four nights of it, she, for her part, limited her hopes to shannies.

Cherry swept them together, and filed them indoors through the trap in righteous wrath, taking her opportunity to box the ears of each. " Come'st along, Hester."

Hester was preparing to follow, when she heard a subdued laugh. It seemed to come from the far side of the parapet, and below her. She drew her dressing-gown close about her and leaned over.

She looked down upon a stout spar overhanging the tide, and thence along a vessel's deck, empty, glimmering in the moonlight; upon mysterious coils of rope; upon the dew-wet roof of a deck-house; upon a wheel twinkling with brass-work, and behind it a white-painted taffrail. Her eyes were travelling forward to the bowsprit again, when, close by the foremast, they were arrested, and she caught her breath sharply.

There, with his naked feet on the bulwarks and one hand against the house-wall, in the shadow of which he leaned out-board, stood a man. His other hand grasped a short stick; and with it he was reaching up to the window above him—her bedroom window. The window, she remembered, was open at the bottom—an inch or two, no more. The man slipped the end of his stick under the sash and prised it up quietly. Next he raised himself on tiptoe, and thrust the stick a foot or so through the opening; worked it slowly along the window-ledge, and hesitated; then pulled with a light jerk, as an angler strikes a fish. And Hester, holding her breath, saw the stick withdrawn, inch by inch; and at the end of it a garment—her petticoat!

" How dare you! "

The thief whipped himself about, jumped back upon deck, and stood smiling up at her, with the petticoat in his hand. It was the young sailor she had danced with.

" How dare you? Oh, I'd be ashamed! "

" Midsummer Eve! " said he, and laughed.

" Give it up at once! " She dared not speak loudly, but felt herself trembling with wrath.

" That's not likely." He unhitched it from the fish-hook he had spliced to the end of his stick. " And after the trouble I've taken! "

" I'll call your captain, and he'll make you give it up."

" The old man's sleeping ashore, and won't be down till nine in the morning. I'm alone here." He stepped to the fore-halliards. " Now I'll just hoist this up to the topmast head, and you'll see what a pretty flag it makes in the morning."

" Oh, please . . . ! "

He turned his back and began to bend the petticoat on the halliards.

"No, no . . . please . . . it's cruel!"

He could hear that she was crying softly; hesitated, and faced round again.

"There now . . . if it teases you so. There
wasn' no harm meant. You shall have it back—
wait a moment!"

He came forward and clambered out on the bowsprit, and from the bowsprit to the jib-boom beneath her. She was horribly afraid he would fall,
and broke off her thanks to whisper him to be careful, at which he laughed. Standing there, and
holding by the fore-topmast stay, he could just
reach a hand up to the parapet, and was lifting it,
but paused.

"No," said he, "I must have a kiss in exchange."

"Please don't talk like that. I thank you so
much. Don't spoil your kindness."

"You've spoilt my joke. See, I can hoist my-
self on the stay here. Bend over as far as you can,
I swear you shall have the petticoat at once, but
I won't give it up without."

"I can't. I shall never think well of you again."

"Oh, yes, you will. Bend lower."

"Don't!" she murmured, but the moonlight,

refracted from the water below, glimmered on her face as she leaned towards him.

"Lower! What queer eyes you've got. Do you know what it means to kiss over running water?" His lips whispered it close to her ear. And with that, as she bent, some treacherous pin gave way, and her loosely knotted hair fell in dark masses across his face. She heard him laugh as he kissed her in the tangled screen of it.

The next moment she had snatched the bundle and sprung to her feet and away. But as she passed by the trapdoor and hurriedly retwisted her hair before descending, she heard him there, beyond the parapet, laughing still.

IV

Three weeks later she married John Penaluna. They spent their honeymoon at home, as sober folks did in those days. John could spare no time for holiday-making. He had entered on his duties as master of Hall, and set with vigour about improving his inheritance. His first step was to clear the long cliff-garden, which had been allowed to drop out of cultivation from the day when he had cast down his mattock there and run away to sea. It was a mere wilderness now. But he fell to work like a navvy.

He fought it single-handed. He had no money to hire extra labour, and apparently had lost his old belief in borrowed capital, or perhaps had grown timid with home-keeping. A single labourer—his father's old hind—managed the cows and the small farmstead. Hester superintended the dairy and the housework, with one small servant-maid at her beck and call. And John tackled the gardens, hiring a boy or two in the fruit-picking season, or to carry water in times of drought. So they lived for two years tranquilly. As for happiness — well, happiness depends on what you expect. It was difficult to know how much John Penaluna (never a demonstrative man) had expected.

As far as folks could judge, John and Hester were happy enough. Day after day, from sunrise to sunset, he fought with Nature in his small wilderness, and slowly won—hewing, digging, terracing, cultivating, reclaiming plot after plot, and adding it to his conquests. The slope was sunny but waterless, and within a year Hester could see that his whole frame stooped with the constant rolling of barrels and carriage of buckets and water-pots up and down the weary incline. It seemed to her that the hill thirsted continually; that no sooner was its thirst slaked than the weeds and brambles took fresh strength and must be driven back with hook and hoe. A small wooden summer-house stood in the upper angle of the cliff-garden. John's father had set it there twenty years before, and given it glazed windows; for it looked down towards the harbour's mouth and the open sea beyond. Before his death the brambles grew close about it, and level with the roof, choking the path to it and the view from it. John had spent the best part of a fortnight in clearing the ground and opening up the view again. And here, on warm afternoons when her house work was over, Hester usually sat with her knitting. She could hear her husband at work on the terraces below; the sound of his pick and mattock mingled with the clank of windlasses or the tick-tack of shipwrights' mallets, as she knitted and watched the smoke of the little town across the water, the knots of idlers on the quay, the children, like emmets, tumbling in and out of the Mayows' doorway, the ships passing out to sea or entering the harbour and coming to their anchorage.

One afternoon in midsummer week John climbed to his wife's summer-house with a big cabbage-leaf in his hand, and within the cabbage-leaf a dozen strawberries. (John's strawberries were known by this time for the finest in the neighbourhood.) He held his offering in at the open window, and was saying he would step up to the house for a dish of cream; but stopped short.

"Hullo!" said he; for Hester was staring at him rigidly, as white as a ghost. "What's wrong, my dear?" He glanced about him, but saw nothing to account for her pallor—only the scorched hill-side, alive with the noise of grasshoppers, the hot air quivering above the bramble-bushes, and beyond, a line of sunlight across the harbour's mouth, and a schooner with slack canvas crawling to anchor on the flood-tide.

"You—you came upon me sudden," she explained.

"Stupid of me!" thought John; and going to the house, fetched not only a dish of cream but the tea-caddy and a kettle, which they put to boil outside the summer-house over a fire of dried brambles. The tea revived Hester and set her tongue going. "'Tis quite a picnic!" said John, and told himself privately that it was the happiest hour they had spent together for many a month.

Two evenings later, on his return from St. Austell market, he happened to let himself in by the door of the walled garden just beneath the house, and came on a tall young man talking there in the dusk with his wife.

"Why, 'tis Zeke Penhaligon! How d'ee do, my

lad? Now, 'tis queer, but only five minutes agone
I was talkin' about 'ee with your skipper, Nummy
Tangye, t'other side o' the ferry. He says you 'm
goin' up for your mate's certificate, and ought to
get it. Very well he spoke of 'ee. Why don't
Hester invite you inside? Come'st 'long in to supper, my son."

Zeke followed them in, and this was the first of
many visits. John was one of those naturally
friendly souls (there are many in the world) who
never go forth to seek friends, and to whom few
friends ever come, and these by accident. Zeke's
talk set his tongue running on his own brief *Wan-
derjahre*. And Hester would sit and listen to the
pair with heightened colour, which made John
wonder why, as a rule, she shunned company—it
did her so much good. So it grew to be a settled
thing that whenever the *Touch-me-not* entered port
a knife and fork awaited Zeke up at Hall, and the
oftener he came the pleasanter was John's face.

V

Three years passed, and in the summer of the
third year Captain Nummy Tangye, of the *Touch-
me-not*, relinquished his command. Captain Tangye's baptismal name was Matthias, and Bideford, in
Devon, his native town. But the *Touch-me-not*,

which he had commanded for thirty-five years, happened to carry for figurehead a wooden Highlander
holding a thistle close to his chest, and against his
thigh a scroll with the motto, *Noli Me Tangere*, and
this being, in popular belief, an effigy of the captain
taken in the prime of life, Mr. Tangye cheerfully
accepted the fiction with its implication of Scottish
descent, and was known at home and in various out-
of-the-way parts of the world as Nolim or Nummy.
He even carried about a small volume of Burns in
his pocket; not from any love of poetry, but to dem-
onstrate, when required, that Scotsmen have their
own notions of spelling.

Captain Tangye owned a preponderance of shares
in the *Touch-me-not*, and had no difficulty in get-
ing Zeke (who now held a master's certificate) appointed to succeed him. The old man hauled
ashore to a cottage with a green door and a brass
knocker and a garden high over the water-side. In
this he spent the most of his time with a glittering
brass telescope of uncommon length, and in the intervals of studying the weather and the shipping,
watched John Penaluna at work across the harbour.

The *Touch-me-not* made two successful voyages
under Zeke's command, and was home again and
discharging beside the Town Quay, when, one summer's day, as John Penaluna leaned on his pitch-

fork beside a heap of weeds arranged for burning, he glanced up and saw Captain Tangye hobbling painfully towards him across the slope. The old man had on his best blue cut-away coat, and paused now and then to wipe his brow.

"I take this as very friendly," said John.

Captain Tangye grunted. "P'rhaps 'tis, p'rhaps 'tisn'. Better wait a bit afore you say it."

"Stay and have a bit of dinner with me and the missus."

"Dashed if I do! 'Tis about her I came to tell 'ee."

"Yes?" John, being puzzled, smiled in a meaningless way.

"Zeke's home agen."

"Yes; he was up here two evenin's ago."

"He was here yesterday; he'll be here again to-day. He comes here too often. I've got a tele-scope, John Penaluna, and I sees what's goin' on. What's more, I guess what'll come of it. So I warn 'ee—as a friend, of course."

John stared down at the polished steel teeth of his pitchfork, glinting under the noonday sun.

"As a friend, of course," he echoed vaguely, still with the meaningless smile on his face.

"I b'lieve she means to be a good 'ooman; but she's listenin' to 'en. Now, I've got 'en a ship up to Runcorn. He shan't sail the *Touch-me-not* no more. 'Tis a catch for 'en—a nice barquentine, five hundred tons. If he decides to take the post (and I reckon he will) he starts to-morrow at latest. Between this an' then there's danger, and 'tis for you to settle how to act."

A long pause followed. The clock across the harbour struck noon, and this seemed to wake John Penaluna up. " Thank 'ee," he said. " I think I'll be going in to dinner. I'll—I'll consider of it. You've took me rather sudden."

" Well, so long! I mean it friendly, of course."

" Of course. Better take the lower path; 'tis shorter, an' not so many stones in it."

John stared after him as he picked his way down the hill; then fell to rearranging his heaps of dried rubbish in an aimless manner. He had forgotten the dinner-hour. Something buzzed in his ears. There was no wind on the slope, no sound in the air. The shipwrights had ceased their hammering, and the harbour at his feet lay still as a lake. They were memories, perhaps, that buzzed so swiftly past his ears—trivial recollections by the hundred, all so little, and yet now immensely significant.

" John, John! "

It was Hester, standing at the top of the slope and calling him. He stuck his pitchfork in the ground, picked up his coat, and went slowly in to dinner.

Next day, by all usage, he should have travelled in to market: but he announced at breakfast that he was too busy, and would send Robert, the hind, in his stead. He watched his wife's face as he said it. She certainly changed colour, and yet she did not seem disappointed. The look that sprang into those grey eyes of her was more like one of relief, or, if not of relief, of a sudden hope suddenly snatched at; but this was absurd, of course. It would not fit in with the situation at all.

At dinner he said: " You'll be up in the sum-merhouse this afternoon? I shouldn't wonder if Zeke comes to say good-bye. Tangye says he 've got the offer of a new berth, up to Runcorn."

" Yes, I know."

If she wished, or struggled, to say more he did not seem to observe it, but rose from his chair, stooped and kissed her on the forehead, and reso-lutely marched out to his garden. He worked that afternoon in a small patch which commanded a view of the ferry and also of the road leading up to Hall: and at half-past three, or a few minutes later, dropped his spade and strolled down to the edge of his property, a low cliff overhanging the ferry-slip.

" Hullo, Zeke! "

Zeke, as he stepped out of the ferry-boat, looked up with some confusion on his face. He wore his best suit, with a bunch of sweet-william in his button-hole.

" Come to bid us good-bye, I s'pose? We've heard of your luck. Here, scramble up this way if you can manage, and shake hands on your fortune."

Zeke obeyed. The climb seemed to fluster him; but the afternoon was a hot one, in spite of a light westerly breeze. The two men moved side by side across the garden-slope, and as they did so John caught sight of a twinkle of sunshine on Captain Tangye's brass telescope across the harbour.

They paused beside one of the heaps of rubbish. " This is a fine thing for you, Zeke."

" Ay, pretty fair."

" I s'pose we sha'n't be seein' much of you now. 'Tis like an end of old times. I reckoned we'd have a pipe together afore partin'." John pulled out a stumpy clay and filled it. " Got a match about you? "

Zeke passed him one, and he struck it on his boot. " There, now," he went on, " I meant to set a light to these here heaps of rubbish this afternoon, and now I've come out without my matches." He waited for the sulphur to finish bubbling, and then began to puff.

Zeke handed him half-a-dozen matches.

"I dunno how many 'twill take, said John. "S'pose we go round together and light up. 'Twont' take us a quarter of an hour, an' we can talk by the way."

Ten minutes later, Captain Tangye, across the harbour, shut his telescope with an angry snap. The smoke of five-and-twenty bonfires crawled up the hillside and completely hid John Penaluna's garden—hid the two figures standing there, hid the little summer-house at the top of the slope. It was enough to make a man swear, and Captain Tangye swore.

John Penaluna drew a long breath.

"Well, good-bye and bless 'ee, Zeke. Hester's up in the summer-house. I won't go up with 'ee; my back's too stiff. Go an' make your adoos to her; she's cleverer than I be, and maybe will tell 'ee what we've both got in our minds."

This was the third rash thing that John Penaluna did.

He watched Zeke up the hill, till the smoke hid him. Then he picked up his spade. "Shall I find her, when I step home this evening? Please God, yes."

And he did. She was there by the supper-table waiting for him. Her eyes were red. John pretended to have dropped something, and went back for a moment to look for it. When he returned, neither spoke.

VI

Years passed—many years. Their life ran on in its old groove.

John toiled from early morning to sunset, as before—and yet not quite as before. There was a difference, and Captain Tangye would, no doubt, have perceived it long before had not Death one day come on him in an east wind and closed his activities with a snap, much as he had so often closed his telescope.

For a year or two after Zeke's departure, John went on enlarging his garden-bounds, though more languidly. Then followed four or five years during which his conquests seemed to stand still. And then little by little, the brambles and wild growth rallied. Perhaps—who knows?—the assaulted wilderness had found its Joan of Arc. At any rate, it stood up to him at length, and pressed in upon him and drove him back. Year by year, on one excuse or another, an outpost, a foot or two, would be abandoned and left to be reclaimed by the weeds. They were the assailants now. And there came a time when they had him at bay, a beaten man, in a patch of not more than fifty square feet, the centre of his former domain. "Time, not Corydon," had conquered him.

He was working here one afternoon when a boy came up the lower path from the ferry, and put a telegram into his hands. He read it over, thought for a while, and turned to climb the old track towards the summer-house, but brambles choked it completely, and he had to fetch a circuit and strike the grass walk at the head of the slope.

He had not entered the summer-house for years, but he found Hester knitting there as usual, and put the telegram into her hands.

"Zeke is drowned." He paused and added—he could not help it—"You'll not need to be looking out to sea any more."

Hester made as if to answer him, but rose instead and laid a hand on his breast. It was a thin hand, and roughened with housework. With the other she pointed to where the view had lain seaward. He turned. There was no longer any view. The brambles hid it, and must have hidden it for many years.

"Then what have you been thinkin' of all these days?"

Her eyes filled; but she managed to say, " Of you, John."

" It's with you as with me. The weeds have us, every side, each in our corner." He looked at his hands, and with sudden resolution turned and left her.

" Where are you going? "

" To fetch a hook. I'll have that view open again before nightfall, or my name's not John Penaluna."

CAPTAIN DICK AND CAPTAIN JACKA

A REPORTED TALE OF TWO FRIGATES AND TWO LUGGERS

I DARE say you've never heard tell of my wife's grandfather, Captain John Tackabird—or Cap'n Jacka, as he was always called. He was a remarkable man altogether, and he died of a seizure in the Waterloo year; an earnest Methody all his days, and towards the end a highly respected class-leader. To tell you the truth, he wasn't much to look at, being bald as a coot and blind of one eye, besides other defects. His mother let him run too soon, and that made his legs bandy. And then a bee stung him, and all his hair came off. And his eye he lost in a little job with the preventive men; but his lid drooped so, you'd hardly know 'twas missing. He'd a way, too, of talking to himself as he went along, so that folks reckoned him silly. It was queer how that maggot stuck in their heads; for in handling a privateer or a Guernsey cargo—sink the crop or run it straight—there wasn't his master in Polperro. The very children could tell 'ee.

I'm telling of the year 'five, when the most of the business in Polperro—free-trade and privateering—was managed (as the world knows) by Mr. Zephaniah Job. This Job he came from St. Ann's —by reason of his having shied some person's child out of a window in a fit of temper—and opened school at Polperro, where he taught rule-of-three and mensuration; also navigation, though he only knew about it on paper. By-and-by he became accountant to all the free-trade companies and agent for the Guernsey merchants; and at last blossomed out and opened a bank with 1*l.* and 2*l.* notes, and bigger ones which he drew on Christopher Smith, Esquire, Alderman of London.

Well, this Job was agent for a company of adventurers called the " Pride o' the West," and had ordered a new lugger to be built for them down at Mevagissey. She was called the *Unity*, 160 tons (that would be about fifty as they measure now), mounting sixteen carriage guns and carrying sixty men, nice and comfortable. She was lying on the ways, ready to launch, and Mr. Job proposed to Cap'n Jacka to sail over to Mevagissey and have a look at her.

Cap'n Jacka was pleased as Punch, of course.

He'd quite made up his mind he was to command
her, seeing that, first and last, in the old *Pride* lugger, he had cleared over 40 per cent. for this very
Company. So they sailed over and took thorough
stock of the new craft, and Jacka praised this and
suggested that, and carried on quite as if he'd got
captain's orders inside his hat—which was where he
usually carried them. Mr. Job looked sidelong
down his nose—he was a leggy old galliganter, with
stiverish grey hair and a jawbone long enough to
make Cap'n Jacka a new pair of shins—and said he,
" What do'ee think of her? "

" Well," said Jacka, " any fool can see she'll run,
and any fool can see she'll reach. I reckon she'll
come about as fast as th' old *Pride*, and if she don't
sit nigher the wind than the new revenue cutter it'll
be your sailmaker's fault."

" That's a first-class report," said Mr. Job. " I
was thinking of offering you the post of mate in
her."

Cap'n Jacka felt poorly all of a sudden. " Aw,"
he asked, " who's to be skipper, then? "

" The Company was thinkin' of young Dick
Hewitt."

" Aw," said Cap'n Jacka again, and shut his
mouth tight. Young Dick Hewitt's father had
shares in the Company and money to buy votes beside.

CAPTAIN DICK AND CAPTAIN JACKA

"What do'ee think?" asked Mr. Job, still slanting his eye down his nose.

"I'll go home an' take my wife's opinion," said
Cap'n Jacka.

So when he got home he told it all to his funny
little wife that he doted on like the apple of his one
eye. She was a small, round body, with beady eyes
that made her look like a doll on a pen-wiper; and
she said, of course, that the Company was a parcel
of rogues and fools together.

"Young Dick Hewitt is every bit so good a seaman as I be," said Cap'n Jacka.

"He's a boaster."

"So he is, but he's a smart seaman for all."

"I declare if the world was to come to an end
you'd sit quiet an' never say a word."

"I dessay I should. I'd leave you to speak up
for me."

"Baint'ee goin' to say *nothin'*, then?"

"Iss; I'm goin' to lay it before the Lord."

So down 'pon their knees these old souls went
upon the limeash, and asked for guidance, and
Cap'n Jacka, after a while, stretched out his hand
to the shelf for Wesley's Hymns. They always
pitched a hymn together before going to bed.
When he'd got the book in his hand he saw that
'twasn't Wesley at all, but another that he never

233

studied from the day his wife gave it to him, because it was called the " Only Hymn Book," * and
he said the name was as good as a lie. Hows'ever,
he opened it now, and came slap on the hymn:—

> *Tho' troubles assail and dangers affright,*
> *If foes all should fail and foes all unite,*
> *Yet one thing assures us, whatever betide,*
> *I trust in all dangers the Lord will provide.*

They sang it there and then to the tune of " O all
that pass by," and the very next morning Cap'n
Jacka walked down and told Mr. Job he was ready
to go for mate under young Dick Hewitt.

More than once, the next week or two, he came
near to repenting; for Cap'n Dick was very loud
about his promotion, especially at the Three Pil-
chards; and when the *Unity* came round and was
fitting—very slow, too, by reason of delay with her
letters of marque—he ordered Cap'n Jacka back
and forth like a stevedore's dog. " There was to
be no ' nigh enough ' on *this* lugger "—that was the
sort of talk; and oil and rotten-stone for the very
gun-swivels. But Jacka knew the fellow, and even
admired the great figure and its loud ways. " He's
a cap'n, anyhow," he told his wife; " 'twon't be
' all fellows to football ' while he's in command.

* Probably " Olney."

234

And I've seen him handle the *Good Intent*, under Hockin."

Mrs. Tackabird said nothing. She was busy making sausages and setting down a stug of butter for her man's use on the voyage. But he knew she would be a disappointed woman if he didn't contrive in some honest way to turn the tables on the Company and their new pet. For days together he went about whistling "Tho' troubles assail . . ."; and the very night before sailing, as they sat quiet, one each side of the hearth, he made the old woman jump by saying all of a sudden, "Coals o' fire!"

"What d'ee mean by that?" she asked.

"Nothin'. I was thinkin' to myself, and out it popped."

"Well, 'tis like a Providence! For, till you said that, I'd clean forgot the sifter for your cuddy fire. Mustn't waste cinders now that you're only a mate."

Being a woman, she couldn't forego that little dig; but she got up there and then and gave the old boy a kiss.

She wouldn't walk down to the quay, though, next day, to see him off, being certain (she said) to lose her temper at the sight of Cap'n Dick carrying on as big as bull's beef, not to mention the sneering shareholders and their wives. So Cap'n Jacka took his congees at his own door, and turned, half-way down the street, and waved a good-bye with the cinder-sifter. She used to say afterwards that this was Providence, too.

The *Unity* ran straight across until she made Ushant Light; and after cruising about for a couple of days, in moderate weather (it being the first week in April) Cap'n Dick laid her head east and began to nose up Channel, keeping an easy little distance off the French coast. You see, the Channel was full of our ships and neutrals in those days, which made fat work for the French priva-teers; but the Frenchies' own vessels kept close over on their coast; and even so, the best our boys could expect, nine times out of ten when they'd crossed over, was to run against a *chasse-marée* dodging between Cherbourg and St. Malo or Mor-laix, with naval stores or munitions of war.

However, Cap'n Dick had very good luck. One morning, about three leagues N.W. of Roscoff, what should he see but a French privateering craft of about fifty tons (new measurement) with an Eng-lish trader in tow—a London brig, with a cargo of all sorts, that had fallen behind her convoy and been snapped up in mid-channel. Cap'n Dick had the weather-gauge, as well as the legs of the French *chasse-marée*. She was about a league to leeward when the morning lifted and he first spied her. By seven o'clock he was close, and by eight had made himself master of her and the prize, with the loss of two men only and four wounded, the Frenchman being short-handed, by reason of the crew he'd put into the brig to work her into Morlaix.

This was first-rate business. To begin with, the brig (she was called the *Martha Edwards*, of London) would yield a tidy little sum for salvage. The wind being fair for Plymouth, Cap'n Dick sent her into that port—her own captain and crew working her, of course, and thirty Frenchmen on board in irons. And at Plymouth she arrived without any mishap.

Then came the *chasse-marée*. She was called the *Bean Pheasant*,* an old craft and powerful leaky; but she mounted sixteen guns, the same as the *Unity*, and ought to have made a better run from her; but first, she hadn't been able to make her mind to desert her prize pretty well within sight of port; and in the second place her men had a fair job to keep her pumps going. Cap'n Dick considered, and then turned to old Jacka.

"I'm thinking," said he, "I'll have to put you aboard with a prize crew to work her back to Polperro."

* Probably *Bienfaisant*.

" The Lord will provide," said Jacka, though he had looked to see a little more of the fun.

So aboard he went with all his belongings, not forgetting his wife's sausages and the stug of butter and the cinder-sifter. Towards the end of the action about fifteen of the Johnnies had got out the brig's large boat and pulled her ashore, where, no doubt, they reached, safe and sound. So Jacka hadn't more than a dozen prisoners to look after, and prepared for a comfortable little homeward trip.

" I'll just cruise between this and Jersey," said Cap'n Dick; " and at the week-end, if there's nothing doing, we'll put back for home and re-ship you."

So they parted; and by half-past ten Cap'n Jacka had laid the *Bean Pheasant's* head north-and-by-west, and was reaching along nicely for home with a stiff breeze and nothing to do but keep the pumps going and attend to his eating and drinking between whiles.

The prize made a good deal of water, but was a weatherly craft for all that, and on this point of sailing shipped nothing but what she took in through her seams; the worst of the mischief being forward, where her stem had worked a bit loose with age and started the bends. Cap'n Jacka, however, thought less of the sea—that was working up into a nasty lop—than of the weather, which turned thick and hazy as the wind veered a little to west of south. But even this didn't trouble him much. He had sausages for breakfast and sausages for dinner, and, as evening drew on, and he knew he was well on the right side of the Channel, he knocked out his pipe and began to think of sausages for tea.

Just then one of the hands forward dropped pumping, and sang out that there was a big sail on the starboard bow. "I b'lieve 'tis a frigate, sir," he said, spying between his hands.

So it was. She had sprung on them out of the thick weather. But now Cap'n Jacka could see the white line on her and the ports quite plain, and not two miles away.

"What nation?" he bawled.

"I can't make out as she carries any flag. Losh me! if there bain't *another!*"

Sure as I'm telling you, another frigate there was, likewise standing down towards them under easy canvas, on the same starboard tack a mile astern, but well to windward of the first.

"Whatever they be," said Cap'n Jacka, "they're bound to head us off, and they're bound to hail us. I go get my tea," he said; "for, if they're Frenchmen, 'tis my last meal for months to come."

So he fetched out his frying-pan and plenty

sausages and fried away for dear life—with butter, too, which was ruinous waste. He shared round the sausages, two to each man, and kept the *Bean Pheasant* to her course until the leading frigate fired a shot across her bows, and ran up the red-white-and-blue; and then, knowing the worst, he rounded-to as meek as a lamb.

The long and short of it was that, inside the hour, the dozen Frenchmen were free, and Cap'n Jacka and his men in their place, ironed hand and foot; and the *Bean Pheasant* working back to France again with a young gentleman of the French navy aboard in command of her.

But 'tis better be lucky born, they say, than a rich man's son. By this time it was blowing pretty well half a gale from sou'-sou'-west, and before midnight a proper gale. The *Bean Pheasant* being kept head to sea, took it smack-and-smack on the breast-bone, which was her leakiest spot; and soon, being down by the head, made shocking weather of it. 'Twas next door to impossible to work the pump forward. Towards one in the morning old Jacka was rolling about up to his waist as he sat, and trying to comfort himself by singing " Tho' troubles assail," when the young French gentleman came running with one of his Johnnies and knocked the irons off the English boys, and told them to be brisk and help work the pumps, or the lugger—that was already hove to—would go down under them.

"But where be you going?" he sings out—or French to that effect. For Jacka was moving aft towards the cuddy there.

Jacka fetched up his best smuggling French, and answered: "This here lugger is going down. Any fool can see that, as you're handling her. And I'm going down on a full stomach."

With that he reached an arm into the cuddy, where he'd stacked his provisions that evening on top of the frying-pan. But the labouring of the ship had knocked everything there of a heap, and instead of the frying-pan he caught hold of his wife's cinder-sifter.

At that moment the Frenchman ran up behind and caught him a kick. "Come out o' that, you old villain, and fall in at the after pump!" said he.

"Aw, very well," said Jack, turning at once— for the cinder-sifter had given him a bright idea; and he went right aft to his comrades. By this time the Frenchmen were busy getting the first gun overboard.

They were so long that Jacka's boys had the after-pump pretty well to themselves, and between spells one or two ran and fetched buckets, making out 'twas for extra baling; and all seemed to be working like niggers. But by-and-by they called out all together with one woeful voice, "The pump is chucked! The pump is chucked!"

At this all the Frenchmen came running, the young officer leading, and crying to know what was the matter.

"A heap of cinders got awash, sir," says Jacka. "The pump's clogged wi' em, and won't work."

"Then we're lost men!" says the officer; and he caught hold by the foremast, and leaned his face against it like a child.

This was Jacka's chance. "'Lost,' is it? Iss, I reckon you *be* lost!—and inside o' ten minutes, unless you hearken to rayson. Here you be, not twenty mile from the English coast, as I make it, and with a fair wind. Here you be, three times that distance and more from any port o' your own, the wind dead on her nose, and you ram-stamming the weak spot of her at a sea that's knocking the bows to Jericho. Now, Mossoo, you put her about, and run for Plymouth. She may do it. Pitch over a couple of guns forr'ad, and quit messing with a ship you don't understand, an' I'll warn she *will* do it."

The young Frenchy was plucky as ginger. "What! Take her into Plymouth, and be made prisoner. I'll sink first!" says he.

But, you see, his crew weren't navy men to listen to him; and they had wives and families, and knew that Cap'n Jacka's was their only chance. In five minutes, for all the officer's stamping and morblewing, they had the *Bean Pheasant* about and were running for the English coast.

Now I must go back and tell you what was happening to the *Unity* in all this while. About four in the afternoon Cap'n Dick, not liking the look of the weather at all, and knowing that, so long as it lasted, he might whistle for prizes, changed his mind and determined to run back to Polperro, so as to re-ship Cap'n Jacka and the prize crew almost as soon as they arrived. By five o'clock he was well on his way, the *Unity* skipping along quite as if she enjoyed it; and ran before the gale all that night.

Towards three in the morning the wind moderated, and by half-past four the gale had blown itself out. Just about then the look-out came to Cap'n Dick, who had turned in for a spell, and reported two ships' lights, one on each side of them. The chances against their being Frenchmen, out here in this part of the Channel, were about five to two; so Cap'n Dick cracked on; and at daybreak—about a quarter after five—found himself right slap between the very two frigates that had called Jacka to halt the evening before.

One was fetching along on the port tack, and the other on the weather side of him, just making ready to put about. They both ran up the white ensign at sight of him; but this meant nothing. And in a few minutes the frigate to starboard fired a shot across his bows and hoisted her French flag.

Cap'n Dick feigned to take the hint. He shortened sail and rounded at a nice distance under the lee of the enemy—both frigates now lying-to quite contentedly with their sails aback, and lowering their boats. But the first boat had hardly dropped a foot from the davits when he sung out, " Wurroo, lads! " and up again went the *Unity's* great lug-sail in a jiffy. The Frenchmen, like their sails, were all aback; and before they could fire a gun the *Unity* was pinching up to windward of them, with Cap'n Dick at the helm, and all the rest of the crew flat on their stomachs. Off she went under a rattling shower from the enemy's bow-chasers and musketry, and was out of range without a man hurt, and with no more damage than a hole or two in the mizzen-lug. The Frenchmen were a good ten minutes trimming sails and bracing their yards for the chase; and by that time Cap'n Dick had slanted up well on their weather bow. Before breakfast-time he was shaking his sides at the sight of seven hundred-odd Johnnies vainly spreading and trimming more canvas to catch up their lee-way (for at first the lazy dogs had barely unreefed courses after the gale, and still had their topgallant masts housed). Likely enough they had work on hand more important than chasing a small lugger all day; for at seven o'clock they gave up and stood away to the south-east, and left the *Unity* free to head back homeward on her old course.

'Twas a surprising feat, to slip out of grasp in this way, and past two broadsides, any gun of which could have sent him to the bottom; and Cap'n Dick wasn't one to miss boasting over it. Even during the chase he couldn't help carrying on in his usual loud and cheeky way, waving good-bye to the Mossoos, offering them a tow-rope, and the like; but now the deck wasn't big enough to hold his swagger, and in their joy of escaping a French prison, the men encouraged him, so that to hear them talk you'd have thought he was Admiral Nelson and Sir Sidney Smith rolled into one.

By nine o'clock they made out the Eddystone on their starboard bow; and a little after—the morning being bright and clear, with a nice steady breeze—they saw a sail right ahead of them, making in for Plymouth Sound. And who should it

be but the old *Bean Pheasant*, deep as a log!
Cap'n Dick cracked along after her, and a picture
she was as he drew up close! Six of her guns had
gone; her men were baling in two gangs, and still
she was down a bit by the head, and her stern yaw-
ing like a terrier's tail when his head's in a rabbit-
hole. And there at the tiller stood Cap'n Jacka,
his bald head shining like a statue of fun, and his
one eye twinkling with blessed satisfaction as he
cocked it every now and then for a glance over his
right shoulder.

"Hullo! What's amiss?" sang out Cap'n Dick,
as the *Unity* fetched within hail.

"Aw, nothin', nothin'. 'Tho' troubles assail an'
dangers'—Stiddy there, you old angletwitch!—
She's a bit too fond o' smelling the wind, that's all."

As a matter of fact she'd taken more water than
Jacka cared to think about, now that the danger
was over.

"But what brings 'ee here? An' what cheer wi'
you?" he asked.

This was Cap'n Dick's chance. "I've had a run
between two French frigates," he boasted, "in
broad day, an' given the slip to both!"

"Dear, now!" said Cap'n Jacka. "So have I
—in broad day, too. They must ha' been the very
same. What did 'ee take out of 'em?"

"Take! They were two war frigates, I tell 'ee!"

"Iss, iss; don't lose your temper. All I managed to take was this young French orcifer here; but I thought, maybe, that you—having a handier craft——"

Jacka chuckled a bit; but he wasn't one to keep a joke going for spite.

"Look-y-here, Cap'n," he said; "I'll hear your tale, when we get into dock, and you shall hear mine. What I want 'ee to do just now is to take this here lugger again and sail along in to Plymouth with her as your prize. I wants, if possible, to spare the feelin's of this young gentleman, an' make it look that he was brought in by force. For so he was, though not in the common way. An' I likes the fellow, too, though he do kick terrible hard."

.   .   .   .   .

They *do* say that two days later, when Cap'n Jacka walked up to his own door, he carried the cinder-sifter under his arm; and that, before ever he kissed his wife, he stepped fore and hitched it on a nail right in the middle of the wall over the chimney-piece, between John Wesley and the weatherglass.

THE POISONED ICE

WE were four in the *patio*. And the *patio* was magnificent, with a terrace of marble running round its four sides, and in the middle a fountain splashing in a marble basin. I will not swear to the marble; for I was a boy of ten at the time, and that is a long while ago. But I describe as I recollect. It was a magnificent *patio*, at all events, and the house was a palace. And who the owner might be, Felipe perhaps knew. But he was not one to tell, and the rest of us neither knew nor cared.

The two women lay stretched on the terrace, with their heads close together and resting against the house wall. And I sat beside them gnawing a bone. The sun shone over the low eastern wall upon the fountain and upon Felipe perched upon the rim of the basin, with his lame leg stuck out straight and his mouth working as he fastened a nail in the end of his beggar's crutch.

I cannot tell you the hour exactly, but it was early morning, and the date the twenty-fourth of February, 1671. I learnt this later. We in the *patio*

248

did not bother ourselves about the date, for the world had come to an end, and we were the last four left in it. For three weeks we had been playing hide-and-seek with the death that had caught and swallowed everyone else; and for the moment it was quite enough for the women to sleep, for me to gnaw my bone in the shade, and for Felipe to fasten the loose nail in his crutch. Many windows opened on the *patio*. Through the nearest, by turning my head a little, I could see into a noble room lined with pictures and heaped with furniture and torn hangings. All of it was ours, or might be, for the trouble of stepping inside and taking possession. But the bone (I had killed a dog for it) was a juicy one, and I felt no inclination to stir. There was the risk, too, of infection—of the plague.

"Hullo!" cried Felipe, slipping on his shoe, with the heel of which he had been hammering. "You awake?"

I put Felipe last of us in order, for he was an old fool. Yet I must say that we owed our lives to him. Why he took so much trouble and spent so much ingenuity in saving them is not to be guessed: for the whole city of Panama comprehended no two lives more worthless than old Doña Teresa's (as we called her) and mine: and as for the Carmelite, Sister Marta, who had joined our adventures two days before, she, poor soul, would have thanked him for putting a knife into her and ending her shame.

But Felipe, though a fool, had a fine sense of irony. And so for three weeks Doña Teresa and I—and for forty-eight hours Sister Marta too—had been lurking and doubling, squatting in cellars, crawling on roofs, breaking cover at night to snatch our food, all under Felipe's generalship. And he had carried us through. Perhaps he had a soft corner in his heart for old Teresa. He and she were just of an age, the two most careless-hearted outcasts in Panama; and knew each other's peccadilloes to a hair. I went with Teresa. Heaven knows in what gutter she had first picked me up, but for professional ends I was her starving grandchild, and now reaped the advantages of that dishonouring fiction.

"How can a gentleman sleep for your thrice-accursed hammering?" was my answer to Felipe Fill-the-Bag.

"The city is very still this morning," he observed, sniffing the air, which was laden still with the scent of burnt cedar-wood. "The English dogs will have turned their backs on us for good. I heard their bugles at daybreak; since then, nothing."

" These are fair quarters, for a change."

He grinned. " They seem to suit the lady, your grandmother. She has not groaned for three hours. I infer that her illustrious sciatica is no longer troubling her."

Our chatter awoke the Carmelite. She opened her eyes, unclasped her hand, which had been locked round one of the old hag's, and sat up blinking, with a smile which died away very pitiably.

" Good morning, Señorita," said I.

She bent over Teresa, but suddenly drew back with a little " Ah! " and stared, holding her breath.

" What is the matter? "

She was on her knees, now; and putting out a hand, touched Teresa's skinny neck with the tips of two fingers.

" What is the matter? " echoed Felipe, coming forward from the fountain.

" She is dead! " said I, dropping the hand which I had lifted.

" Jesu——" began the Carmelite, and stopped: and we stared at one another, all three.

With her eyes wide and fastened on mine, Sister Marta felt for the crucifix and rope of beads which usually hung from her waist. It was gone: but her hands fumbled for quite a minute before the loss came home to her brain. And then she removed her face from us and bent her forehead to the pavement. She made no sound, but I saw her feet writhing.

"Come, come," said Felipe, and found no more to say.

I can guess now a little of what was passing through her unhappy mind. Women are women, and understand one another. And Teresa, unclean and abandoned old hulk though she was, had stood by this girl when she came to us flying out of the wrack like a lost ship. "Dear, dear, dear"—I remembered scraps of her talk—"the good Lord is debonair, and knows all about these things. He isn't like a man, as you might say": and again, "Why bless you, He's not going to condemn you for a matter that I could explain in five minutes. 'If it comes to that,' I should say—and I've often noticed that a real gentleman likes you all the better for speaking up—'If it comes to that, Lord, why did You put such bloody-minded pirates into the world?' Now to my thinking"—and I remember her rolling a leaf of tobacco as she said it—"it's a great improvement to the mind to have been through the battle, whether you have won or lost; and that's why, when on earth, He chose the likes of us for company."

This philosophy was not the sort to convince

252

a religious girl: but I believe it comforted her. Women are women, as I said; and when the ship goes down a rotten plank is bettter than none. So the Carmelite had dropped asleep last night with her hand locked round Teresa's: and so it happened to Teresa this morning to be lamented, and sincerely lamented, by one of the devout. It was almost an edifying end; and the prospect of it, a few days ago, would have tickled her hugely.

"But what did she die of?" I asked Felipe, when we had in delicacy withdrawn to the fountain, leaving the Carmelite alone with her grief.

He opened his mouth and pointed a finger at it.

"But only last evening I offered to share my bone with her: and she told me to keep it for myself."

"Your Excellency does not reason so well as usual," said Felipe, without a smile on his face. "The illustrious defunct had a great affection for her grandchild, which caused her to overlook the ambiguity of the relationship—and other things."

"But do you mean to say——"

"She was a personage of great force of character, and of some virtues which escaped recognition, being unusual. I pray," said he, lifting the rim of his rusty hat, "that her soul may find the last peace! I had the honour to follow her career al·

253

most from the beginning. I remember her even as a damsel of a very rare beauty: but even then, as I say, her virtues were unusual, and less easily detected than her failings. I, for example, who supposed myself to know her thoroughly, missed reckoning upon her courage, or I had spent last night in seeking food. I am a fool and a pig."

"And consequently, while we slept——"

"Excuse me, I have not slept."

"You have been keeping watch?"

"Not for the buccaneers, my Lord. They left before daybreak. But the dogs of the city are starving, even as we: and like us they have taken to hunting in company. Now this is a handsome courtyard, but the gate does not happen to be too secure."

I shivered. Felipe watched me with an amiable grin.

"But let us not," he continued, "speak contemptuously of our inheritance. It is, after all, a very fair kingdom for three. Captain Morgan and his men are accomplished scoundrels, but careless: they have not that eye for trifles which is acquired in our noble profession, and they have no instinct at all for hiding-places. I assure you this city yet contains palaces to live in, linen and silver plate to keep us comfortable. Food is scarce, I grant, but we shall have wines of the very first quality. We

254

shall live royally. But, alas! Heaven has exacted more than its tithe of my enjoyment. I had looked forward to seeing Teresa in a palace of her own. What a queen she would have made, to be sure!"

"Are we three the only souls in Panama?"

Felipe rubbed his chin. "I think there is one other. But he is a philosopher, and despises purple and linen. We who value them, within reason, could desire no better subject." He arose and treated me to a regal bow. "Shall we inspect our legacy, my brother, and make arrangements for the coronation?"

"We might pick up something to eat on the way," said I.

Felipe hobbled over to the terrace. "Poor old ———," he muttered, touching the corpse with his staff, and dwelling on the vile word with pondering affection. "Señorita," said he aloud, "much grief is not good on an empty stomach. If Juan here will lift her feet———"

We carried Doña Teresa into the large cool room, and laid her on a couch. Felipe tore down the silken hangings from one of the windows and spread them over her to her chin, which he tied up with the yellow kerchief which had been her only headgear for years. The Carmelite meanwhile detached two heavy silver sconces from a great candelabrum and set them by her feet. But we could find no tinder-box to light the candles—big enough for an altar.

"She will do handsomely until evening," said Felipe, and added under his breath, "but we must contrive to fasten the gate of the *patio*."

"I will watch by her," said Sister Marta.

Felipe glanced at us and shook his head. I knew he was thinking of the dogs. "That would not do at all, Señorita. 'For the living, the living,' as they say. If we live, we will return this evening and attend to her; but while my poor head remains clear (and Heaven knows how long that will be) there is more important work to be done."

"To bury the dead——"

"It is one of the Seven Corporal Acts of Mercy, Señorita, and it won Raphael to the house of Tobit. But in this instance Raphael shuts himself up and we must go to him. While Teresa lived, all was well: but now, with two lives depending on my wits, and my wits not to be depended on for an hour, it does not suit with my conscience to lose time in finding you another protector."

"But *they—they* have gone?"

"The Lutheran dogs have gone, and have taken the city's victuals with them."

"I do not want to live, my friend."

THE POISONED ICE

"Granted: but I do not think that Juanito, here, is quite of your mind."

She considered for a moment. "I will go with you," she said: and we quitted the *patio* together.

The gate opened upon a narrow alley, encumbered now with charred beams and heaps of refuse from a burnt house across the way. The fury of the pirates had been extravagant, but careless (as Felipe had said). In their lust of robbing, firing, murdering, they had followed no system; and so it happened that a few houses, even wealthy ones, stood intact, like islands, in the general ruin. For the most part, to be sure, there were houses which hid their comfort behind mean walls. But once or twice we were fairly staggered by the blind rage which had passed over a mansion crowded with valuables and wrecked a dozen poor habitations all around it. The mischief was that from such houses Felipe, our forager, brought reports of wealth to make the mouth water, but nothing to stay the stomach. The meat in the larders was putrid; the bread hard as a stone. We were thankful at last for a few oranges, on which we snatched a breakfast in an angle of ruined wall on the north side of the Cathedral, pricking up our ears at the baying of the dogs as they hunted their food somewhere in the northern suburbs.

I confess that the empty houses gave me the
creeps, staring down at me with their open windows
while I sucked my orange. In the rooms behind
those windows lay dead bodies, no doubt: some
mutilated, some swollen with the plague (for during
a fortnight now the plague had been busy); all
lying quiet up there, with the sun staring in on
them. Each window had a meaning in its eye, and
was trying to convey it. "If you could only look
through me," one said. "The house is empty—
come upstairs and see." For me that was an un-
comfortable meal. Felipe, too, had lost some of
his spirits. The fact is, we had been forced to step
aside to pass more than one body stretched at length
or huddled in the roadway, and—well, I have told
you about the dogs.

Between the Cathedral and the quays scarcely a
house remained: for the whole of this side of the
city had been built of wood. But beyond this
smoking waste we came to the great stone warehouses by the waterside, and the barracks where the
Genoese traders lodged their slaves. The shells of
these buildings stood, but every one had been gutted
and the roofs of all but two or three had collapsed.
We picked our way circumspectly now, for here
had been the buccaneers' headquarters. But the
quays were as desolate as the city. Empty, too,

were the long stables where the horses and mules had used to be kept for conveying the royal plate from ocean to ocean. Two or three poor beasts lay in their stalls—slaughtered as unfit for service; the rest, no doubt, were carrying Morgan's loot on the road to Chagres.

Here, beside the stables, Felipe took a sudden turn to the right and struck down a lane which seemed to wind back towards the city between long lines of warehouses. I believe that, had we gone forward another hundred yards, to the quay's edge, we should have seen or heard enough to send us along that lane at the double. As it was, we heard nothing, and saw only the blue bay, the islands shining green under the thin line of smoke blown on the land breeze—no living creature between us and them but a few sea-birds. After we had struck into the lane I turned for another look, and am sure that this was all.

Felipe led the way down the lane for a couple of gun-shots; the Carmelite following like a ghost in her white robes, and I close at her heels. He halted before a low door on the left; a door of the most ordinary appearance. It opened by a common latch upon a cobbled passage running between two warehouses, and so narrow that the walls almost met high over our heads. At the end of this passage—

which was perhaps forty feet long—we came to a second door, with a grille, and, hanging beside it, an iron bell-handle, at which Felipe tugged.

The sound of the bell gave me a start, for it seemed to come from just beneath my feet. Felipe grinned.

"Brother Bartolomé works like a mole. But good wine needs no bush, my Juanito, as you shall presently own. He takes his own time, though," Felipe grumbled, after a minute. "It cannot be that——"

He was about to tug again when somebody pushed back the little shutter behind the grille, and a pair of eyes (we could see nothing of the face) gazed out upon us.

"There is no longer need for caution, reverend father," said Felipe, addressing the grille. "The Lutheran dogs have left the city, and we have come to taste your cordial and consult with you on a matter of business."

We heard a bolt slid, and the door opened upon a pale emaciated face and two eyes which clearly found the very moderate daylight too much for them. Brother Bartolomé blinked without ceasing, while he shielded with one hand the thin flame of an earthenware lamp.

"Are you come all on one business?" he asked,

his gaze passing from one to another, and resting at length on the Carmelite.

"When the forest takes fire, all beasts are cousins," said Felipe sententiously. Without another question the friar turned and led the way, down a flight of stairs which plunged (for all I could tell) into the bowels of earth. His lamp flickered on bare walls upon which the spiders scurried. I counted twenty steps, and still all below us was dark as a pit; ten more, and I was pulled up with that peculiar and highly disagreeable jar which everyone remembers who has put forward a foot expecting a step, and found himself suddenly on the level. The passage ran straight ahead into darkness: but the friar pushed open a low door in the left-hand wall, and, stepping aside, ushered us into a room, or paved cell, lit by a small lamp depending by a chain from the vaulted roof.

Shelves lined the cell from floor to roof; chests, benches, and work-tables occupied two-thirds of the floor-space: and all were crowded with books, bottles, retorts, phials, and the apparatus of a laboratory. "Crowded," however, is not the word; for at a second glance I recognised the beautiful order that reigned. The deal work-benches had been scoured white as paper; every glass, every metal pan and basin sparkled and shone in the double light of the lamp and of a faint beam of day conducted down from the upper world by a kind of funnel and through a grated window facing the door.

In this queer double light Brother Bartolomé faced us, after extinguishing the small lamp in his hand.

" You say the pirates have left? "

Felipe nodded. " At daybreak. We in this room are all who remain in Panama."

" The citizens will be returning, doubtless, in a day or two. I have no food for you, if that is what you seek. I finished my last crust yesterday."

" That is a pity. But we must forage. Meanwhile, reverend father, a touch of your cordial——"

Brother Bartolomé reached down a bottle from a shelf. It was heavily sealed and decorated with a large green label bearing a scarlet cross. Bottles similarly sealed and labelled lined this shelf and a dozen others. He broke the seal, drew the cork, and fetched three glasses, each of which he held carefully up to the lamplight. Satisfied of their cleanliness, he held the first out to the Carmelite. She shook her head.

" It is against the vow."

He grunted and poured out a glassful apiece for Felipe and me. The first sip brought tears into my

eyes: and then suddenly I was filled with sunshine
—golden sunshine—and could feel it running from
limb to limb through every vein in my small body.

Felipe chuckled. " See the lad looking down at
his stomach! Button your jacket, Juanito; the
noonday's shining through! Another sip, to the
reverend father's health! His brothers run away—
the Abbot himself runs: but Brother Bartolomé
stays. For he labours for the good of man, and
that gives a clear conscience. Behold how just,
after all, are the dispositions of Heaven: how blind
are the wicked! For three weeks those bloody-
minded dogs have been grinning and running about
the city: and here under their feet, as in a mine,
have lain the two most precious jewels of all—a
clear conscience and a liquor which, upon my faith,
holy father, cannot be believed in under a second
glass."

Brother Bartolomé was refilling the glass, when
the Carmelite touched his arm.

" You have been here—all the while? "

" Has it been so long? I have been at work, you
see."

" For the good of man," interrupted Felipe.
" Time slips away when one works for the good of
man."

" And all the while you were distilling this? "

" This—and other things."

" Other things to drink? "

" My daughter, had they caught me, they might have tortured me. I might have held my tongue: but, again, I might not. Under torture one never knows what will happen. But the secret of the liquor had to die with me—that is in the vow. So to be on the safe side I made—other things."

" Father, give me to drink of those other things."

She spoke scarcely above her breath: but her fingers were gripping his arm. He looked straight into her eyes.

" My poor child! " was all he said, very low and slow.

" I can touch no other sacrament," she pleaded. " Father, have mercy and give me that one! " She watched his eyes eagerly as they flinched from hers in pity and dwelt for a moment on a tall chest behind her shoulder, against the wall to the right of the door. She glanced round, stepped to the chest, and laid a hand on the lid. " Is it here? " she asked.

But he was beside her on the instant; and stooping, locked down the lid, and drew out the key abruptly.

" Is it here? " she repeated.

" My child, that is an ice-chest. In the liquor,

for perfection, the water used has first to be frozen. That chest contains ice, and nothing else."

" Nothing else? " she persisted.

But here Felipe broke in. " The Señorita is off her hinges, father. Much fasting has made her light-headed. And that brings me to my business. You know my head, too, is not strong: good enough for a furlong or two, but not for the mile course. Now if you will shelter these two innocents whilst I forage, we shall make a famous household. You have rooms here in plenty; the best-hidden in Panama. But none of us can live without food, and with these two to look after I am hampered. There are the dogs, too. But Felipe knows a trick or two more than the dogs, and if he do not fill your larder by sunset, may his left leg be withered like his right! "

Brother Bartolomé considered. " Here are the keys," said he. " Choose your lodgings and take the boy along with you, for I think the sister here wishes to talk with me alone."

Felipe took the keys and handed me the small lamp, which I held aloft as he limped after me along the dark corridor, tapping its flagged pavement with the nail of his crutch. We passed an iron-studded door which led, he told me, to the crypt of the chapel; and soon after mounted a flight of steps and found ourselves before the great folding doors of the ante-chapel itself, and looked in. Here was daylight again: actual sunlight, falling through six windows high up in the southern wall and resting in bright patches on the stall canopies within. We looked on these bright patches through the interspaces of a great carved screen: but when I would have pressed into the chapel for a better view, Felipe took me by the collar.

"Business first," said he, and pointed up the staircase, which mounted steeply again after its break by the chapel doors. Up we went, and were saluted again by the smell of burnt cedar-wood wafted through lancet windows, barred but unglazed, in the outer wall. The inner wall was blank, of course, being the northern side-wall of the chapel: but we passed one doorway in it with which I was to make better acquaintance. And, about twenty steps higher, we reached a long level corridor and the cells where the brothers slept.

Felipe opened them one by one and asked me to take my choice. All were empty and bare, and seemed to me pretty much alike.

"We have slept in worse, but that is not the point. Be pleased to remember, Juanito, that we are kings now: and as kings we are bound to find the reverend fathers' notions of bedding inadequate. Suppose you collect us half-a-dozen of these mattresses apiece, while I go on and explore."

I chose three cells for Sister Marta, Felipe, and myself, and set about dragging beds and furniture from the others to make us really comfortable. I dare say I spent twenty minutes over this, and, when all was done, perched myself on a stool before the little window of my own bed-room, for a look across the city. It was a very little window indeed, and all I saw was a green patch beyond the northern suburbs, where the rich merchants' gardens lay spread like offerings before a broken-down shrine. Those trees no doubt hid trampled lawns and ruined verandahs: but at such a distance no scar could be seen. The suburbs looked just as they had always looked in early spring.

I was staring out of window, so, and just beginning to wonder why Felipe did not return as he had promised, when there came ringing up the staircase two sharp cries, followed by a long, shrill, blood-freezing scream.

My first thought (I cannot tell you why) was that Felipe must have tumbled downstairs: and without any second thought I had jumped off my chair and was flying down to his help, three stairs at a bound, when another scream and a roar of laughter fetched me up short. The laugh was not Felipe's;

nor could I believe it Brother Bartolomé's. In fact it was the laugh of no one man, but of several. The truth leapt on me with a knife, as you might say. The buccaneers had returned.

I told you, a while back, of a small doorway in the inner wall of the staircase. It was just opposite this door that I found myself cowering, trying to close my ears against the abhorrent screams which filled the stairway and the empty corridor above with their echoes. To crawl out of sight—had you lived through those three weeks in Panama you would understand why this was the only thought in my head, and why my knees shook so that I actually crawled on them to the little door, and finding that it opened easily, crept inside and shut it before looking about me.

But even in the act of shutting it I grew aware that the screams and laughter were louder than ever. And a glance around told me that I was not in a room at all, but in the chapel, or rather in a gallery overlooking it, and faced with an open balustrade.

As I crouched there on my knees, they could not see me, nor could I see them; but their laughter and their infernal jabber—for these buccaneers were the sweepings of half-a-dozen nations—came to my ears as distinct as though I stood among them.

And under the grip of terror I crawled to the front of the gallery and peered down between its twisted balusters.

I told you, to start with, that Felipe was a crazy old fool: and I dare say you have gathered by this time what shape his craziness took. He had a mania for imagining himself a great man. For days together he might be as sane as you or I; and then, all of a sudden—a chance word would set him off —he had mounted his horse and put on all the airs of the King of Spain, or his Holiness the Pope, or aṇy grandissimo you pleased, from the Governor of Panama upwards. I had known that morning, when he began to prate about our being kings, that the crust of his common-sense was wearing thin. I suppose that after leaving me he must have come across the coffers in which the Abbot kept his robes of state, and that the sight of them started his folly with a twist; for he lay below me on the marble floor of the chapel, arrayed like a prince of the Church. The mitre had rolled from his head; but the folds of a magnificent purple cope, embroidered with golden lilies and lined with white silk, flowed from his twisted shoulders over the black and white chequers of the pavement. And he must have dressed himself with care, too: for beneath the torn hem of the alb his feet and ankles stirred feebly, and caught my eye: and they were clad in silken stockings. He was screaming no longer. Only a moan came at intervals as he lay there, with closed eyes, in the centre of that ring of devils: and on the outer edge of the ring, guarded, stood Brother Bartolomé and the Carmelite. Had we forgotten or been too careless to close the door after us when Brother Bartolomé let us in? I tried to remember, but could not be sure.

The most of the buccaneers—there were eight of them—spoke no Spanish: but there was one, a cross-eyed fellow, who acted as interpreter. And he knelt and held up a bundle of keys which Felipe wore slung from a girdle round his waist.

" Once more, Master Abbot—will you show us your treasures, or will you not? "

Felipe moaned.

" I tell you," Brother Bartolomé spoke up, very short and distinct, " there are no treasures. And if there were, that poor wretch could not show them. He is no Abbot, but a beggar who has lived on charity these twenty years to my knowledge."

" That tongue of yours, friar, needs looking to. I promise you to cut it out and examine it when I have done with your reverend father here. As for the wench at your side——"

" You may do as your cruelty prompts you,"

Brother Bartolomé interrupted. But that man is no Abbot."

" He may be Saint Peter himself, and these the keys of Heaven and Hell. But I and my camarados are going to find out what they open, as sure as my name is Evan Evans." And he knotted a cord round Felipe's forehead and began to twist. The Carmelite put her hands over her eyes and would have fallen: but one of her guards held her up, while another slipped both arms round her neck from behind and held her eyelids wide open with finger and thumb. I believe—I hope—that Felipe was past feeling by this time, as he certainly was past speech. He did not scream again, and it was only for a little while that he moaned. But even when the poor fool's head dropped on his shoulder, and the life went out of him, they did not finish with the corpse until, in their blasphemous sport, they had hoisted it over the altar and strapped it there with its arms outstretched and legs dangling.

" Now I think it is your turn," said the scoundrel Evans, turning to Brother Bartolomé with a grin. " I regret that we cannot give you long, for we returned from Tavoga this morning to find Captain Morgan already on the road. It will save time if you tell us at once what these keys open."

" Certainly I will tell you," said the friar, and

stretched out a hand for the bunch. "This key, for instance, is useless: it opens the door of the wicket by which you entered. This opens the chest which, as a rule, contains the holy vessels; but it, too, is useless, since the chest is empty of all but the silver chalices and a couple of patens. Will you send one of your men to prove that I speak truth? This, again, is the key of my own cell——"

"Where your reverence entertains the pretty nuns who come for absolution."

"After *that*," said Brother Bartolomé, pointing a finger towards the altar and the poor shape dangling, "you might disdain small brutalities."

The scoundrel leaned his back against a carved bench-end and nodded his head slowly. "Master friar, you shall have a hard death."

"Possibly. This, as I was saying, is the key of my cell, where I decoct the liquor for which this house is famous. Of our present stock the bulk lies in the cellars, to which this"—and he held up yet another key—"will admit you. Yes, that is it," as one of the pirates produced a bottle and held it under his nose.

"Eh? Let me see it." The brute Evans snatched the bottle. "Is this the stuff?" he demanded, holding it up to the sunlight which streamed down red on his hand from the robe of a martyr in one of the painted windows above. He pulled out his heavy knife, and with the back of it knocked off the bottle-neck.

"I will trouble you to swear to the taste," said he.

"I taste it only when our customers complain. They have not complained now for two-and-twenty years."

"Nevertheless you will taste it."

"You compel me?"

"Certainly I compel you. I am not going to be poisoned if I can help it. Drink, I tell you!"

Brother Bartolomé shrugged his shoulders. "It is against the vow . . . but, under compulsion . . . and truly I make it even better than I used," he wound up, smacking his thin lips as he handed back the bottle.

The buccaneer took it, watching his face closely. "Here's death to the Pope!" said he, and tasted it, then took a gulp. "The devil, but it is hot!" he exclaimed, the tears springing into his eyes.

"Certainly, if you drink it in that fashion. But why not try it with ice?"

"Ice?"

"You will find a chestful in my cell. Here is the key; which, by the way, has no business with this bunch. Felipe, yonder, who was always light-fingered, must have stolen it from my work-bench."

" Hand it over. One must go to the priests to learn good living. Here, Jacques le Bec! " He rattled off an order to a long-nosed fellow at his elbow, who sualted and left the chapel, taking the key.

" We shall need a cup to mix it in," said Brother Bartolomé quietly.

One of the pirates thrust the silver chalices into his hands: for the bottle had been passed from one man to another, and they were thirsty for more. Brother Bartolomé took it, and looked at the Carmelite. For the moment nobody spoke: and a queer feeling came over me in my hiding. This quiet group of persons in the quiet chapel—it seemed to me impossible they could mean harm to one another, that in a minute or two the devil would be loose among them. There was no menace in the posture of any one of them, and in Brother Bartolomé's there was certainly no hint of fear. His back was towards me, but the Carmelite stood facing my gallery, and I looked straight into her eyes as they rested on the cups, and in them I read anxiety indeed, but not fear. It was something quite different from fear.

The noise of Jacques le Bec's footstep in the ante-chapel broke this odd spell of silence. The man Evans uncrossed his legs and took a pace to

meet him. " Here, hand me a couple of bottles.
How much will the cups hold?"

" A bottle and a half, or thereabouts: that is, if
you allow for the ice."

Jacques carried the bottles in a satchel, and a
block of ice in a wrapper under his left arm. He
handed over the satchel, set down the ice on the
pavement and began to unwrap it. At a word from
Evans he fell to breaking it up with the pommel of
his sword.

" We must give it a minute or two to melt,"
Evans added. And again a silence fell, in which I
could hear the lumps of ice tinkling as they knocked
against the silver rims of the chalices.

" The ice is melted. Is it your pleasure that I
first taste this also?" Brother Bartolomé spoke
very gravely and deliberately.

" I believe," sneered Evans, " that on these occasions the religious are the first to partake."

The friar lifted one of the chalices and drank.
He held it to his lips with a hand that did not shake
at all; and, having tasted, passed it on to Evans without a word or a glance. His eyes were on. the
Carmelite, who had taken half a step forward with
palms held sidewise to receive the chalice he still
held in his right hand. He guided it to her lips, and
his left hand blessed her while she drank. Almost

before she had done, the Frenchman, Jacques le Bec, snatched it.

The Carmelite stood, swaying. Brother Bartolomé watched the cups as they went full circle.

Jacques le Bec, wiping his mouth with the back of his hand, spoke a word or two rapidly in French.

Brother Bartolomé turned to Evans. "Yes, I go with you. For you, my child!"—— He felt for his crucifix and held it over the Carmelite, who had dropped on her knees before him. At the same time, with his left hand, he pointed towards the altar. "For these, the mockery of the Crucified One which themselves have prepared!"

I saw Evans pull out his knife and leap. I saw him like a man shot, drop his arm and spin right-about as two screams rang out from the gallery over his head. It must have been I who screamed: and to me, now, that is the inexplicable part of it. I cannot remember uttering the screams: yet I can see Evans as he turned at the sound of them.

Yet it was I who screamed, and who ran for the door and, still screaming, dashed out upon the staircase. Up the stairs I ran: along the corridor: and up a second staircase.

"The sunshine broke around me. I was on the leads of the roof, and Panama lay spread at my feet like a trodden garden. I listened: no footsteps

were following. Far away from the westward came
the notes of a bugle—faint, yet clear. In the northern suburbs the dogs were baying. I listened again.
I crept to the parapet of the roof and saw the
stained eastern window of the chapel a few yards
below me, saw its painted saints and martyrs, out-
lined in lead, dull against the noonday glow. And
from within came no sound at all.

D'ARFET'S VENGEANCE

The Story is Told by Dom Bartholomew Perestrello,
Governor of the Island of Porto Santo.

It was on the fifteenth day of August, 1428, and
about six o'clock in the morning, that while taking
the air on the seaward side of my house at Porto
Santo, as my custom was after breaking fast, I
caught sight of a pinnace about two leagues distant, and making for the island.

I dare say it is commonly known how I came to
the governance of Porto Santo, to hold it and pass
it on to my son Bartholomew; how I sailed to it
in the year 1420 in company with the two honour-
able captains John Gonsalvez Zarco and Tristram
Vaz; and what the compact was which we made
between us, whereby on reaching Porto Santo these
two left me behind and passed on to discover the
greater island of Madeira. And many can tell with
greater or less certainty of our old pilot, the Spaniard Morales, and how he learned of such an island
in his captivity on the Barbary coast. Of all this
you shall hear, and perhaps more accurately, when

278

I come to my meeting with the Englishman. But I shall tell first of the island itself, and what were my hopes of it on the morning when I sighted his pinnace.

In the first warmth of discovering them we never doubted that these were the Purple Islands of King Juba, the very Garden of the Hesperides, found anew by us after so many hundreds of years; or that we had aught to do but sit still in our governments and grow rich while we feasted. But that was in the year 1420, and the eight years between had made us more than eight years sadder. In the other island the great yield of timber had quickly come to an end: for Count Zarco, returning thither with wife and children in the month of May, 1421, and purposing to build a city, had set fire to the woods behind the fennel-fields on the south coast, with intent to clear a way up to the hills in the centre: and this fire quickly took such hold on the mass of forest that not ten times the inhabitants could have mastered it. And so the whole island burned for seven years, at times with a heat which drove the settlers to their boats. For seven years as surely as night fell could we in Porto Santo count on the glare of it across the sea to the south-west, and for seven years the caravels of our prince and master, Dom Henry, sighted the

flame of it on their way southward to Cape Bojador.

In all this while Count Zarco never lost heart;
but, when the timber began to fail, planted his
sugar-canes on the scarcely cooled ashes, and his
young plants of the Malmsey vine—the one sent
from Sicily, the other from Candia, and both by
the care of Dom Henry. While he lives it will
never be possible to defeat my friend and old comrade: and he and I have both lived to see his island
made threefold richer by that visitation which in
all men's belief had clean destroyed it.

This planting of vines and sugar-canes began in
1425, the same year in which the Infante gave me
colonists for Porto Santo. But if I had little of
Count Zarco's merit, it is certain I had none of
his luck: for on my small island nothing would
thrive but dragon-trees; and we had cut these in
our haste before learning how to propagate them,
so that we had at the same moment overfilled the
market with their gum, or " dragon's blood," and
left but a few for a time of better prices. And,
what was far worse, at the suggestion surely of
Satan I had turned three tame rabbits loose upon
the island; and from the one doe were bred in
two or three years so many thousands of these pesti-
lent creatures that when in 1425 we came to plant

the vines and canes, not one green shoot in a million escaped. Thus it happened that by 1428 my
kingdom had become but a barren rock, dependent
for its revenues upon the moss called the orchilla
weed, of which the darker and better kind could
be gathered only by painful journeys inland.

You may see, therefore, that I had little to comfort me as I paced before my house that morning.
I was Governor of an impoverished rock on which
I had wasted the toil and thought of eight good
years of my prime: my title was hereditary, but
I had in those days no son to inherit it. And
when I considered the fortune I had exchanged for
this, and my pleasant days in Dom Henry's service
at Sagres, I accused myself for the most miserable
among men.

Now, at the north-western angle of my house,
and a little below the terrace where I walked, there
grew a plantation of dragon-trees, one of the few
left upon the island. Each time this sentry-walk
of mine brought me back to the angle I would halt
before turning and eye the trees, sourly pondering
on our incredible folly. For, on my first coming
they had grown everywhere, and some with trunks
great enough to make a boat for half a dozen men:
but we had cut them down for all kinds of uses,
whenever a man had wanted wood for a shield or

281

a bushel for his corn, and now they scarce grew
fruit enough to fatten the hogs. It was standing
there and eyeing my dragon-trees that over the tops
of them I caught sight of the pinnace plying towards the island. I remember clearly what manner
of day it was; clear and fresh, the sea scarce heaving, but ruffled under a southerly breeze. The
small vessel, though well enough handled, made a
sorry leeway by reason of her over-tall sides, and
lost so much time at every board through the labour
of lowering and rehoisting her great lateen yard
that I judged it would take her three good hours
before she came to anchor in the port below.

I could not find that she had any hostile appearance, yet—as my duty was—sent down word to the
guard to challenge her business before admitting
her; and a little before nine o'clock I put on my
coat and walked down to the haven to look after
this with my own eyes. I arrived almost at the
moment when she entered and her crew, with sail
partly lowered, rounded her very cleverly up in the
wind.

The guard-boat put off at once and boarded her;
and by-and-by came back with word that the pinnace was English (which by this time I had
guessed), by name the *George of Bristol*, and owned
by an Englishman of quality, who, by reason of his

extreme age, desired of my courtesy that I would
come on board and confer with him. This at first
I was unwilling to risk: but seeing her moored well
under the five guns of our fort, and her men so
far advanced with the furling of her big sail that
no sudden stroke of treachery could be attempted
except to her destruction, I sent word to the gun-
ners to keep a brisk look-out, and stepping into the
boat was pulled alongside.

At the head of the ladder there met me an aged
gentleman, lean and bald and wrinkled, with narrow eyes and a skin like clear vellum. For all the
heat of the day he wore a furred cloak which
reached to his knees; also a thin gold chain around
his neck: and this scrag neck and the bald head
above it stood out from his fur collar as if they had
been a vulture's. By his dress and the embroidered
bag at his girdle, and the clasps of his furred shoes,
I made no doubt he was a rich man; and he leaned
on an ebony staff or wand capped with a pretty de-
vice of ivory and gold.

He stood thus, greeting me with as many bobs
of the head as a bird makes when pecking an apple; and at first he poured out a string of salutations (I suppose) in English, a language with which
I have no familiarity. This he perceived after a
moment, and seemed not a little vexed; but cover-

ing himself and turning his back shuffled off to a door under the poop.

"Martin!" he called in a high broken voice. "Martin!"

A little man of my own country, very yellow and foxy, came running out, and the pair talked together for a moment before advancing towards me.

"Your Excellency," the interpreter began, "this is a gentleman of England who desires that you will dine with him to-day. His name is Master Thomas d'Arfet, and he has some questions to put to you, of your country, in private."

"D'Arfet?" I mused: and as my brows went up at the name I caught the old gentleman watching me with an eye which was sharp enough within its dulled rim. "Will you answer that I am at his service, but on the one condition that he comes ashore and dines with *me*."

When this was reported at first Master d'Arfet would have none of it, but rapped his staff on the desk and raised a score of objections in his scolding voice. Since I could understand none of them, I added very firmly that it was my rule; that he could be carried up to my house on a litter without an ache of his bones; and, in short, that I must either have his promise or leave the ship.

He would have persisted, I doubt not; but it is ill disputing through an interpreter, and he ended by giving way with a very poor grace. So ashore we rowed him with the man Martin, and two of my guard conveyed him up the hill in a litter, on which he sat for all the world like a peevish cross'd child. In my great airy dining-room he seemed to cool down and pick up his better humour by degrees. He spoke but little during the meal, and that little was mainly addressed to Martin, who stood behind his chair: but I saw his eyes travelling around the panelled walls and studying the portraits, the furniture, the neat table, the many comforts which it clearly astonished him to find on this forsaken island. Also he as clearly approved of the food and of my wine of Malmsey. Now and then he would steal a look at my wife Beatrix, or at one or the other of my three daughters, and again gaze out at the sea beyond the open window, as though trying to piece it all together into one picture.

But it was not until the womenfolk had risen and retired that he unlocked his thoughts to me. And I hold even now that his first question was a curious one.

" Dom Bartholomew Perestrello, are you a happy man? "

Had it come from his own lips it might have

found me better prepared: but popped at me through the mouth of an interpreter, a servant who (for all his face told) might have been handing it on a dish, his question threw me out of my bearings.

"Well, Sir," I found myself answering, "I hope you see that I have much to thank God for." And while this was being reported to him I recalled with a twinge my dejected thoughts of the morning. "I have made many mistakes," I began again.

But without seeming to hear, Master d'Arfet began to dictate to Martin, who, after a polite pause to give me time to finish if I cared to, translated in his turn.

"I have told you my name. It is Thomas d'Arfet, and I come from Bristol. You have heard my name before?"

I nodded, keeping my eyes on his.

"I also have heard of you, and of the two captains in whose company you discovered these islands."

I nodded again. "Their names," said I, "are John Gonsalvez Zarco and Tristram Vaz. You may visit them, if you please, on the greater island, which they govern between them."

He bent his head. "The fame of your discovery, Sir, reached England some years ago. I heard at the time, and paid it just so much heed as one does pay to the like news—just so much and no more. The *manner* of your discovery of the greater island came to my ears less than a twelvemonth ago, and then but in rumours and broken hints. Yet here am I, close on my eightieth year, voyaging more than half across the world to put those broken hints together and resolve my doubts. Tell me "—he leaned forward over the table, peering eagerly into my eyes—" there was a tale concerning the island—concerning a former discovery———"

" Yes," said I, as he broke off, his eyes still searching mine, " there was a tale concerning the island."

" Brought to you by a Spanish pilot, who had picked it up on the Barbary coast? "

" You have heard correctly," said I. " The pilot's name was Morales."

" Well, it is to hear that tale that I have travelled across the world to visit you."

" Ah, but forgive me, Sir! " I poured out another glassful of wine, drew up my chair, rested both elbows on the table, and looked at him over my folded hands. " You must first satisfy me what reason you have for asking."

" My name is Thomas d'Arfet," he said.

" I do not forget it: but maybe I should rather

287

have said—What aim you have in asking. I ought
first to know that, methinks."

In his impatience he would have leapt from his
chair had his old limbs allowed. Pressing the table
with white finger-tips, he sputtered some angry
words of English, and then fell back on the interpreter Martin, who from first to last wore a coun-
tenance fixed like a mask.

"Mother of Heaven, Sir! You see me here, a
man of eighty, broken of wind and limb, palsied,
with one foot in the grave: you know what it
costs to fit out and victual a ship for a voyage: you
know as well as any man, and far better than I,
the perils of these infernal seas. I brave those
perils, undergo those charges, drag my old limbs
these thousands of miles from the vault where they
are due to rest—and you ask me if I have any reason for coming!"

"Not at all," I answered. "I perceive rather
that you must have an extraordinarily strong reason—a reason or a purpose clean beyond my power
of guessing. And that is just why I wish to hear
it."

"Men of my age——" he began, but I stopped
Martin's translation midway.

"Men of your age, Sir, do not threaten the peace
of such islands as these. Men of your age do not

288

commonly nurse dangerous schemes. All that I
can well believe. Men of your age, as you say, do
not chase a wild goose so far from their chimney-
side. But men of your age are also wise enough to
know that governors of colonies—ay," for my
words were being interpreted to him a dozen at a
time, and I saw the sneer grow on his face, " even
of so poor a colony as this—do not give up even a
small secret to the very first questioner."

"But the secret is one no longer. Even in England I had word of it."

"And your presence here," said I, "is proof
enough that you learned less than you wanted."

He drew his brows together over his narrow eyes.
I think what first set me against the man was the
look of those eyes, at once malevolent and petty.
You may see the like in any man completely un-
generous. Also the bald skin upon his skull was
drawn extremely tight, while the flesh dropped in
folds about his neck and under his lean chaps, and
the longer I pondered this the more distasteful I
found him.

"You forget, Sir," said he—and while Martin
translated he still seemed to chew the words—" the
story is not known to you only. I can yet seek out
the pilot himself."

"Morales? He is dead these three years."

" Your friends, then, upon the greater island.
Failing them, I can yet put back to Lagos and appeal to the Infante himself—for doubtless he knows.
Time is nothing to me now." He sat his chin obstinately, and then, not without nobility, pushed his
glass from him and stood up. " Sir," said he, " I
began by asking if you were a happy man. I am
a most unhappy one, and (I will confess) the un-
happier since you have made it clear that you cannot or will not understand me. In my youth a
great wrong was done me. You know my name,
and you guess what that wrong was: but you ask
yourself, ' Is it possible this old man remembers,
after sixty years?' Sir, it is possible, nay, certain;
because I have never for an hour forgotten. You
tell yourself, ' It cannot be this only: there must
be something behind.' There is nothing behind;
nothing. I am the Thomas d'Arfet whose wife betrayed him just sixty years ago; that, and no more.
I come on no State errand, I! I have no son, no
daughter; I never, to my knowledge, possessed a
friend. I trusted a woman, and she poisoned the
world for me. I acknowledge in return a duty to
no man but myself; I have voyaged thus far out of
that duty. You, Sir, have thought it fitter to baffle
than to aid me—well and good. But by the Christ
above us I will follow that duty out; and, at the

worst, death, when it comes, shall find me pursuing it!"

He spoke this with a passion of voice which I
admired before his man began to interpret: and
even when I heard it repeated in level Portuguese,
and had time to digest it and extract its monstrous
selfishness, I could look at him with compassion,
almost with respect. His cheeks had lost their flush
almost as rapidly as they had taken it on, and he
stood awkwardly pulling at his long bony fingers
until the joints cracked.

"Be seated, Sir," said I. "It is clear to me that
I must be a far happier man than I considered myself only this morning, since I find nothing in myself which, under any usage of God, could drive me
on such a pursuit as yours would seem to be. I
may perhaps, without hypocrisy, thank God that I
cannot understand you. But this, at any rate, is
clear—that you seek only a private satisfaction: and
although I cannot tell you the story here and now,
something I will promise. As soon as you please
I will sail with you to the greater island, and we
will call together on Count Zarco. In his keeping
lies one of the two copies of Morales' story as we
took it down from his lips at Sagres, or, rather,
compiled it after much questioning. It shall be for
the Count to produce or withhold it, as he may

decide. He is a just man, and neither one way nor the other will I attempt to sway him."

Master d'Arfet considered for a while. Then said he, " I thank you: but will you sail with me in my pinnace or in your own ? "

" In my own," said I, " as I suspect you will choose to go in yours. I promise we shall outsail you; but I promise also to await your arriving, and give the Count his free choice. If you knew him," I added, " you would know such a promise to be superfluous."

II

My own pinnace arrived in sight of Funchal two mornings later, and a little after sunrise. We had outsailed the Englishman, as I promised, and lay off-and-on for more than two hours before he came up with us. I knew that Count Zarco would be sitting at this time in the sunshine before his house and above the fennel plain, hearing complaints and administering justice: I knew, moreover, that he would recognise my pinnace at once: and from time to time I laughed to myself to think how this behaviour of ours must be puzzling my old friend.

Therefore I was not surprised to find him already arrived at the quay when we landed; with a groom at a little distance holding his magnificent black stallion. For I must tell you that my friend was ever, and is to this day, a big man in all his ways —big of stature, big of voice, big of heart, and big to lordliness in his notions of becoming display. None but Zarco would have chosen for his title, " Count of the Chamber of the Wolves," deriving it from a cave where his men had started a herd of sea-calves on his first landing and taking seizin of the island. And the black stallion he rode when another would have been content with a mule; and the spray of fennel in his hat; and the ribbon, without which he never appeared among his dependents; were all a part of his large nature, which was guileless and simple withal as any child's.

Now, for all my dislike, I had found the old Englishman a person of some dignity and command: but it was wonderful how, in Zarco's presence, he shrank to a withered creature, a mere applejack without juice or savour. The man (I could see) was eager to get to business at once, and could well have done without the ceremony of which Zarco would not omit the smallest trifle. After the first salutations came the formal escort to the Governor's house; and after that a meal which lasted us two hours; and then the Count must have us visit his new sugar-mills and inspect the Candia vines freshly pegged out, and discuss them. On all manner of

trifles he would invite Master d'Arfet's opinion:
but to show any curiosity or to allow his guests to
satisfy any, did not belong to his part of host—a
part he played with a thoroughness which diverted
me while it drove the Englishman well-nigh mad.

But late in the afternoon, and after we had
worked our way through a second prodigious meal,
I had compassion on the poor man, and taking (as
we say) the bull by both horns, announced the business which had brought us. At once Zarco became
grave.

"My dear Bartholomew," said he, "you did
right, of course, to bring Master d'Arfet to me.
But why did you show any hesitation?" Before I
could answer he went on: "Clearly, as the lady's
husband, he has a right to know what he seeks.
She left him: but her act cannot annul any rights
of his which the Holy Church gave him, and of
which, until he dies, only the Holy Church can de-
prive him. He shall see Morales' statement as we
took it down in writing: but he should have the
story from the beginning: and since it is a long
one, will you begin and tell so much as you know?"

"If it please you," said I, and this being conveyed to Master d'Arfet, while Zarco sent a servant
with his keys for the roll of parchment, we drew
up our chairs to the table, and I began.

D'ARFET'S VENGEANCE

"It was in September, 1419," said I, "when the two captains, John Gonsalvez Zarco and Tristram Vaz, returned to Lagos from their first adventure in these seas. I was an equerry of our master, the Infante Henry, at that time, and busy with him in rebuilding and enlarging the old arsenal on the neck of Cape Sagres; whence, by his wisdom, so many expeditions have been sent forth since to magnify God and increase the knowledge of mankind.

"We had built already the chapel and the library, with its map-room, and the Prince and I were busy there together on the plans for his observatory in the late afternoon when the caravels were sighted: and the news being brought, his Highness left me at work while he rode down to the port to receive his captains. I was still working by lamplight in the map-room when he returned, bringing them and a third man, the old Spaniard Morales.

"Seating himself at the table, he bade me leave my plans, draw my chair over, and take notes in writing of the captains' report. Zarco told the story —he being first in command, and Tristram Vaz a silent man, then and always: and save for a question here and there, the Prince listened without comment, deferring to examine it until the whole had been related.

" Now, in one way, the expedition had failed, for
the caravels had been sent to explore the African
coast beyond Cape Bojador, and as far south as
might be; whereas they had scarcely put to sea
before a tempest drove them to the westward, and
far from any coast at all. Indeed, they had no hope
left, nor any expectation but to founder, when they
sighted the island; and so came by God's blessing
to the harbour which, in their joy, they named
Porto Santo. There, finding their caravels strained
beyond their means to repair for a long voyage, and
deeming that this discovery well outweighed their
first purpose, they stayed but a sufficient time to
explore the island, and so put back for Lagos. But
their good fortune was not yet at an end: for off
the Barbary coasts they fell in with and captured a
Spaniard containing much merchandise and two
score of poor souls ransomed out of captivity with
the Barbary corsairs. ' And among them,' said my
friend Gonsalvez, ' your Highness will find this one
old man, if I mistake not, to be worth the charges
of two such expeditions as ours.'

" Upon this we all turned our eyes upon the
Spaniard, who had been shrinking back as if to
avoid the lamplight. He must have been a tall, up-
standing man in his prime; but now, as Tristram
Vaz drew him forward, his knees bowed as if he

cringed for some punishment. 'Twas a shock, this
fawning carriage of a figure so venerable: but
when Tristram Vaz drew off the decent doublet he
wore and displayed his back, we wondered no longer.
Zarco pushed him into a chair and held a lamp
while the Prince examined the man's right foot,
where an ankle-ring had bitten it so that to his
death (although it scarcely hindered his walking)
the very bone showed itself naked between the
healed edges of the wound.

"Moreover, when Zarco persuaded him to talk
in Spanish it was some while before we could understand more than a word or two here and there.
The man had spent close upon thirty years in captivity, and his native speech had all but dried up
within him. Also he had no longer any thought
of difference between his own country and another:
it was enough to be among Christians again: nor
could we for awhile disengage that which was of
moment from the rambling nonsense with which he
wrapped it about. He, poor man! was concerned
chiefly with his own sufferings, while we were
listening for our advantage: yet as Christians we
forbore while he muttered on, and when a word or
two fell from him which might be of service, we
recalled him to them (I believe) as gently as we
could.

" Well, the chaff being sifted away, the grain came to this: His name was Morales, his birthplace Cadiz, his calling that of pilot: he had fallen (as I have said) into the hands of the Moors about thirty years before: and at Azamor, or a little inland, he had made acquaintance with a fellow-prisoner, an Englishman, by name Roger Prince, or Prance. This man had spent the best part of his life in captivity, and at one time had changed his faith to get better usage: but his first master dying at a great age, he passed to another, who cruelly ill-treated him, and under whose abominable punishments he quickly sank. He lay, indeed, at the point of death when Morales happened upon him. Upon some small act of kindness such as one slave may do for another, the two had made friends: and thus Morales came to hear the poor Englishman's story."

Here I broke off and nodded to the Count, who called for a lamp. And so for a few minutes we all sat without speech in the twilight, the room silent save for the cracking of Master d'Arfet's knuckles. When at length the lamp arrived, Zarco trimmed it carefully, unfolded his parchment, spread it on the table, and began to read very deliberately in his rolling voice, pausing and looking up between the sentences while the man Martin translated—

D'ARFET'S VENGEANCE

"*This is the statement made to me by Roger Prance, the Englishman, Anno MCCCCIX., at various times in the month before he died.*

"He said: My name is Roger Prance. I come from St. Lawrence on the River Jo,* in England. From a boy I followed the sea in the ships of Master Canynge,† of Bristol, sailing always from that port with cargoes of wool, and mostly to the Baltic, where we filled with stock-fish: but once we went south to your own city of Cadiz, and returned with wines and a little spice purchased of a Levantine merchant in the port. My last three voyages were taken in the *Mary Radclyf* or *Redcliffe*. One afternoon" [the year he could not remember, but it may have been 1373 or 1374] "I was idle on the Quay near Vyell's tower, when there comes to me Gervase Hankock, master, and draws me aside, and says he: 'The vessel will be ready sooner than you think,' and named the time—to wit, by the night next following. Now I, knowing that she had yet not any cargo on board, thought him out of his mind: but said he, 'It is a secret business, and double pay for you if you are ready and hold your tongue between this and then.'

"So at the time he named I was ready with the

---

* Wick St. Lawrence on the Yeo, in Somerset.
† Grandfather of the famous merchant, William Canynge.

most of our old crew, and all wondering; with the
ship but half ballasted as she came from the Baltic,
and her rigging not seen to, but moored down between the marshes at the opening of the River
Avon.

"At ten o'clock then comes a whistle from the
shore, and anon in a shore-boat our master with a
young man and woman well wrapped, and presently
cuts the light hawser we rode by; and so we
dropped down upon the tide and were out to sea by
morning.

"All this time we knew nothing of our two pas-
sengers; nor until we were past the Land's End
did they come on deck. But when they did, it was
hand in hand and as lovers; the man a mere
youngster, straight, and gentle in feature and dress,
but she the loveliest lady your eyes ever looked
upon. One of our company, Will Tamblyn, knew
her at once—as who would not that had once seen
her?—and he cried out with an oath that she was
Mistress d'Arfet, but newly married to a rich man
a little to the north of Bristol. Afterwards, when
Master Gervase found that we knew so much, he
made no difficulty to tell us more; as that the name
of her lover was Robert Machin or Macham, a
youth of good family, and that she it was who had
hired the ship, being an heiress in her own right.

"We held southward after clearing the land; with intent, as I suppose, to make one of the Breton ports. But about six leagues from the French coast a tempest overtook us from the north-east and drove us beyond Channel, and lasted with fury for twelve days, all of which time we ran before it, until on the fourteenth day we sighted land where never we looked to find any, and came to a large island, thickly wooded, with high mountains in the midst of it.

"Coasting this island we soon arrived off a pretty deep bay, lined with cedar-trees: and here Master Machin had the boat lowered and bore his mistress to land: for the voyage had crazed her, and plainly her time for this world was not long. Six of us went with them in the boat, the rest staying by the ship, which was anchored not a mile from shore. There we made for the poor lady a couch of cedar-boughs with a spare sail for awning, and her lover sat beside her for two nights and a day, holding of her hand and talking with her, and wiping her lips or holding the cup to them when she moaned in her thirst. But at dawn of the second day she died.

"Then we, who slept on the beach at a little distance, being waked by his terrible cry, looked up and supposed he had called out for the loss of the ship. Because the traitors on board of her, considering how that they had the lady's wealth, had weighed or slipped anchor in the night (for certainly there was not wind enough to drag by), and now the ship was nowhere in sight. But when we came to Master Machin he took no account of our news: only he sat like a statue and stared at the sea, and then at his dead lady, and ' Well,' he said; ' is she gone?' We knew not whether he meant the lady or the ship: nor would he taste any food though we offered it, but turned his face away.

" So that evening we buried the body, and five days later we buried Master Machin beside her, with a wooden cross at their heads. Then, not willing to perish on the island, we caught and killed four of the sheep which ran wild thereon, and having stored the boat with their flesh (and it was bitter to taste), and launched it, steered, as well as we could contrive, due east. And so on the eleventh day we were cast on the coast near to Mogador: but two had died on the way. Here (for we were starving and could offer no fight) some Moors took us, and carrying us into the town, sold us into that slavery in which I have passed all my miserable life since. What became of the *Mary Radclyf* I have never heard: nor of the three who came ashore with me have I had tidings since the day we were sold."

D'ARFET'S VENGEANCE

Here Zarco came to the end of his reading: and facing again on Master d'Arfet (who sat pulling his fingers while his mouth worked as if he chewed something) I took up the tale.

" All this, Sir, by little and little the pilot Morales told us, there in the Prince's map-room: and you may be sure we kept it to ourselves. But the next spring our royal master must fit out two caravels to colonise Porto Santo; with corn and honey on board, and sugar-canes and vines and (that ever I should say it!) rabbits. Gonsalvez was leader, of course, with Tristram Vaz: and to my great joy the Prince appointed me third in command.

" We sailed from Lagos in June and reached Porto Santo without mishap. Here Gonsalvez found all well with the colonists he had left behind on his former visit. But of one thing they were as eager to tell as of their prosperity: and we had not arrived many hours before they led us to the top of the island and pointed to a dark line of cloud (as it seemed) lying low in the south-west. They had kept watch on this (they said) day by day, until they had made certain it could not be a cloud, for it never altered its shape. While we gazed at it I heard the pilot's voice say suddenly at my shoulder, ' That will be the island, Captain—the Englishman's island! ' and I turned and saw that he was trembling. But Gonsalvez, who had been musing, looked up at him sharply. ' All my life,' said he, ' I have been sailing the seas, yet never saw landfall like yonder. That which we look upon is cloud and not land.' ' But who,' I asked, ' ever saw a fixed cloud?' ' Marry, I for one,' he answered, ' and every seaman who has sailed beside Sicily! But say nothing to the men; for if they believe a volcano lies yonder we shall hardly get them to cross.' ' Yet,' said Morales, ' by your leave, Captain, that is no volcano, but such a cloud as might well rest over the thick moist woodlands of which the Englishman told me.' ' Well, that we shall discover by God's grace,' Gonsalvez made answer. ' You will cross thither?' I asked. ' Why to be sure,' said he cheerfully, with a look at Tristram Vaz; and Tristram Vaz nodded, saying nothing.

" Yet he had no easy business with his sailors, who had quickly made up their own minds about this cloud and that it hung over a pit of fire. One or two had heard tell of Cipango, and allowed this might be that lost wandering land. ' But how can we tell what perils await us there?' ' Marry, by going and finding out,' growled Tristram Vaz, and this was all the opinion he uttered. As for Morales, they would have it he was a Castilian, a foreigner, and only too eager to injure us Portuguese.

"But Gonsalvez had enough courage for all: and on the ninth morning he and Tristram set sail, with their crews as near mutiny as might be. Me they left to rule Porto Santo. 'And if we never come back,' said Gonsalvez, 'you will tell the Prince that *something* lies yonder which we would have found, but our men murdered us on the way——' "

"My dear brother Bartholomew," Gonsalvez broke in, "you are wearying Master d'Arfet, who has no wish to hear about *me*." And taking up the tale he went on: "We sailed, Sir, after six hours into as thick a fog as I have met even on these seas, and anon into a noise of breakers which seemed to be all about us. So I prayed to the Mother of Heaven and kept the lead busy, and always found deep water: and more by God's guidance than our management we missed the Desertas, where a tall bare rock sprang out of the fog so close on our larboard quarter that the men cried out it was a giant in black armour rising out of the waves. So we left it and the noises behind, and by-and-by I shifted the helm and steered towards the east of the bank, which seemed to me not so thick thereabouts: and so the fog rolled up and we

305

saw red cliffs and a low black cape, which I named
the Cape of St. Lawrence. And beyond this, where
all appeared to be marshland, we came to a forest
shore with trees growing to the water's edge and
filling the chasms between the cliffs. We were now
creeping along the south of the island, and in clearer
weather, but saw no good landing until Morales
shouted aft to me that we were opening the Gulf of
Cedars. Now I, perceiving some recess in the cliffs
which seemed likely to give a fair landing, let him
have his way: for albeit we could never win it out
of him in words, I knew that the Englishman must
have given him some particular description of the
place, from the confidence he had always used in
speaking of it. So now we had cast anchor, and
were well on our way shoreward in the boat before
I could be certain what manner of trees clothed
this Gulf: but Morales never showed doubt or hesi-
tancy; and being landed, led us straight up the
beach and above the tide-mark to the foot of a low
cliff, where was a small pebbled mound and a plain
cross of wood. And kneeling beside them I prayed
for the sculs' rest of that lamentable pair, and so
took seizin of the island in the names of our King
John, Prince Henry, and the Order of Christ.
That, Sir, is the story, and I will not weary you
by telling how we embarked again and came to

this plain which lies at our feet. So much as I believe will concern you you have heard: and the
grave you shall look upon to-morrow."

Master d'Arfet had left off cracking his joints,
and for a while after the end of the story sat drumming with his finger-tips on the table. At length
he looked up, and says he—

" I may suppose, Count Zarco, that as governor
of this island you have power to allot and sell estates
upon it on behalf of the King of Portugal?"

" Why, yes," answered Gonsalvez; " any new
settler in Funchal must make his purchase through
me: the northern province of Machico I leave to
Tristram Vaz."

" I speak of your southern province, and indeed
of its foreshore, the possession of which I suppose
to be claimed by the crown of Portugal."

" That is so."

" To be precise I speak of this Gulf of Cedars,
as you call it. You will understand that I have
not seen it: I count on your promise to take me
thither to-morrow. But it may save time, and I
shall take it as a favour if—without binding yourself or me to any immediate bargain—you can give
me some notion of the price you would want for it.
But perhaps "—here he lifted his eyes from the
table and glanced at Gonsalvez cunningly—" you

307

have already conveyed that parcel of land, and I must deal with another."

Now Gonsalvez had opened his mouth to say something, but here compressed his lips for a moment before answering.

"No: it is still in my power to allot."

"In England just now," went on Master d'Arfet, "we should call ten shillings an acre good rent for unstocked land. We take it at sixpence *per annum* rent and twenty years' purchase. I am speaking of reasonably fertile land, and hardly need to point out that in offering any such price for mere barren foreshore I invite you to believe me half-witted. But, as we say at home, he who keeps a fancy must pay a tax for it: and a man of my age with no heir of his body can afford to spend as he pleases."

Gonsalvez stared at him, and from him to me, with a puzzled frown.

"Bartholomew," said he, "I cannot understand this gentleman. What can he want to purchase in the Gulf of Cedars but his wife's grave? And yet of such a bargain how can he speak as he has spoken?"

I shook my head. "It must be that he is a merchant, and is too old to speak but as a haggler. Yet I am sure his mind works deeper than this

308

haggling." I paused, with my eyes upon Master
d'Arfet's hands, which were hooked now like claws
over the table which his fingers still pressed: and
this gesture of his put a sudden abominable thought
in my mind. "Yes, he wishes to buy his wife's
grave. Ask him——" I cried, and with that I
broke off.

But Gonsalvez nodded. "I know," said he
softly, and turned to the Englishman. "Your desire, Sir, is to buy the grave I spoke of?"

Master d'Arfet nodded.

"With what purpose? Come, Sir, your one
chance is to be plain with us. It may be the difference in our race hinders my understanding you:
it may be I am a simple captain and unused to the
ways and language of the market. In any case
put aside the question of price, for were that all
between us I would say to you as Ephron the Hit-
tite said to Abraham. 'Hear me, my lord,' I
would say, 'what is four hundred shekels of silver
betwixt me and thee? Bury therefore thy dead.'
But between you and me is more than this: something I cannot fathom. Yet I must know it before
consenting. I demand, therefore, what is your purpose?"

Master d'Arfet met him straightly enough with
those narrow eyes of his, and said he, "My pur-

pose, Count, is as simple as you describe your mind to be. Honest seaman, I desire that grave only that I may be buried in it."

"Then my thought did you wrong, Master d'Arfet, and I crave your pardon. The grave is yours without price. You shall rest in the end beside the man and woman who wronged you, and at the Last Day, when you rise together, may God forgive you as you forgave them!"

The Englishman did not answer for near a minute. His fingers had begun to drum on the table again and his eyes were bent upon them. At length he raised his head, and this time to speak slowly and with effort—

"In my country, Count, a bargain is a bargain. When I seek a parcel of ground, my purpose with it is my affair only: my neighbour fixes his price, and if it suit me I buy, and there's an end. Now I have passed my days in buying and selling and you count me a huckster. Yet we merchants have our rules of honour as well as you nobles: and if in England I bargain as I have described, it is because between me and the other man the rules are understood. But I perceive that between you and me the bargain must be different, since you sell on condition of knowing my purpose, and would not sell if my purpose offended you. Therefore to leave you in error concerning my purpose would be cheating: and, Sir, I have never cheated in my life. At the risk then, or the certainty, of losing my dearest wish I must tell you this—*I do not forgive my wife Anne or Robert Machin:* and though I would be buried in their grave, it shall not be beside them."

" How then?" cried Gonsalvez and I in one voice.

" I would be buried, Sirs, not beside but between them. Ah? Your eyes were moist, I make no doubt, when you first listened to the pretty affecting tale of their love and misfortune? Not yet has it struck either of you to what a hell they left *me.* And I have been living in it ever since! Think! I loved that woman. She wronged me hatefully, meanly: yet she and he died together, feeling no remorse. It is I who keep the knowledge of their vileness which shall push them asunder as I stretch myself at length in my cool dead ease, content, with my long purpose achieved, with the vengeance prepared, and nothing to do but wait securely for the Day of Judgment. Pardon me, Sirs, that I say ' this shall be,' whereas I read in your faces that you refuse me. I have cheered an unhappy life by this one promise, which at the end I have thrown away upon a little scruple." He

311

passed a hand over his eyes and stood up. " It is curious," he said, and stood musing. " It is curious," he repeated, and turning to Gonsalvez said in a voice empty of passion, " You refuse me, I understand? "

" Yes," Gonsalvez answered. " I salute you for an honest gentleman; but I may not grant your wish."

" It is curious," Master d'Arfet repeated once more, and looked at us queerly, as if seeking to excuse his weakness in our judgment. " So small a difficulty! "

Gonsalvez bowed. " You have taught us this, Sir, that the world speaks at random, but in the end a man's honour rests in no hands but his own."

Master d'Arfet waited while Martin translated; then he put out a hand for his staff, found it, turned on his heel and tottered from the room, the interpreter following with a face which had altered nothing during our whole discourse.

. . . .

Master d'Arfet sailed at daybreak, having declined Gonsalvez' offer to show him the grave. My old friend insisted that I must stay a week with him, and from the terrace before his house we watched the English pinnace till she rounded the point to eastward and disappeared.

"After all," said I, "we treated him hardly."

But Gonsalvez said: "A husk of a man! All the blood in him sour! And yet," he mused, "the husk kept him noble after a sort."

And he led me away to the warm slopes to see how his young vines were doing.

MARGERY OF LAWHIBBET

A Story of 1644

I PRAY God to deal gently with my sister Margery
Lantine; that the blood of her twin-brother Mark,
though it cry out, may not prevail against her on
the Day of Judgment.

We three were all the children of Ephraim Lantine, a widower, who owned and farmed (as I do
to-day) the little estate of Lawhibbet on the right
shore of the Fowey River, above the ford which
crosses to St. Veep. The whole of our ground slopes
towards the river; as also does the neighbour estate
of Lantine, sometime in our family's possession,
but now and for three generations past yielding us
only its name. Three miles below us the river
opens into Fowey Harbour, with Fowey town beside it and facing across upon the village of Pol-
ruan, and a fort on either shore to guard the entrance. Three miles above us lies Lostwithiel, a
neat borough, by the bridge of which the tidal
water ceases. But the traffic between these two
towns passes behind us and out of sight, by the

high-road which after climbing out of Lostwithiel
runs along a narrow neck of land dividing our valley from Tywardreath Bay. This ridge comes to
its highest and narrowest just over the chimneys of
Lawhibbet, and there the old Britons once planted
an earthwork overlooking the bay on one hand and
the river-passage on the other. Castle Dore is its
name; a close of short smooth turf set within two
circular ramparts and two fosses choked with brambles. Thither we children climbed, whether to be
alone with our games—for I do not suppose my
father entered the earthwork twice in a year, and
no tillage ever disturbed it, though we possessed a
drawerful of coins ploughed up from time to time
in the field outside—or to watch the sails in the
bay and the pack-horses jingling along the ridge,
which contracted until it came abreast of us and
at once began to widen towards Fowey and the
coast; so that it came natural to feign ourselves
robbers sitting there in our fastness and waiting
to dash out upon the rich convoys as they passed
under our noses.

I talk as if we three had played this game with
one mind. But indeed I was six years younger than
the others, and barely nine years old when my
brother Mark tired of it and left me, who hitherto
had been his obedient scout, to play at the game

315

alone. For Margery turned to follow Mark in this,
as in everything, although with her it had been
more earnest play. For him the fun began and
ended with the ambush, the supposed raid and its
swashing deeds of valour; for her all these were
but incident to a scheme, long brooded on, by which
we were to amass plunder sufficient to buy back the
family estate of Lantine with all the consequence
due to an ancient name in which the rest of us forgot to feel any pride. But this was my sister Margery's way; to whom, as honour was her passion,
so the very shadows of old repute, dead loyalties,
perished greatness, were idols to be worshipped. By
a ballad, a story of former daring or devotion, a
word even, I have seen her whole frame shaken and
her eyes brimmed with bright tears; nay, I have
seen tears drop on her clasped hands, in our pew
in St. Sampson's Church, with no more cause than
old Parson Kendall's stuttering through the prayer
for the King's Majesty—and this long before the
late trouble had come to distract our country. She
walked our fields beside us, but in company with
those who walked them no longer; when she looked
towards Lantine 'twas with an angry affection. In
the household she filled her dead mother's place,
and so wisely that we all relied on her without
thinking to wonder or admire; yet had we stayed

to think, we had confessed to ourselves that the love
in which her care for us was comprehended reached
above any love we could repay or even understand
—that she walked a path apart from us, obedient to
a call we could not hear.

In her was born the spirit which sends men to
die for a cause; but since God had fashioned her
a girl and condemned her to housework, she took
(as it were) her own hope in her hands and laid
it all upon her twin brother. They should have
been one, not twain. He had the frame to do, and
for him she nourished the spirit to impel. With
her own high thoughts she clothed him her hero,
and made him mine also. And Mark took our hom-
age easily enough, without doubting he deserved
it. He was in truth a fine fellow, tall, upright, and
handsome, with the delicate Lantine hands and a
face in which you saw his father's features refined
and freshly coloured to the model of the Lantine
portraits which hung in the best sitting-room to
remind us of our lost glories. For me, I take after
my mother, who was a farmer's daughter of no
lineage.

I remember well the Christmas Eve of 1643,
when the call came for Mark; a night very clear
and crisp, with the stars making a brave show
against the broad moon, and a touch of frost against

which we wrapped ourselves warmly before the
household sallied down to the great Parc an Wollas
orchard above the ford, to bless the apple-trees.
My father led the way as usual with his fowling-
piece under his arm, Mark following with another;
after them staggered Lizzie Pascoe, the serving
maid, with the great bowl of lamb's wool; Margery
followed, I at her side, and the men after us with
their wives, each carrying a cake or a roasted apple on a string. We halted as usual by the bent
tree in the centre of the orchard, and there, having
hung our offerings on the bough, formed a circle,
took hands and chanted, while Lizzie splashed cider
against the trunk—

> " *Here's to thee, old apple-tree*
> *Whence to bud and whence to blow,*
> *And whence to bear us apples enow—*
> *Hats full, packs full,*
> *Great bushel sacks full,*
> *And every one a pocket full—*
> *With hurrah ! and fire off the gun !* "

I remember the moment's wait on the flint-lock
and the flame and roar of my father's piece, shat-
tering echoes across the dark water and far up the
creek where the herons roosted. And out of the
echoes a voice answered—a man's voice hailing
across the ford.

Mark took a torch, and, running down to the water's edge, waved it to guide the stranger over. By-and-by we caught sight of him, a tall trooper on horseback with the moonlight and torchlight flaming together on his steel morion and gorget. He picked his way carefully to shore and up the bank, and reined up his dripping horse in the midst of us with a laugh.

"Hats full, pockets full, eh? Good-evenin', naybours, and a merry Christmas, and I'm sure I wish you may get it. Which of 'ee may happen to be Master Ephr'm Lantine?"

My father announced himself, and the trooper drew out a parchment and handed it.

"'Tisn' no proper light here," said my father, fumbling with the packet, and not caring to own that he could not read. "Come to the house, honest man, and we'll talk it over; for thou'lt sleep with us, no doubt?"

"Ay, and drink to your apple-trees too," the trooper answered very heartily. So my father led the way and we followed, Margery gripping my hand tight, and the rest talking in loud whispers. They guessed what the man's business was.

An hour later, when the ashen faggot had been lit and the cider-drinking and carolling were fairly started in the kitchen, Margery packed me off to bed; and afterwards came and sat beside me for a while, very silent, listening with me to the voices below.

"Where is Mark?" I asked, for I missed his clear tenor.

"In the parlour. He and father and the soldier are talking there."

"Is Mark going to fight?"

She bent down, slipped an arm round my neck and caught me to her in a sudden breathless hug.

"But he may be killed," I objected.

"No, no; we must pray against that." She said it confidently, and I knew Margery had a firm belief that what was prayed for fitly must be granted. "I will see to that, morning and evening: we will pray together. But you must pray sometimes between whiles, when I am not by to remind you— many times a day—promise me, Jack."

I promised, and it made me feel better. Margery had a way of managing things, a way which I had learned to trust. We said no more but Good-night: in a little while she left me and I jumped out of bed and punctually started to keep my new promise.

Next morning—Christmas Day—we all attended church together; that is to say, all we of the family, for our guest chose rather to remain in the parlour with the cider-mug. Parson Kendall

.

preached to us at length on Obedience and the authority delegated by God upon kings; and working back to his text, which was I. Samuel, xvii. 42, wound up with some particular commendation of " the young man to-day going forth from amongst us "—which turned all heads towards the Lawhibbet pew and set Mark blushing and me almost as shamefacedly, but Margery, after the first flow of colour, turned towards her brother with bright proud eyes.

That same afternoon between three and four o'clock—so suddenly was all decided—Mark rode away from us on the young sorrel, and the trooper beside him, to join the force Sir Bevill Grenvill was collecting for Sir Ralph Hopton at Liskeard. To his father he said good-bye at the yard-gate, but Margery and I walked beside the horses to the ford and afterwards stood and watched their crossing, waving many times as Mark turned and waved a hand back, and the red sun over behind us blinked on the trooper's cap and shoulder-piece. Just before they disappeared we turned away together— for it is unlucky to watch anyone out of sight— and I saw that Margery was trembling from head to foot.

" But he will come back," said I, to comfort her.
" Yes," she answered, " he will come back."

With that she paused, and broke forth, twisting her handkerchief, " Jack, if I were a man——" and so checked herself.

" Why, you think more of the Cause than Mark does, I believe! " I put in.

" Not more than Mark—not more than Mark! Jack, you mustn't say that: you mustn't think it! "

" And a great deal more of our name," I went on sturdily, disregarding her tone, which I considered vehement beyond reason. " 'Tis a strange thing to me, Margery, that of us three you should be the one to think everything of the name of Lantine, who are a girl and must take another when you marry."

She halted and turned on me with more anger than I had ever seen on her face. She even stamped her foot. " Never! " she said, and again " Never! "

" Oh, well——" I began; but she had started walking rapidly, and although I caught her up, not another word would she say to me until we reached home.

For a year we saw no more of our brother, and received of him only two letters (for he hated pen-work), the both very cheerful. Yet within a month of his going, on a still clear day in January, we listened together to the noise of a pitched battle in

which he was fighting, a short six miles from us as
the crow flies. I have often admired how men who
were happily born too late to witness the troubles
of those times will make their own pictures of war-
fare, as though it changed at once the whole face
of the country and tenour of folk's lives; whereas
it would be raging two valleys away and men upon
their own farms ploughing to the tune of it, with
nothing seen by them then or afterwards; or it
would leap suddenly across the hills, filling the
roads with cursing weary men, and roll by, leaving a sharp track of ruin for the eye to follow and
remember it by. So on this afternoon, when Hopton and the Cornish troops were engaging and
defeating Ruthen on Braddock Down, Margery and
I counted the rattles of musketry borne down to us
on the still reaches of the river and, climbing to
the earthwork past the field where old Will Retal-
lack stuck to his ploughing with an army of gulls
following and wheeling about him as usual, spied
the smoke rolling over the edge of Boconnoc woodland to the northeast; but never a soldier we saw
that day or for months after.

A little before the end of the day the rebel army
broke and began to roll back through Liskeard and
towards the passes of the Tamar, and Mark followed
with his troops to Saltash, into Devonshire, and as

far as Chagford, where he rode by Mr. Sydney
Godolphin in the skirmish which gave that valiant
young gentleman his mortal wound. Soon after,
the whole of the King's forces retired upon Tavis-
tock, where a truce was patched up between the
opposing factions in the West. But this did not
release Mark, who was kept at duty on the border
until May—when the strife burst out again—and
joined the pursuit after Stratton Heath. There-
after he fought at Lansdowne, and in the operations
against Bristol, and later in the same year, having
won a cornetcy in the King's Horse, bore his part
in the many brisk expeditions led by Hopton
through Dorsetshire and Hampshire into Sussex.

'Twas from Worthing he came back to us a few
days before Christmas, and his mission was to beat
up recruits for his troop in the season of slackness
before the Spring campaign. He had grown almost
two inches, his chest was fuller, his voice manly,
and his handsome face not spoiled (Margery declared it improved) by a scar across the cheek, won
in a raid upon Poole. He had borne himself gallantly, and our prayers had prevailed with God to
save him from serious hurt even in the furious
charge at Lansdowne, when of two thousand horse
no more than six hundred reached the crest of the
hill. He greeted us all lovingly and made no dis-

guise of his joy to be at home again, though but on a short furlough.

And yet even on the first happy evening, when we walked up through the dusk together to the old earthwork, and he told us the first chapter of his adventures, I seemed to see, or rather to feel, that our brother was not wholly a better man for his campaigning. To be sure, a soldier must be allowed an oath or two; but Mark slipped out one before his sister which took me like a slap across the cheek. He bit his lip the moment it was out, and talked rapidly and at random for a while, with a dark flush on his face. Margery pretended that she had not heard, and for the rest he told his story with a manly carelessness which became him. Once only, when he described the entry of the troops into Bristol and their behaviour there—while Margery turned her eyes aside for a moment, that were dim for the death of Slanning and Trevanion—he came to a pause with a grin that invited me to be knowing beyond my years. The old Mark would never have looked at me with that meaning.

On the whole he behaved well, and took Margery's adoration with great patience. He had the wit to wish to fall nothing in her eyes. His new and earthlier view of war, as a game with coarse rewards, he confided to me; and this not in words but in a smile now and then and a general air, when safe from his sister's eyes, of being passably amused by her high-fangled nonsense. His business of beating up recruits took him away from us for days together; and we missed him on Christmas Eve when we christened the apple-trees as usual. It was I who discovered and kept it from Margery—who supposed him as far away as St. Austell, and tried to find that distance a sufficient excuse—that he had spent the night a bare mile away, hobnobbing with the owner of Lantine, a rich man who had used to look down on our family but thought it worth while to make friends with this promising young soldier.

"And I mean to be equal with him and his likes," said Mark to me afterwards by way of excuse. "A man may rise by soldiering as by any other calling—and quicker too, perhaps, in these days."

The same thought clearly was running in his head a week later, when he took leave of us once more by the ford.

"Come back to us, Mark!" Margery wept this time, with her arms about his neck.

"Ay, sweetheart, and with an estate in my pocket."

"Ah, forget that old folly! Come back with

body safe and honour bright, and God may take the rest."

He slapped his pocket with a laugh as he shook up the reins.

Then followed five quiet anxious months. 'Twas not until early in June that, by an express from Ashburton in Devon, we heard that our brother's fortune was still rising, he having succeeded to the command of his company made vacant by the wounding of Captain Sir Harry Welcome. " And this is no mean achievement for a poor yeoman's son," he wrote, " in an army where promotion goes as a rule to them that have estates to pawn. But I hope in these days some few may serve his Majesty and yet prosper, and that my dear Margery may yet have her wish and be mistress in Lantine." Margery read this letter and knit her brow thoughtfully. " It was like Mark to think of writing so," said she; " but I have not thought of Lantine for this many a day."

" And he might have left thinking of it," said I, " until these troubles are over and the King's peace established."

" Tut," she answered smiling, " he does not think of it but only to please me. 'Tis his way to speak what comes to his tongue to give us pleasure."

" For all that, he need not have misjudged us,"
I grumbled; and then was sorry for the pain with
which she looked at me.

" It is you, Jack, who misjudged! " She spoke
it sharply. We still prayed together for our brother
twice a day; but she knew—and either dared not
or cared not to ask why—that since his first home-
coming my love had cooled towards him. Very
likely she believed me to be jealous.

The hay-harvest found and passed us in peace,
and the wheat was near ripe, when, towards the
close of July, rumours came to us of an army
marching towards Cornwall under command of the
Earl of Essex; by persuasion (it was said) of the
Lord Robarts, whose seat of Lanhydrock lies on
our bank of the river about three miles above Lostwithiel, facing the Lord Mohun's house of Boconnoc
across the valley. My Lord Mohun, after some
wavering at first, had cast in his fortune with the
King's party, to which belonged well nigh all the
gentry of our neighbourhood; and had done so in
good time for his reputation. But the Lord Robarts was an obstinate clever man who chose the
other side and stuck to it in despite of first mis-
fortunes. We guessed therefore that if the Parlia-
mentarians came by his invitation they would not
neglect a district on which he staked so much for

mastery; and sure enough, about July 25th, we heard that Essex had reached Bodmin with the mass of his forces, Sir Richard Grenvill having retired before him and moved hastily with the Queen's troop to Truro. After this, Margery and I used to climb every morning to the earthwork and spy all the country round for signs of the hated troopers. Yet day passed after day with nought to be seen, and little to be heard but further rumours, of which the most constant said that the King himself was following Essex with an army, and had already seized and crossed the passes of the Tamar.

'Twas on the 2nd of August that the bolt fell; when after mounting the slope at daybreak with nothing to warn us, we stepped through the dykes into the old camp. A heavy dew hung in beads on the brambles, and at the second dyke I had turned and was holding aside a brier to let Margery pass, when a short cry from her fetched me right-about and staring into the face of a tall soldier grinning at us over the bank. In the enclosure behind him (as we saw through a gap) were a number of men in mud-coloured jerkins, quietly mounting a couple of cannon.

" Good morning! " said the soldier amiably, with an up-country twang in his voice, " Good-morning, my pretty dears! And if you come from the farm below, what may be the name of it?"

"Lawhibbet," I answered, seeing that Margery closed her lips tight.

"Ay, Lawhibbet; that's the name I was told." He nodded in the friendliest manner.

"Are you the rebels?" I blurted out, while Margery gripped my arm; but this boldness only fetched a laugh from the big man.

"Some of 'em," said he; "though you'll have to unlearn that name, my young whipstercock, seein' we're here to stay for a while. The Earl marched down into Fowey last night while you were asleep, and is down there now making it right and tight. Do you ever play at blind-man's buff in these parts?"

Three or four soldiers had gathered behind him by this, and were staring down on us. One of them blew a clumsy kiss to Margery.

"Do you mean the child's game?" I asked, wondering whatever he could be driving at.

"I do; but perhaps, sir, you are too old to remember it." He winked at the men and they guffawed. "It begins, 'How many horses has your father got?' 'Six,' says you; 'black, red, and grey' —or that's the number according to our instructions. 'Very good then,' says we; 'turn round three times and catch which you may.' And the moral is, don't be surprised if you find the stable empty when you get home. There's a detachment gone to attend to it after seizing the ford below; hungry men, all of them. No doubt they'll be visiting the bacon-rack after the stable, and if missy knows where to pick up the new-laid eggs she might put a score aside for us poor artillery-men."

We turned from them and hurried down the slope. "Rebels!" said Margery once, under her breath; but the blow had stunned us and we could not talk. In the stable yard we found, as the artillerymen had promised, a company of soldiers leading out the horses, and my father watching them with that patient look which never deserted him. He turned to Margery—

"Go into the kitchen, my dear. They will want food next, and we have to do what we can. They have been civil, and promise to pay for all they take. I do not think they will show any rough-ness."

Margery obeyed with a set face. For the next hour she and Lizzie were busy in the kitchen, fry-ing ham and eggs, boiling great pans of milk, cut-ting up all the bread of the last baking, and heating the oven for a fresh batch. The men, I am bound to say, took their food civilly, that morning and afterwards; and for a fortnight at least they paid reasonably for all they took. For several days I hung closer about the ingle than ever I had done in my life; not that a boy of fourteen could be any protection to the women-folk, but to be ready at least to give an alarm should insult be offered. But we had to do with decent men, who showed themselves friendly not only in the house but in their camp down by the ford, whither, after the first morning, Lizzie and I trudged it twice a day with baskets of provisions. Lizzie indeed talked freely with them, but I held my tongue and glowered (I dare say) in my foolish hate. Margery kept to the house.

'Twas, I think, on August 15th that the first hope of release came to us, by the King's troops seizing the ford-head across the river; and this happened as suddenly as our first surprise. Lizzie and I were carrying down our baskets at four o'clock that day, when we heard a sound of musketry on the St. Veep shore and on top of it a bugle twice blown. Running to the top of a knoll from which the river spread in view, I saw some rebels of our detachment splashing out from shore in a hurry. The leaders reached mid-stream or thereabouts, and paused. Doubtless they could see bet-

ter than I what was happening; for after they had
stood there a couple of minutes, holding their fire
—the musketry on the St. Veep bank continuing
all the while—some twenty men came running out
of the woods there and fled across towards us, many
bullets splashing into the water behind them. They
reached their comrades in the river-bed, and the
whole body stood irresolute, facing the shore where
nothing showed but a glint of steel here and there
between the trees. Thus for ten further minutes,
perhaps, they hesitated; then turned and came sullenly back across the rising water. In this manner
the royal troops won the ford-head, and kept it;
for although the two cannon opened fire that evening from the earthwork above us, and dropped many
balls among the trees, they did not dislodge the
regiment (Colonel Lloyd's) which lay there and
held one of the few passes by which the rebels could
break away.

For—albeit I knew nothing of this at the time
—by withdrawing his headquarters to Lostwithiel
and holding our narrow ridge with Fowey at the
end of it seaward, the Earl had led his army into
a trap, and one which his Majesty was now fast closing. Already he had drawn his troops across the
river-meadows above Lostwithiel; and, whatever
help the Earl might have hoped to fetch from the

sea at his base, he was there prevented by the quickness of Sir Jacob Astley in seizing a fort on the
other side of the harbour's mouth as well as a battery commanding the town from that shore, and in
flinging a hundred men into each, who easily beat
off all ships from entering. From this comfortable
sea-entrance then Essex perforce turned for his
stores to Twyardreath Bay on the western side of
the ridge, where he landed a couple of cargoes at
the mouth of the little river Par; but on the 25th
the Prince Maurice sent down 2,000 horse and
1,000 foot, and after sharp skirmishing blocked this
inlet also. So now we had the whole rebel army
cooped around us and along the two sides of the
ridge, trampling our harvest and eating our larders
bare, with no prospect but a surrender; which yet
the Earl refused, although his Majesty thrice offered
to treat with him.

This (I say) was the position, though we at Lawhibbet knew not how desperate 'twas for the rebels
our guests; only that our food was pinched to short
rations of bread and that payment had ceased,
though the sergeants still gave vouchers duly for
the little we could supply. The battery above us
kept silence day after day, save twice when the
Royalists made a brief show of forcing the pass;
but at intervals each day we would hear a brisk play

of artillery a little higher up the stream, where they had planted a fort on the high ground by St. Nectan's Chapel, to pound at Lostwithiel in the valley. For my part I could have pitied the rebels, so worn they were with weeks of hunger and watching, to which the weather added another misery, turning at the close of the month to steady rain with heavy fogs covering land and sea, and no wind to disperse them. Margery had no pity; but I believed would have starved cheerfully—if that could have helped —to see these poor sodden wretches in worse plight.

I think 'twas on the morning of the 28th that the Royalists across the ford showed a flag of truce; which having been answered, a small party of horse came riding over, the leader with a letter for the Earl of Essex which he was suffered to carry to Fowey, riding thither in the midst of an escort of six and leaving his own men behind on the near side of the ford.

While they waited by their horses I drew near to one of them and asked him if he knew aught of my brother, Captain Mark Lantine. He answered, after eyeing me sharply, that he knew my brother well—a very gallant officer, now serving with the Earl of Cleveland's brigade.

" That will be on the slope beneath Boconnoc," said I.

"How know you that?" he asked briskly, and
I was telling him that the dispositions of the Royal
troops were no secret to the rebels (warning of all
fresh movements being brought daily to the ford
from Lostwithiel), when a sergeant interrupted
and, forbidding any further converse, packed me
off homeward, yet not unkindly.

For what came of this talk Margery—to whom
I reported it that same evening—must bear the
credit. For two days she brooded over it, keeping
silence even beyond her wont, and then on the night
of the 30th, at nine o'clock, when I was scarce abed,
she tapped at my door and bade me arise and dress
myself. She had an expedition to propose, no less
than that we should cross the river and pay Mark
a visit in his quarters.

Her boldness took away my breath: yet as she
whispered her plan it did not seem impossible or,
bating the chance of being shot by a stray outpost,
so very dangerous. A heavy fog lay over the hills,
as it had lain for nights. The tide was flowing.
My father's boat had been dragged ashore and lay
bottom upwards under a cliff about three hundred
yards above the ford. If we could reach and right
it without being discovered, either one of us was
clever enough, with an oar over the stern, to scull
noiselessly across to the entrance of a creek where

336

the current would take us up towards Boconnoc
between banks held on either side by Royalists; to
whom, if they surprised us, we could tell our business.

The plan (I say) was a promising one. It miscarried only after we had righted the boat and were
dragging it across the strip of shingle between the
meadow bank and the water's edge. A quick-eared
sentry caught the sound and challenged at two gun-
shots' distance. I had the boat's nose afloat as I
heard his feet stumbling over the uneven foreshore:
but the paddles and even the bottom-boards were
lying on the beach behind us. There was no help
for it. Margery stepped on board swiftly and
silently, and I pushed well out into the stream, following until the water rose to my middle and so
standing while the fellow challenged again. For a
minute we kept mute as mice. The footsteps hesitated and came to a halt by the water's edge a full
twenty yards below, and I guessed that the fog had
blurred for him the distance as well as the direction of the sound. Very quietly I heaved myself
over the stern and into the boat, which swung
broadside to the current and so was borne up and
beyond danger from him. But the mischief was,
we were drifting up the main channel which ended
in the Lostwithiel marshes and must pretty cer-

tainly lead us into the enemy's hands, unless before striking the moors below the town we could by some means push across to the farther bank. We leaned over, dipped our arms in the water, and with the least possible noise began to paddle. Even in the darkness the tall banks were familiar, and between skill and good fortune we came to shore on the left bank below a coppice and just within sight of the town lights. Between us and them lay a broad marsh-land through which the river wound, and along the edge of which, under the trees skirting this shore, we started at a timorous run, pulling up now and again to listen.

So we had come abreast of the town without challenge, when the sky almost on a sudden grew lighter, and we saw the church spire glimmering and the weather-cock above it, and knew that the moon had risen over the woodland in the shadow of which we crouched. And with that Margery glanced back and plucked at my arm.

The moor we had skirted was full of horsemen, drawn up in rank and motionless. They loomed through the river fog like giants—rank behind rank, each man stiff and upright and silent in his saddle—as it were a vale full of mounted ghosts awaiting the dreadful trumpet, and in my terror I forgot to tremble at the nearness of our escape (for we had all but blundered into them). But while I stared, and the wreaths of fog hid and again disclosed them, I heard Margery's whisper—

" They are escaping to-night. It can only be by the bridge and across Boconnoc downs. If we can win to Mark and warn him! "

She drew me off into the wood at a sharp angle, and we began to climb beneath the branches. They dripped on us, soaking us to the skin; but this we scarcely felt. We knew that we must be moving along the narrow interval between the two lines of outposts. Beneath us, in the centre of a basin of fog, a cluster of lights marked Lostwithiel: above, the moon and the glow of Royalist camp-fires threw up the outline of the ridge. Alongside of this we kept, and a little below it, crossing the high-road which leads east from Lostwithiel bridge, and, beyond that, advancing more boldly under the lee of a hedge beside a by-road which curves towards the brow of Boconnoc downs. I began to find it strange that, for all our secrecy, no one challenged us here. At a bend of the lane, we came in view of a solitary cottage with one window lit and blurring its light on the mist. We crept close, still on the far side of the hedge, and, parting the bushes, peered at it.

It must be here or hereabouts (by all information) that the Earl of Cleveland kept his quarters.

The light shone into our eyes through a drawn blind which told nothing; and Margery was dragging me forward to knock at the door when it opened and two men stepped quickly across the threshold and passed down the lane. They crossed the bar of light swiftly and were gone into the dark; and they trod softly—so softly that we listened in vain for their footfalls.

Then, almost before I knew it, Margery had dragged me across a gap in the hedge and was rapping at the cottage door. No one answered. She lifted the latch and entered, I at her heels. The kitchen—an ordinary cottage kitchen—was empty. A guttered candle stood on the table to the right, and beside it lay a feathered cap. Margery stepped toward this and had scarce time to touch the brim of it before a voice hailed us in the doorway behind my shoulder.

" Hullo! "

It was our brother Mark.

" Well, of all——" he began, and came to a stop; his face white as a sheet, as well it might be.

Margery rounded upon him. She must have been surprised, but she began without explanation, running to him and kissing him swiftly—

" Mark—dear Mark, we have news for thee, instant news! Sure, Heaven directed us to-night that

you should be the first to hear it. Mark, we passed
the rebel cavalry in the valley, and for certain they
will attempt to break through to-night."

"Yes, yes," said he peevishly, pulling at an end
of his long love-locks, "we have had that scare often
enough, these last few nights."

"But we passed them close—saw them plainly
in rank below Lostwithiel bridge, and every man in
saddle. Even now they will be moving——"

Mark swung about and passed out at the open
door. He had not returned Margery's kiss. "I
must be off, then, to visit my videttes," said he
quickly, and then paused as if considering. "For
you, the cottage here will not be safe: it stands close
beside the line of march and I must get down a
company of musketeers. You had best follow
me——" he took a step and paused again: "No,
there will not be time."

"Tell us in what direction to go and we will fend
for ourselves and leave you free."

"Through the garden, then, at the back and into
the woods—the fence has a gap and from it a path
leads up to a quarry among the trees; you cannot
miss. The quarry is full of brambles—good hiding,
in case we have trouble. No cavalryman will win
so far, you may be sure."

Margery gathered her skirts about her, and we

stole out into the darkness. At the door she turned
up her face to Mark. " Kiss me, my brother." He
kissed her, and breaking away (as I thought) with
a low groan, strode from us up the lane.

" Now why should he go up the lane? " mused
Margery: and I too wondered. For the first alarm
must needs come from the lower end towards which
he had been walking with his other visitor, when we
first spied on the cottage through the bushes.

But 'twas not for us to guess how the troops were
disposed or where the outposts lay. We made our
escape through the little garden, and, blundering
along the woodland path behind it, came at length
to a thicket of brambles over which hung the scarp
of the quarry with a fringe of trees above it pitch-
black against the foggy moonlight. Here on the
soaked ground I found a clear space and a tumbled
stone or two, on which we crouched together, sleep-
less and intently listening.

For an hour we heard no sound. Then the valley
towards Lostwithiel shook with a dull explosion,
which puzzled us a great deal. (But the meaning,
I have since learnt was this:—Two prisoners in the
church there had contrived to climb up into the
steeple and, pulling the ladder after them, jeered
down upon the rebels' Provost Marshal, who was
now preparing for a night retreat of the Infantry

upon Fowey and in a hurry to be gone. " I'll fetch you down," said he, and with a barrel of powder blew most of the slates off the roof but without harming the defiant pair who were found still perched on the steeple next morning.)

After this the hours passed without sound. It seemed incredible, this silence in the ring of wakeful outposts. Margery shivered now and again, and I knew that her eyes were open, though she said nothing. For me, towards morning, I dropped into a doze, and woke to the tightening of her hand upon my arm.

" Hist! "

I listened with her. The sky had grown grey about us, and up through the dripping trees came a soft and regular footfall, as of a body of horse moving past. " It will be Mark's troop," I whispered, and listened again. It seemed to me that the noise moved away to our right instead of towards Lostwithiel. A quick suspicion took me then: I scaled the right-hand side of the quarry at a run, burst through the fringe of pines, and came out suddenly upon a knoll in full view of the down. The first gleam of sunshine was breaking over this slope, and towards it at an easy trot rode the whole body of rebel cavalry, in number above a thousand.

" Escaped! "

While I stood and stared, Margery caught up
with me. We looked into each other's face. Then
without a word she went from me. I lingered there
for perhaps ten minutes; for now, from behind the
trees above, a squadron of Royalist horse charged
across the slope at a gallop. They were less than
four hundred, however, and as the rebel rearguard
turned to face them, drew rein and exchanged but
a few harmless shots. I watched the host as it
wound slowly over the crest with its pursuers hanging sullenly at heel: then I turned and descended
in search of Margery. As I reached the gap in the
hedge, Mark entered the garden by the little gate
opposite. He came hastily, but halted as if shot,
with his hand on the gatepost to steady him—yet
not at sight of me. I looked across the gap into
the garden between us. Beside a heap of freshly
turned mould, with her back to the currant-bush,
stood Margery, her hands stained with soil; and on
the ground before her lay a small chest with its lid
open.

I lifted my eyes from the glinting coins and
sought Mark's gaze: but it was fastened on Margery, who walked slowly forward and straight up
to him. Though he shrank, he could not retreat.
She went to him, I following a pace behind. She
put out a hand and touched the pistol in his sling.

"Redeem." The voice was Margery's and yet not hers. "Redeem," she repeated—"*not Lantine.*"

With a groan he ran round the gable of the cottage. A moment later we heard the gallop of his horse down the lane.

At seven o'clock that morning the King's forlorn hope of foot, in number about 1,000, entered Lostwithiel after a smart skirmish with the rebel rearguard at the bridge; and not long after, the rebel reserve of foot, perceiving their comrades giving ground and being themselves galled by two or three pieces of cannon which began to play upon them from the captured leaguer, moved away from the hill they had been holding: so that now we had the whole force falling back towards Fowey along the ridge, with our forlorn hope following in chase from field to field.

Before eight the King himself with two troops of horse (one of them my brother's) passed over a ford a little to the south of the town, with intent to catch this movement in flank: and there, by the ford's edge, I believe, took a cartload of muskets with five abandoned pieces, two of them very long guns. The river being too deep, with a rising tide, for Margery to wade, we made our crossing by the bridge, where the fighting had been, but where there was now no soldiery, only a many dead bodies, some huddled into the coigns of the parapet, more laid out upon a patch of turf at the bridge end, the mud caked on their faces. It made me shiver to see: but my sister went by with scarce a glance and, once past the river, caught my hand and set off running after the troops.

The beginning of the retreat had been brisk enough—so brisk that it outpaced his Majesty's movement in flank: who, breasting the hill with his cavalry (after some minutes lost at the ford in collecting the cannon and muskets which might well have been gleaned later) found himself, if anything, in the rear of his victorious footmen. But after two miles, coming to that part of the ridge where it narrows above Lawhibbet, and in view of our old earthwork which was yet pretty strongly held by their artillery, the enemy made a more forcible resistance, fighting the several hedges and, even when dislodged, holding them with a hot skirmishing fire while the main body found the next cover. By these checks we two, who had lost ground at the start, now regained it fast; and by and by (towards ten o'clock as I guess) were forced to pick our way under shelter of the hedges, to avoid the enemy's bullets and espial by any of the King's men, who would doubtless have cursed and driven us back out of the way of danger.

It was Margery who bethought her here of a sunken cart-road descending along the right of the ridge and crossed on its way by another which would lead us to the summit again and within two gunshots of the great earthwork. By following these two roads we might outflank the soldiery while keeping the crown of the ridge between us; for the fighting still followed along the left-hand slope, above the river.

This way, to be sure, was reasonably safe for a while; but must lead us out, if we persisted, into close danger—perhaps into the very interval between the fighting lines, and if at the rebels' rear, then certainly between them and their artillery on the earthwork. As we ran I tried to prove this to Margery. She would not listen: indeed I doubt that she heard me. " He must," " he must," she kept saying: and I thought sure she had taken leave of her wits.

It happened as I warned her. The second cart-track, mounting from the valley bottom, led us up to the high road on the ridge; and there, peering out cautiously, I spied the backs of a rebel company posted across it, a bare two hundred yards away towards Lostwithiel. Their ranks parted and

I had time enough, and no more, to push Margery
into the ditch and fling myself beside her among
the brambles before a team of horses swept by at
a gallop, with a cannon bumping on its carriage behind them and dragging a long cloud of dust.

"Quick!" called Margery as it passed: sprang
to her feet and across the road in the noise and
smother. Choking with dust and anger I followed,
almost on all-fours.

"But what folly is this?" I demanded, overtaking her by the opposite hedge.

"I know what I am doing," she said. "They
did not see—the dust hid us. Now quick again, and
help me up to this hazel-bush."

I swung her up, and myself after her. The bush
was one which I myself had polled two years before; an old stump set thickly about with young
shoots, in the cover of which we huddled, staring
down the slope of our own great grass-field (the larg-
est on Lawhibbet farm) now filled with rebels withdrawing in good order upon the earthwork on Castle
Dore. This earthwork stood in the very next field
on our right, behind what had used to be a hedge
but where was now a gap some twenty yards wide
(levelled a few days before by Essex's cannoniers),
and through this gap, towards which the regiments
were streaming, drifted the smoke of the guns as

they flung their round shot high over our heads,
and over the hedge on our left which hid from us
all of the royal troops save now and then the flash
of a steel cap behind the top-growth of hazel ash
and bramble.

The line of this hedge, on the near side to us,
was yet held by musketeers who had spread themselves along it very closely and seemed to be using
every bush. Indeed I wondered how they were to
be forced from such cover, when a party of them
by the gate suddenly gave back and began running,
and through the gateway a small troop of horse
came pouring at their heels. And albeit these
cavaliers must have suffered desperately in so charging up to a covered foe (and many riderless chargers
came galloping with them), yet the remnant held
such good order that in pouring through they
seemed to divide by agreement, a part wheeling to
right and a part to left to drive the skirmishers,
while the main troop held on across the field nor
drew rein until they had chased the rebel rearguard
to the gap. But as the gap cleared ahead and
showed the earthwork and the muzzles of the guns
now lowered right in their path, their leader checked
his horse, wheeled about in as pretty a curve as you
would wish to see, and his troop following cantered
back towards the gate.

It was gallantly done and clearly won high approval from a horseman who at the moment came at a trot through the gate, with a second troop behind him, and was saluted by the returning squadron with one flash of sword-blades, all together, hilt brought to chin and every blade pointing straight in air—a flourish almost as pretty as the feat it concluded. He too held his sword before him with point upright, but awkwardly; and though he sat his saddle well, his bearing had more of civil authority than of soldierlike precision. I was wondering, indeed, what his business might be on this field of arms—for his men hung back somewhat, as escorting rather than charging at his lead, when Margery plucked at my elbow.

" The King! "

I stared at her stupidly. And reading awe in her wide eyes, I had almost turned to follow their gaze when my own fell on a rider who had detached himself from the escort and was coming towards us along the hedge row, whipping it idly with the flat of his sword, and now and again thrusting at it with the point, as if beating for hidden skirmishers. It was our brother Mark, and he frowned as he rode.

I held my breath as he drew near. Margery's eyes were on the King; but she must needs recognise her brother when he came abreast of us.

And so it was. She gave him an idle glance, and with that she let out a short choking cry, and leapt down from the hedge right in his path, dragging me after her by the sleeve.

" Mark! " she cried.

He swerved his horse round with a curse. But she caught at the bridle and pointed towards the gap through which, though hidden from us by the angle, pointed the muzzles of the rebel artillery. " You must! Oh, if you fear, I will run with you and die with you—I your sister! There is no other way. You *must*, Mark! "

He pushed past her sullenly, moving towards the group where the King stood.

" Mark, if you do not, the King shall know! Redeem, brother; or I swear—and when did I break word?—here and now the King shall know who lost him the rebel horse."

She spoke it fast and low, with a dead-white face. We were close now to the royal group; close enough to hear the King's words.

" I must needs," he was saying, " envy her Majesty, Captain Brett. Under your leading her troop has done that which my own can only envy."

He turned at what seemed at first a murmur among his own men, and no doubt was framing a compliment from them too. But their murmur

351

grew to a growl of mere astonishment as a thud of hoofs drew all eyes after my brother riding at full gallop for the gap.

"But what is the madman after?" began the King, and broke off with a sharp exclamation as his eyes fell on Margery, who had picked up her skirts and was running after Mark. She was perhaps a hundred yards behind him when the cannon roared and, almost in the entrance of the gap, he flung up both arms, and horse and rider rolled over together. A moment later she too staggered and fell sideways —stunned by the wind of a round-shot.

The firing ceased as suddenly as it began. I heard a voice saying as if it continued a discussion —"And Lantine of all men! I'd have picked him for the levellest-headed man in the troop. By the way, he comes from these parts, I've heard say."

And with that I ran to my sister's side.

Two days later by the earthwork where we had played as children his Majesty received the surrender of the rebel foot; while, on the slope below, the house which should have been Mark's heritage blazed merrily, fired by the last shot of the campaign.

PHŒBUS ON HALZAPHRON

" God! of whom music
And song and blood are pure,
The day is never darkened
That had thee here obscure. "

EARLY in 1897 a landslip on the tall cliffs of Halzaphron—which face upon Mount's Bay, Cornwall,
and the Gulf Stream of the Atlantic—brought to
light a curiosity. The slip occurred during the
night of January 7th to 8th, breaking through the
roof of a cavern at the base of the cliff and carrying
many hundreds of tons of rock and earth down into
deep water. For some weeks what remained of the
cavern was obliterated, and in the rough weather
then prevailing no one took the trouble to examine
it; since it can only be approached by sea. The
tides, however, set to work to sift and clear the
detritus, and on Whit-Monday a party of pleasure-
seekers from Penzance brought their boat to shore,
landed, and discovered a stairway of worked stone
leading up from the back of the cavern through
solid rock. The steps wound spirally upward, and
were cut with great accuracy; but the drippings

353

from the low roof of the stairway had worn every tread into a basin and filled it with water. Green slippery weeds coated the lowest stairs; those immediately above were stained purple and crimson by the growth of some minute fungus; but where darkness began, these colors passed through rose-pink into a delicate ivory-white—a hard crust of lime, crenelated like coral by the ceaseless trickle of water which deposited it.

At first the explorers supposed themselves on the track of a lost holy well. They had no candles, but by economising their stock of matches they followed up the mysterious and beautiful staircase until it came to a sudden end, blocked by the fallen mass of cliff. Still in ignorance whither it led or what purpose it had served, they turned back and descended to the sunshine again; when one of the party, scanning the cliff's face, observed a fragment —three steps only—jutting out like a cornice some sixty or seventy feet overhead.

This seemed to dispose of the holy well theory, and suggested that the stairway had reached to the summit, where perhaps an entrance might be found. The party returned to Penzance, and their report at once engaged the attention of the local Antiquarian Society; a small subscription list was opened, permission obtained from the owner of the property, and within a week a gang of labourers began to excavate on the cliff-top directly above the jutting cornice. The ground here showed a slight depression, and the soil proved unexpectedly deep and easy to work. On the second day, at a depth of seven feet, one of the men announced that he had come upon rock. But having spaded away the loose earth, they discovered that his pick had struck upon the edge of an extremely fine tessellated pavement, the remains apparently of a Roman villa.

Yet could this be a Roman villa? That the Romans drove their armies into Cornwall is certain enough; their coins, ornaments, and even pottery, are still found here and there; their camps can be traced. That they conquered and colonised it, however, during any of the four hundred years they occupied Britain has yet to be proved. In other parts of England the plough turns up memorials of that quiet home life with its graces which grew around these settlers and comforted their exile; and the commonest of these is the tessellated pavement with its emblems of the younger gods, the vintage, the warm south. But in the remote west, where the Celts held their savage own, no such traces have ever been found.

Could this at last be one? The pavement, cleared with care, proved of a disappointing size, measuring

8 feet by 4 at the widest. The *tessellæ* were exceptionally beautiful and fresh in color; and each separate design represented some scene in the story of Apollo. No Bacchus with his panther-skin and Mænads, no Triton and Nymphs, no loves of Mars and Venus, no Ganymede with the eagle, no Leda, no Orpheus, no Danaë, no Europa—but always and only Apollo! He was guiding his car; he was singing among the Nine; he was drawing his bow; he was flaying Marsyas; above all—the only repeated picture—he was guiding the oxen of Admetus, goad in hand, with the glory yet vivid about his hair. Could it (someone suggested) be the pavement of a temple? And, if so, how came a temple of the sun-god upon this unhomely coast?

The discovery gave rise to a small sensation and several ingenious theories, one enthusiastic philologer going so far as to derive the name Halzaphron from the Greek, interpreting it as " the salt of the west winds " or " Zephyrs," and to assert roundly that the temple (he assumed it to be a temple) dated far back beyond the Roman Invasion. This contention, though perhaps no more foolish than a dozen others, undoubtedly met with the most ridicule.

And yet in my wanderings along that coast I have come upon broken echoes, whispers, fragments of a tale, which now and again, as I tried to piece them together, wakened a suspicion that the derided philologer, with his false derivation, was yet " hot," as children say in the game of hide-and-seek.

For the stretch of sea overlooked by Halzaphron covers the lost land of Lyonnesse. Take a boat upon a clear, calm day, and, drifting, peer over the side through its shadow, and you will see the tops of tall forests waving below you. Walk the shore at low water and you may fill your pockets with beech-nuts, and sometimes—when a violent tide has displaced the sand—stumble on the trunks of large trees. Geologists dispute whether the Lyonnesse disappeared by sudden catastrophe or gradual subsidence, but they agree in condemning the fables of Florence and William of Worcester, that so late as November, 1099, the sea broke in and covered the whole tract between Cornwall and the Scillies, overwhelming on its way no less than a hundred and forty churches! They prove that, however it befell, we must date the inundation some centuries earlier. Now if my story be true—But let it be told:

In the year of the great tide Graul, son of Graul, was king in the Lyonnesse. He lived at peace in his city of Maenseyth, hard by the Sullêh, where the foreign traders brought their ships to anchor—

sometimes from Tyre itself, oftener from the Tyrian colonies down the Spanish coast; and he ruled over a peaceful nation of tinners, herdsmen, and charcoal-burners. The charcoal came from the great forest to the eastward where Cara Clowz in Cowz, the gray rock in the wood, overlooked the Cornish frontier; his cattle pastured nearer, in the plains about the foot of the Wolves' Cairn; and his tinners camped and washed the ore in the valley-bottoms—for in those days they had no need to dig into the earth for metal, but found plenty by puddling in the river-beds.

So King Graul ruled happily over a happy people until the dark morning when a horseman came galloping to the palace of Maenseyth with a cry that the tide had broken through Crebawethan and was sweeping north and west upon the land, drowning all in its path. " Hark! " said he, " already you may hear the roar of it by Bryher! "

Yann, the King's body-servant, ran at once to the stables and brought three horses—one for Queen Niotte; one for her only child, the Princess Gwennolar; and for King Graul the red stallion, Rubh, swiftest and strongest in the royal stalls, one of the Five Wonders of Lyonnesse. More than six leagues lay between them and the Wolves' Cairn, which surely the waters could never cover; and toward it the three rode at a stretch gallop, King Graul only tightening his hand on the bridle as Rubh strained to outpace the others. As he rode he called warnings to the herdsmen and tinners who already had heard the far roar of waters and were fleeing to the hills. The cattle raced ahead of him, around him, beside him; he passed troop after troop; and among them, in fellowship, galloped foxes, badgers, hares, rabbits, weasels; even small field-mice were skurrying and entangling themselves in the long grasses, and toppling head over heels in their frenzy to escape.

But before they reached the Wolves' Cairn the three riders were alone again. Rubh alone carried his master lightly, and poised his head to sniff the wind. The other two leaned on their bridles and lagged after him, and even Rubh bore against the left-hand rein until it wearied the King's wrist. He wondered at this; but at the base of the cairn he wondered no longer, for the old gray wolf, for whose head Graul had offered a talent of silver, was loping down the hill-side in full view, with her long family at her heels. She passed within a stone's throw of the King and gave him one quiet, disdainful look out of her green eyes as she headed her pack to the southward.

Then the King understood. He looked southward and saw the plain full of moving beasts. He looked northward, and two miles away the rolling downs were not, but in their place a bright line stretched taut as a string, and the string roared as if a great finger were twanging it.

Queen Niotte's horse had come to a standstill. Graul lifted and set her before him on Rubh's crupper, and called to Gwennolar to follow him. But Gwennolar's horse, too, was spent, and in a little while he drew rein and lifted her, too, and set her on the stallion's broad back behind him. Then forward he spurred again and southward after the wolves—with a pack fiercer than wolves shouting at Rubh's heels, nearer and yet nearer.

And Rubh galloped, yet not as before; for this Gwennolar was a witch—a child of sixteen, golden-tressed, innocent to look upon as a bird of the air. Her parents found no fault in her, for she was their only one. None but the Devil, whom she had bound to serve her for a year and a day, knew of her lovers—the dark young sailors from the ships of Tyre, who came ashore and never sailed again nor were seen—or beneath what beach their bodies lay in a row. To-day his date was up, and in this flood he was taking his wages.

Gwennolar wreathed her white arms around her father and clung to him, while her blown hair streamed like gold over his beard. And King Graul set his teeth and rode to save the pair whom he knew to be dearest and believed to be best. But if Niotte weighed like a feather, Gwennolar with her wickedness began to weigh like lead—and more heavily yet, until the stallion could scarcely heave his strong loins forward, as now the earth grew moist about his hoofs. For far ahead of the white surge-line the land was melting and losing its features; trickles of water threading the green pastures, channelling the ditches, widening out into pools among the hollows—traps and pitfalls to be skirted, increasing in number while the sun sank behind and still the great rock of Cara Clowz showed far away above the green forest.

Rubh's head was leaning and his lungs throbbed against the King's heels. Yet he held on. He had overtaken the wolves; and Graul, thinking no longer of deliverance, watched the pack streaming beside him but always falling back and a little back until even the great gray dam dropped behind. A minute later a scream rang close to his ear; the stallion leaped as if at a water-brook, and as suddenly sank backward with a dozen wolves on his haunches.

" Father! " shrieked Gwennolar. " Father! "

He felt her arms dragged from around his neck.

With an arm over his wife Niotte he crouched, waiting for the fangs to pierce his neck. And while he waited, to his amazement the horse staggered up, shook himself, and was off with a bound, fleet as an arrow, fleeter than ever before, yet not fleeter than the pack now running again and fresh beside him. He looked back. Gwennolar rose to her knees on the turf where the wolves had pulled her down and left her unhurt; she stretched out both arms to him, and called once. The sun dipped behind her, and between her and the sun the tide —a long bright-edged knife—came sweeping and cut her down. Then it seemed as if the wolves had relinquished to the waters not their prey only but their own fierce instinct; for the waves paused at the body and played with it, nosing and tumbling it over and over, lifting it curiously, laying it down again on the green knoll, and then withdrawing in a circle while they took heart to rush upon it all together and toss it high, exultant and shouting. And during that pause the fugitives gained many priceless furlongs.

They reached the skirts of the great forest and dashed into its twilight, crouching low while Rubh tore his way between the gray beech-trunks and leaped the tangles of brier, but startled no life from bough or undergrowth. Beast and reptile had fled inland; and the birds hung and circled over the tree-tops without thought of roosting. Graul's right arm tightened about his wife's waist, but his left hand did no more than grasp the rein. He trusted to the stallion, and through twilight and darkness alike Rubh held his course.

When at length he slackened speed and came to a halt with a shudder, Graul looked up and saw the stars overhead and a glimmering scarp of granite, and knew it for the gray rock, Cara Clowz. By the base of it he lowered Niotte to the ground, dismounted, and began to climb, leading Rubh by the bridle and seeking for a pathway. Behind him the voices of crashing trees filled the windless night. He found a ledge at length, and there the three huddled together—Niotte between swooning and sleep, Graul seated beside her, and Rubh standing patient, waiting for the day. When the crashing ceased around them, the King could hear the soft flakes of sweat dripping from the stallion's belly, and saw the stars reflected now from the floor where his forest had stood. Day broke, and the Lyonnesse had vanished. Forest and pasture, city, mart and haven—away to the horizon a heaving sea covered all. Of his kingdom there remained only a thin strip of coast, marching beside the Cornish border, and this sentinel rock, standing as it stands to-day, then called Cara Clowz, and now St. Michael's Mount.

If you have visited it, you will know that the mount stands about half a mile from the mainland; an island except at low water, when you reach it by a stone causeway. Here, on the summit, Graul and Niotte built themselves a house, asking no more of life than a roof to shelter them; for they had no child to build for, and their spirit was broken. The little remnant of their nation settled in Marazion on the mainland, or southward along the strip of coast, and set themselves to learn a new calling. As the sea cast up the bodies of their drowned cattle and the trunks of uprooted trees, they took hides and timber and fashioned boats and launched forth to win their food. They lowered nets and wicker pots through the heaving floor deep into the twilight, and, groping across their remembered fields, drew pollack and conger, shellfish and whiting from rocks where shepherds had sat to watch their sheep, or tinners gathered at noonday for talk and dinner. At first it was as if a man returning at night to his house and, finding it unlit, should feel in the familiar cupboard for food and start back from touch of a monstrous body, cold and unknown. Time and use deadened the shock. They were not happy, for they remembered days of old; but they endured, they fought off hunger, they earned sleep; and their King, as he watched from Cara Clowz their dark sails moving out against the sunset, could give thanks that the last misery had been spared his people.

But there were dawns which discovered one or two missing from the tale of boats, home-comings with heavy news for freight, knots of women and children with blown wet hair awaiting it, white faces and the wails of widow and orphan. The days drew in and this began to happen often—so often that a tale grew with it and spread, until it had reached all ears but those of King Graul and Queen Niotte.

One black noon in November a company of men crossed the sands at low-water and demanded to speak with the King.

"Speak, my children," said Graul. He knew that they loved him and might count on his sharing the last crust with them.

"We are come," said the spokesman, "not for ourselves, but for our wives and children. For us life is none too pleasant; but they need men's hands to find food for them, and at this rate there will soon be no men of our nation left."

"But how can I help you?" asked the King.

"That we know not; but it is your daughter

Gwennolar who undoes us. She lies out yonder
beneath the waters, and through the night she calls
to men, luring them down to their death. I myself—all of us here—have heard her; and the
younger men it maddens. With singing and witch
fires she lures our boats to the reefs and takes toll
of us, lulling even the elders to dream, cheating
them with the firelight and voices of their homes."

Now the thoughts of Graul and Niotte were with
their daughter continually. That she should have
been lost and they saved, who cared so little for life
and nothing for life without her—that was their
abiding sorrow and wonder and self-reproach. Why
had Graul not turned Rubh's head perforce and
ridden back to die with her, since help her he could
not? Many times a day he asked himself this; and
though Niotte's lips had never spoken it, her eyes
asked it too. At night he would hear her breath
pause at his side, and knew she was thinking of
their child out yonder in the cold waters.

" She calls to us also," he answered, and checked
himself.

" So it is plain her spirit is alive yet, and she must
be a witch," said the spokesman, readily.

The King rent his clothes. " My daughter is no
witch!" he cried. " But I left her to die, and she
suffers."

366

" Our lads follow her. She calls to them and they perish."

" It is not Gwennolar who calls, but some evil thing which counterfeits her. She was innocent as the day. Nevertheless your sons shall not perish, nor you accuse her. From this day your boats shall have a lantern on this rock to guide them, and I and my wife will tend it with our own hands."

Thenceforward at sunset with their own hands Graul and Niotte lit and hung out a lantern from the niche which stands to this day and is known as St. Michael's Chair; and trimmed it, and tended it the night through, taking turns to watch. Niotte, doited with years and sorrow, believed that it shone to signal her lost child home. Her hands trembled every night as Graul lit the wick, and she arched her palms above to shield it from the wind. She was happier than her husband.

Gwennolar's spell defied the lantern and their tottering pains. Boats were lost, men perished as before. The people tried a new appeal. It was the women's turn to lay their grief at the King's door. They crossed the sands by ones and twos—widows, childless mothers, maids betrothed and bereaved— and spread their dark skirts and sat before the gate- way. Niotte brought them food with her own hands; they took it without thanks. All the day they sat silent, and Graul felt their silence to be heavier than curses—nay, that their eyes did indeed curse as they sat around and watched the lighting of the lantern, and Niotte, nodding innocently at her arched hands, told them, " See, I pray; cannot you pray too? "

But the King's prayer was spoken in the morning, when the flame and the stars grew pale together and the smoke of the extinguished lamp sickened his soul in the clean air. His gods were gone with the oaks under which he had worshipped; but he stood on a rock apart from the women and, lifting both hands, cried aloud: " If there be any gods above the tree-tops, or any in the far seas whither the old fame of King Graul has reached; if ever I did kindness to a stranger or wayfarer, and he, returning to his own altars, remembered to speak of Graul of Lyonnesse: may I, who ever sought to give help, receive help now! From my youth I have believed that around me, beyond sight as surely as within it, stretched goodness answering the goodness in my own heart; yea, though I should never travel and find it, I trusted it was there. O trust, betray me not! O kindness, how far soever dwelling, speak comfort and help! For I am afflicted because of my people."

Seven mornings he prayed thus on his rock: and

on the seventh, his prayer ended, he stood watching while the sunrays, like dogs shepherding a flock, searched in the mists westward and gathered up the tale of boats one by one. While he counted them, the shoreward breeze twanged once like a harp, and he heard a fresh young voice singing from the base of the cliff at his feet—

> *" There lived a king in Argos,—*
> *A merchantman in Tyre*
> *Would sell the King his cargoes,*
> *But took his heart's desire :*
> *Sing Io, Io, Io !— "*

Graul looked toward his wife. " That will be the boy Laian," said Niotte; " he sits on the rock below and sings at his fishing."

" The song is a strange one," said Graul; " and never had Laian voice like that."

The singer mounted the cliff—

> *" The father of that merry may*
> *A thousand towns he made to pay,*
> *And lapp'd the world in fire ! "*

He stood before them—a handsome, smiling youth, with a crust of brine on his blue sea-cloak, and the light of the morning in his hair. " Salutation, O Graul ! " said he, and looked so cordial and well-willing that the King turned to him from the dead lamp and the hooded women as one turns to daylight from an evil dream.

"Salutation, O Stranger!" he answered. "You come to a poor man, but are welcome—you and your shipmates."

"I travel alone," said the youth; "and my business——"

But the King put up his hand. "We ask no man his business until he has feasted."

"I feast not in a house of mourning; and my business is better spoken soon than late, seeing that I heal griefs."

"If that be so," answered Graul, "you come to those who are fain of you." And then and there he told of Gwennolar. "The blessing of blessings rest on him who can still my child's voice and deliver her from my people's curse!"

The Stranger listened, and threw back his head. "I said I could heal griefs. But I cannot cure fate; nor will a wise man ask it. Pain you must suffer, but I can soothe it; sorrow, but I can help you to forget; death, but I can brace you for it."

"Can death be welcomed," asked Graul, "save by those who find life worse?"

"You shall see." He stepped to the mourning women, and took the eldest by the hand. At first he whispered to her—in a voice so low that Graul heard nothing, but saw her brow relax, and that she listened while the blood came slowly back to her cheeks.

" Of what are you telling her? " the King demanded.

" Hush! " said the Stranger, " Go, fetch me a harp."

Graul brought a harp. It was mute and dusty, with a tangle of strings; but the Stranger set it against his knee, and began to mend it deftly, talking the while in murmurs as a brook talks in a covert of cresses. By and by as he fitted a string he would touch and make it hum on a word— softly at first, and with long intervals—as though all its music lay dark and tangled in chaos, and he were exploring and picking out a note here and a note there to fit his song. There was trouble in his voice, and restlessness, and a low, eager striving, and a hope which grew as the notes came oftener, and lingered and thrilled on them. Then his fingers caught the strings together, and pulled the first chord: it came out of the depths with a great sob—a soul set free. Other souls behind it rose to his fingers, and he plucked them forth, faster and faster—some wailing, some laughing fiercely, but each with the echo of a great pit, the clang of doors,

and the mutter of an army pressing at its heels.
And now the mourners leaned forward, and forgot
all except to listen, for he was singing the Creation.
He sang up the stars and set them in procession; he
sang forth the sun from his chamber; he lifted the
heads of the mountains and hitched on their man-
tles of green forest; he scattered the uplands with
sheep, and the upper air with clouds; he called the
west wind, and it came with a rustle of wings; he
broke the rock into water and led it dancing down
the cliffs, and spread it in marshes, and sent it
spouting and hurrying in channels. Flowers
trooped to the lip of it, wild beasts slunk down to
drink; armies of corn spread in rank along it, and
men followed with sickles, chanting the hymn of
Linus; and after them, with children at the breast,
women stooped to glean or strode upright bearing baskets of food. Over their heads days and
nights hurried in short flashes, and the seasons overtook them while they rested, and drowned them in
showers of bloom, and overtopped their bodies with
fresh corn: but the children caught up the sickles
and ran on. To some—shining figures in the host
—he gave names; and they shone because they
moved in the separate light of divine eyes watching
them, rays breaking the thickets or hovering down
from heights where the gods sat at their ease.

But before this the men had brought their boats
to shore, and hurried to the Mount, drawn by his
harping. They pressed around him in a ring; and
at first they were sad, since of what he sang they
remembered the like in Lyonnesse—plough and
sickle and flail, nesting birds and harvest, flakes of
ore in the river-beds, dinner in the shade, and the
plain beyond winking in the noon-day heat. They
had come too late for the throes of his music, when
the freed spirit trembled for a little on the threshold,
fronting the dawn, but with the fire of the pit behind it and red on its trailing skirt. The song rolled
forward now like a river, sweeping them past shores
where they desired to linger. But the Stranger
fastened his eyes on them, and sang them out to
broad bars and sounding tumbling seas, where the
wind piped, and the breeze came salt, and the spray
slapped over the prow, hardening men to heroes.
Then the days of their regret seemed to them good
only for children, and the life they had loathed took
a new face; their eyes opened upon it, and they
saw it whole, and loved it for its largeness. " Beyond! beyond! beyond! "—they stared down on
the fingers plucking the chords, but the voice of the
harp sounded far up and along the horizon.

And with that quite suddenly it came back, and
was speaking close at hand, as a friend telling them

a simple tale; a tale which all could understand, though of a country unknown to them. Thus it ran:

"*In Hellas, in the kingdom of Argos, there lived two brothers, Cleobis and Biton—young men, well to do, and of great strength of body, so that each had won a crown in the public games. Now, once, when the Argives were keeping a festival of the goddess Hera, their mother had need to be driven to the temple in her chariot, but the oxen did not return from the field in time. The young men, therefore, seeing that the hour was late, put the yoke on their own necks, and drew the car in which their mother sat, and brought her to the temple, which was forty-five stades away. This they did in sight of the multitude assembled; and the men commended their strength, while the women called her blessed to be the mother of such sons. But she, overjoyed at the deed and its renown, entered the temple and, standing before the image of Hera, prayed the goddess to grant her two sons, Cleobis and Biton, the greatest boon which could fall to man. After she had prayed, and they had sacrificed and eaten of the feast, the young men sat down in the temple and fell asleep, and never awoke again, but so made an end with life. In this wise the blessing of Hera came to them; and the men of Argos caused statues to be made of them and set up at Delphi, for a memorial of their piety and its reward.*"

374

Thus quietly the great song ended, and Graul, looking around on his people, saw on their faces a cheerfulness they had not known since the day of the flood.

"Sir," said he, "yours is the half of my poor kingdom and yours the inheritance, if you will abide with us and sing us more of these songs."

"For that service," answered the Stranger, "I am come; but not for the reward. Give me only a hide of land somewhere upon your cliffs, and there will I build a house and sing to all who have need of me."

So he did; and the fable goes on to say that never were known in the remnant of Lyonnesse such seasons as followed, nor ever will be. The fish crowded to the nets, the cliffs waved with harvest. Heavy were the nets to haul and laborious was the reaping, but the people forgot their aches when the hour came to sit at the Stranger's feet and listen, and drink the wine which he taught them to plant. For his part he toiled not at all, but descended at daybreak and nightfall to bathe in the sea, and returned with the brine on his curls and his youth renewed upon him. He never slept; and they, too, felt little need of sleep, but drank and sang the night away, refreshed by the sacred dews, watching for the moon to rise over the rounded cornfields, or for her feet to touch the sea and shed silver about the boats in the offing. Out yonder Gwennolar sang and took her toll of life as before; but the people heeded less, and soon forgot even when their dearest perished. Other things than sorrow they began to unlearn. They had been a shamefaced race: the men shy and the women chaste. But the Stranger knew nothing of shame; nor was it possible to think harm where he, their leader, so plainly saw none. Naked he led them from the drinking-bout down the west stairway to the bathing-pool, and naked they plunged in and splashed around him and laughed as the cool shock scattered the night's languor and the wine-fumes. What mattered anything?—what they did, or what they suffered, or what news the home-coming boats might bring? They were blithe for the moment and lusty for the day's work, and with night again would come drink and song of the amorous gods; or if by chance the Singer should choose another note and tell of Procris or of Philomela, they could weep softly for others' woes and, so weeping, quite forget their own.

And the fable goes on to say that for three years by these means the Stranger healed the griefs of the people of Lyonnesse, until one night when they sat around he told them the story of Ion; and if the Stranger were indeed Phœbus Apollo himself, shameless was the telling. But while they listened, wrapped in the story, a cry broke on the night above the murmur of the beaches—a voice from the cliff below them, calling " Repent! Repent! "

They leaped to their feet at once, and hurried down the stairway. But the beach was empty; and though they hunted for an hour, they found no one. Yet the next night and every night after the same voice called " Repent! Repent! " They hurled down stones upon it and threatened it with vengeance; but it was not to be scared. And by and by the Stranger missed a face from his circle, then another. At length came a night when he counted but half of his company.

He said no word of the missing ones; but early next morning, when the folk had set out to their labors in the fields, he took a staff and walked along the shore toward the Mount. A little beyond Parc-an-als, where a spring gushes from the face of the cliff, he came upon a man who stood under it catching the trickle in a stone basin, and halted a few paces off to watch him. The man's hair and beard were long and unkempt, his legs bare, and he wore a tattered tunic which reached below the knees and was caught about his waist with a thong girdle.

For some minutes he did not perceive the Singer; but turned at length, and the two eyed each other awhile.

Then the Singer advanced smiling, while the other frowned.

"Thou hast followed me," he said.

"I have followed and found thee," the other answered.

"Thy name?"

"Leven," said the man. "I come out of Ireland."

"The Nazarite travels far; but this spot He overlooked on his travels, and the people had need. I brought them help; but they desert me now—for thee doubtless?"

The Saint bent his head. The Singer laughed.

"He is strong, but the old gods bear no malice. I go to-night to join their sleep, but I have loved this folk in a fashion. I pitied their woes and brought them solace: I taught them to forget—and in the forgetting maybe they have learned much that thou wilt have to unteach. Yet deal gently with them. They are children, and too often you holy men come with bands of iron. Shall we sit and talk awhile together, for their sakes?"

And the fable says that for a long day St. Leven sat on the sands of the Porth which now bears his

378

name, and talked with the Singer; and, that in consequence, to this day the descendants of the people of Lyonnesse praise God in cheerfuller hymns than the rest of the world uses—so much so that a company of minstrels visiting them not long ago were surprised in the midst of a drinking-chorus to find the audience tittering, and to learn afterward that they had chanted the most popular local burying-tunes!

Twilight had fallen before the Stranger rose and took his farewell. On his way back he spied a company approaching along the dusky shore, and drew aside behind a rock while they passed toward the Saint's dwelling. He found his own deserted. Of his old friends either none had come or none had waited; and away on a distant beach rose the faint chant of St. Patrick's Hymn of the Guards-man:

> " *Christ the eye, the ear, the heart,*
> *Christ above, before, behind me ;*
> *From the snare, the sword, the dart,*
> *On the Trinity I bind me—*
> > *Christi est salus,*
> > *Christi est salus,*
> *Salus tua, Domine, sit semper nobiscum !* "

www.ingramcontent.com/pod-product-compliance
Lightning Source LLC
Chambersburg PA
CBHW030354030726
47497CB00002B/336